JASON *and the* ARGONAUTS

TONY WHITEFIELD

Published by Karpasi Press.
whitefield.tony@gmail.com
Printed by Print Strategy Management.

**Also available from Amazon, Book Depository, Booktopia
and other online booksellers.**

First published in Australia 2023
This edition published 2023

Cover design, typesetting: WorkingType (www.workingtype.com.au)
Cover image: Public domain image sourced from *Tanglewood Tales*, Nathaniel
Hawthorne; Edmund Dulac. London ; New York : Hodder and Stoughton. c. 1919

ISBN: 978-0-6459600-1-3

A catalogue record for this
book is available from the
National Library of Australia

To Rae

ALSO BY TONY WHITEFIELD

The Queen of Limnos
George's Cafe

INTRODUCTION

T he story of Jason and the Argonauts is a mythical story from ancient Greece, set around 1250 BCE. Emerging from a time where knowledge was passed down through the agency of oral tradition, it is impossible to establish just what details were ignored, deleted, generalised, distorted or added over time. What evidence of oral tradition did the first authors, some 800 years later, who detailed these stories in writing have at their disposal?

Many academics over the years have attempted to answer these important literary questions. Today, the story of Jason and the Argonauts is still popular and a quick Google search produces many hits. Movies, television mini-series, operas, books, scholarly articles, and a host of school projects fill the internet with references to this myth.

But it had a beginning at some point in time.

The Jason story appears to be an amalgamation of many different tales, rituals, histories and anecdotes. From around

1500 BCE, these verbally edited snippets were passed on by word of mouth through a succession of storytellers. Over the centuries, word of mouth stories tended to change with each telling. Gods were required to help people make sense of and to explain the natural world, where a scientific explanation had not yet gained a foothold. The gods played an important role in their daily lives, and these stories often included the gods as direct players with physical influences in the actions and deeds of people. The story of Jason was no exception. The gods had to be appeased.

But what if we attempt to unravel the Jason story; take away the direct influence of the gods, and re-write the narrative? For example – is there a natural way that the young boy Phrixus ended up in Colchis other than on the back of a flying ram? Could the golden fleece have a much simpler and logical explanation, other than from a flying sheep? What if the gods were deities to be feared, to give thanks to, to pray to, give libations to and build temples for, but who had no physical role to play in men's and women's lives? How might the Jason story have originated? How might the story now be told?

In my first novel, The Queen of Limnos, I introduced Peter the storyteller, a man who made his living travelling the Greek speaking world telling stories, that often took many days, and many glasses of wine to complete. In this book, Peter returns to tell the tale of Jason, approximately three generations after the events took place. He is acutely aware that storytellers before him have already begun to distort events, so he is proud to be the one to set the record straight, due to his extensive research based upon conversations with those who met key participants.

The year is approximately 1190 BCE, and Peter is speaking to a group of unknown people, gathered to hear the famous storyteller talk of Jason and the Argonauts.

PROLOGUE

One of my most requested stories is that of Jason, the man from Iolchus who travelled the length of the known world with a band of warriors and a feisty woman to undertake the most dangerous of quests. Their journey has already reached that of legendary status, where facts seem to have been replaced by myth. If you believe the wildly outrageous tales of flying rams, talking serpents, winged men soaring high above the clouds, wicked witches with dangerous potions, shifting cliffs of sheer rock ready to crush any man or boat, centaurs with special powers to heal, and meddling gods who delight in playing games with their most favourite of toys – man, then you will believe in almost anything.

As usual, I am here to uncover the authentic story. To help separate the man from the myth, and to paint a realistic picture of the factual Jason, not a concocted conglomeration of ill-informed half-baked ideas formed by dim-witted individuals who claimed to be eyewitnesses or storytellers.

Jason's story has been told to me by people who knew some of the principal participants. I have not relied on only one individual with a solid tale to tell before I have taken to the road to visit good people like you. This is my life's work. My stories are well researched, and free from mythological overtones.

Now you will learn that truth is much stranger, and by far, more interesting than fiction. I am often asked if my stories are truthful. My response is always the same. 'You can't make this shit up!'

CHAPTER 1

Jason's family

The city of Iolchus was founded by Jason's grandfather, Cretheus, on the northern coast of the Pagasitic Gulf in central Greece. Cretheus was born nearby in a village close to the sea. The son of a sheep farmer, Cretheus was destined to continue in the family farming business. He had three brothers and two sisters, and they all lived within half a day's walk from their parents after moving away from home. Each brother was a shepherd, and each sister married a shepherd. For young Cretheus growing up, he learned everything there was about rearing sheep, milking them, making cheese, spinning wool into clothing and cooking all parts of the animal. He especially loved sheep's heart and liver in preference to the normal meat others liked. He was different that way. His brothers loved the village life with their flocks and had no interest in travelling more than a few days' walk from their homes.

But Cretheus had other grander ideas and wanted to see the world. Once he was old enough, he married Tyro. Unknown to him at the time of their marriage, his new wife had given birth to twin boys long before they met.

Tyro was incredibly young when she gave birth to the twins, and her mother Alcidice and father Salmoneus said they would look after the boys due to the immaturity and age of their daughter. I know this sounds like I am heading down a dead-end goat path but stay with me here. Tyro was told the boys were abandoned by her parents, and were then found by a passing herdsman who raised them as his own. Tyro ceased all contact with her parents not knowing whether her boys were indeed alive. She fell into a deep depression, only to be rescued by the young shepherd, Cretheus. Tyro never told Cretheus about the twins and married him at the start of their first summer together. While blissfully happy with her new husband, Tyro never did forget about her first-born babies, who were named Pelias and Neleus.

Cretheus was anxious to leave his birthplace and move closer to the sea, so he and Tyro agreed to move their flock of sheep and goats nearer the coast. The area they chose was a short distance away from the base of Mt Pelion, and overlooking the sea where Cretheus envisaged the potential for a new village, or perhaps even a city. They took almost ten days to walk with their flock to the sea, sleeping on the bare ground wherever they could. Once they reached their destination, Cretheus and Tyro fell in love with the smells, feel and sound of small waves lapping the sandy shores.

The animals loved their new home too. Suddenly, milk production seemed to increase, and the quality of cheese improved. Cretheus had no trouble selling his produce, and with the gradual migration of new arrivals, a small village sprung up around the idyllic geographical position. Newcomers planted grapevines, vegetables, and fruit trees. Olive and fig trees were also introduced, and thrived in the coastal areas surrounding the new village.

Fascinated by his new love of all things to do with the sea, Cretheus expanded his interests to include fishing, and arranged for a small boat to be built by one of his friends so that he could fish in the shallow waters of the gulf. The wood from nearby Mt Pelion was perfect for boat building, and in no time at all, it appeared that Cretheus had been the impetus for a thriving boat building business, along with flocks of sheep and goats grazing on the lush plains between Mt Pelion and the coast. New people arrived almost daily to join the existing families in the area. The quality of boats constructed using locally sourced wood was news that travelled far and wide in a relatively short time. As the population grew, Cretheus and other men commenced construction of a stone acropolis with bulky defense walls in the sea to create a safe harbour from all kinds of adverse weather events.

Cretheus became the first King of Iolchus. He and Tyro gave birth to three boys; Aeson, Pheres and Amythaon. For a while, life for the young family was idyllic. A growing local population gave rise to many new challenges. Cretheus was always busy with matters needing the attention of a king, and Tyro was struggling to control three boisterous young lads. King Cretheus was spending more time away from home, and it became apparent to all that he and Tyro were becoming distant from each other. The palace built for them was large enough to live under the one roof, but still lead separate lives. After fifteen years together, and with Tyro's approval, Cretheus took a new wife Sidero.

Tyro remained in the servant's quarters, but her boys lived with their father in the palace. On the face of it, the new living conditions for all involved seemed harmonious enough. Cretheus and Sidero immediately set about having children, but Tyro was still able to see her boys. Sidero proved to be excellent at producing girls, and together with Cretheus, delivered seven daughters in the space of ten years. Their eldest daughter Myrina was later promised in marriage to Thoas of Crete. Thoas and Myrina became the first royal family on the island of Limnos. Thoas and Myrina had a daughter named Hypsipyle and are the subject of my other popular story. Where was I? Oh yes, but get me a drink of your finest wine. This story telling is thirsty business!

Cretheus' sons were growing into fine young men, and Sidero was becoming increasingly jealous of them. The cause of her jealously was simple. Sidero knew Cretheus wanted to install Aeson as his heir apparent upon his death, and having only daughters with him, was aware that none of their daughters had a chance of becoming Queen in their own right. These thoughts manifested in Sidero's behaviour towards Tyro. Placing pressure on her husband, Sidero was influential in ostracising the boys from their father.

Seemingly unaware of the twins Pelias and Neleus, Sidero was further enraged when she learned secretly that Tyro was their mother.

Far away from the palace in Iolchus, Pelias and his twin brother Neleus had grown into manhood. The boys had lived a quiet life as herdsmen with their parents. The boy's personalities were distinctly different. As kind and good natured as Neleus was, his brother was opposite in all regards. Manipulative, and hard-nosed were some of Pelias' better characteristics. Growing tired of life as a herder of sheep and goats, Pelias had an inkling he was destined for grander things in life.

One day while the brothers were far away from home with their herd gently grazing on the grassy plains, they spotted a lone figure walking across the fields towards them carrying a shepherd's crook and leather satchel. This person was not known to the brothers and was dressed like a slave. Thinking the slave had escaped its masters' confines, the twins were immediately suspicious. When the slave approached, he asked them if they were the twins Pelias and Neleus. They answered in the affirmative and the next thing the slave said shook the twins very foundation of who they believed they were.

The slave told them that the people they called mother and father were in fact their adoptive parents. Their birth father was not known to the slave, but he told them their natural mother was alive and wanted to meet them.

"Your mother is Tyro, and was married to King Cretheus of Iolchus."

"You say *was* married to a king" asked Pelias inquisitively.

"Yes, *was* married. The king has re-married, and his new wife is mistreating your mother."

"Who are you and how do you know this?"

"My name is unimportant, but I am the head of slaves in Iolchus where your mother now resides. She remains in the palace, but lives in the slave quarters with us, and her three sons."

Before Neleus could ask a question, the slave produced a

clay tablet with an imprint of King Cretheus firmly stamped as evidence of his association with the palace.

"Your mother is desperate to know of your lives and would like me to report back to her anything you may wish to say."

Neleus did not know what to say. He was very happy with his life, and even the news of his birth mother did not change his love for the parents who raised him. Peleus took the news as proof of his premonition that he was destined for greater achievements.

"Are you saying our mother, our birth mother wants to know if we are alive?"

"Yes."

"Does she want to meet us?"

"Yes."

Peleus did not know if he wanted to speak to the woman who abandoned him, but the slave spoke more.

"Your mother did not abandon you. She gave birth under very trying circumstances. She was only a child herself, and unable to care for you. Your adoptive parents could not have children of their own, so when the opportunity arose for them to care for you, they took that as a sign from the gods to protect and nurture you both."

"But there is one more thing you should know."

"What is that?" asked Peleus.

"I fear for your mother's life. Not from the king, who is too busy with his life to even recognise her, but from Sidero, the king's wife."

Peleus told the slave that the brothers would accompany him to the palace in Iolchus to meet their mother. Neleus was hesitant, but before he decided to leave on this journey, his adoptive parents gave them their full blessing.

I will go over the next part of this story very quickly. The twins met their mother, and disguised themselves as slaves so as not to arouse any suspicion from the king or from Sidero. They instantly liked their mother and felt a deep connection to her. But Pelias had ulterior motives. He hatched a plan to kill Sidero, banish the king's three sons, and even to banish his own brother. All this in the hope he would usurp the kingdom of Iolchus from Cretheus' choice of Aeson as the rightful heir.

His plan worked to a perfection. Sidero was killed, and driven by grief at the sudden loss of his second wife, King Cretheus died shortly after. Tyro regained access to the palace, the daughters of the former king and queen were permitted to remain, and the banishment of his half-brothers, Aeson, Pheres and Amython, and of his full brother Neleus was instantaneous. Pelias succeeded in becoming king of Iolchus.

Tyro was in no hurry to convince her son that he should not be king, because she had been restored to the palace and her life was looking positive once more. She did not fear Sidero and Cretheus' daughters at all and saw them as no threat to her son's rise to the top, and Pelias too must have thought that nothing could interfere with his ascension to the throne.

Aeson, Pelias' half-brother and Cretheus' choice to take over the kingdom, returned to Iolchus on hearing of his fathers' death. Thinking this would not be a difficult task, Aeson was immediately taken in chains and swiftly thrown in prison.

Pelias enjoyed his rapid rise to the throne. His days of herding sheep and goats were a distant memory, as were the two loving parents who raised him. All his plans were in place, and he saw no potential problems with Aeson rotting away in prison. Feeling somewhat comfortable and convinced no living relative was a threat to his position, Pelias softened slightly and granted Aeson permission to marry. Aeson miraculously persuaded his half-brother to set him free and was released soon after to marry Polymede. Pelias' power was now at its peak, and soon after the wedding to Polymede, Aeson was summoned to the palace for a meeting with the king. King Pelias told Aeson that he could remain in Iolchus for as long as he wanted, and even hinted that one day, he would give up the kingship for Aeson. Aeson firmly believed this, but in reality, the king had no intention of doing so.

To keep Aeson at bay, Pelias secretly told Polymede that if she and Aeson had any male children, the child would be taken from them by force and bashed against rocks. She was also instructed not to inform her husband of the details of this conversation, on fear of death.

Aeson and Polymede quickly became pregnant, and as you can guess, Pelias was eagerly awaiting the outcome of the pregnancy. He had installed a spy as Polymede's nurse and was kept informed of all the tribulations of the impending birth. What Pelias did not know, was that the woman he had installed as a spy, was an old, dear friend of Polymede. The nurse was disgusted with his instructions, and hid her anger well. She risked her own life in deciding to inform Polymede if indeed a male child was born. The nurse was now acting as a double spy.

Sure enough, a male child was born, and Aeson and Polymede were given a few precious moments to hold their son. The nurse relayed the threat of immediate and a gory death to the boy should King Pelias discovered the truth. Polymede and Aeson were heartbroken at the same time as being elated at the birth of a healthy baby boy. Naming the child Jason, Aeson quickly rushed the boy to a safe place, far away on Mt Pelion where his identity could be kept secret for many years. Polymede, Aeson and the nurse conducted a mock funeral and buried a log of wood in place of a fake dead child. Pelias did not check the accuracy of this, trusting the news from his spy.

Polymede and Aeson were so convincing at disguising their grief, Pelias believed them without question. In a magnanimous gesture, Pelias permitted Aeson and his wife to live on the edge of Iolchus, if they agreed to stay away from the palace. Aeson was genuinely terrified of Pelias, and kept his word for many years, living a simple farm life. If anyone knew him to be the son of Cretheus and asked why he wasn't king, Aeson would simply say that Pelias was a better leader, and he preferred to live a simpler life. But, Aeson always knew that his own son would one day return, and claim the throne legitimately.

Meanwhile, baby Jason was sent to Mt Pelion, to a safe boy's home run by Chiron and his wife Chariklo and their three daughters Pelionides, Okyro and Karysto. Chiron's mother, Philyra started the home as a place for young men to learn valuable life skills, when the boys' own parents were not able to do so. As the boys grew older, the lessons taught by Chiron progressed from basic survival skills to those necessary to live in the modern adult world, and competition for places at the home were eagerly sought after. Lessons started as soon as boys arrived, and within no time, all boys learned how to dress themselves, collect wood, make fire, prepare meals and wash clothes. Once they mastered these basic competences, hunting skills using javelins, bows, swords, and slingshots commenced.

It was one thing to catch an animal with a javelin or by bow, but to prepare the animal for food was vitally important. Butchering skills, use of animal skins and fur for clothing or basic household items, and weapon making were then mastered. Herb gathering, knowing which plants to eat, how to grow vegetables and make wine were deemed as important as knowing how to light a fire.

Quite often, boys had to spend time on their own, away from others, and learn how to survive wild conditions in all kinds of weather. Survival skills like weapon making, shelter construction and food preparation became necessary for existence.

Chiron taught the difference with what he called immature and mature hunting. Immature hunting took place at night where the boys hunted alone utilising nets and snares. Jason learned at a young age to construct his own nets and snares with whatever material was available. Once they had mastered this form, mature hunting took place during daylight, when the hunters stalked an animal and killed it. In contrast to the night-time immature, alone hunt, daylight hunting often necessitated the boys working together for a common cause.

Once the boys were old enough, which was at the age of twelve, lessons progressed to include arts and science, philosophy, the art of war, language, rhetoric and the history of the world. However, the most valuable lesson Chiron taught his boys was the art of healing. By this age, the boys had an extensive knowledge of herbs, vegetables, fruit and which animals were safe to cook. They could prepare any herbs to add to other food for taste, but now it was time to put these herbs to another use – pharmacological and medicinal. Chiron was an expert healer of physical injuries and he demanded that all his charges knew as much as he did by the time of their ultimate release into the wider community. Chiron passed on his knowledge and experience to the boys, but perhaps the main lesson he taught was the dangers associated with these drugs in addition to the healing practices associated with them.

Their home was amongst the rough and gentle slopes of Mt Pelion, and over many years, countless boys had been sent to them, for a fee of course. Jason spent the first twenty years of his life with Chiron as his mentor, Chariklo as his mother, and the girls as his sisters. In addition to this, Jason had hundreds of 'brothers' who he called family.

One of Chiron's hard and fast rules was that no boy he took in was to learn of his true parentage until he had seen twenty summers. Each boy was told this, and each parent too. Aeson sent Chiron payments through a slave runner he employed. Chiron could trust this slave, and would not trust any parents' nominated slave to be discreet with this knowledge.

On reaching the required age, Chiron would allow each boy to make up his own mind about reuniting with his true family, and each parent had to face the distinct possibility that their son may not wish to be reunited with them. It was a risk all parents accepted. Twenty summers was the maximum time a boy stayed with Chiron. Some boys only were indentured for five. Some for ten and some for a little as two. Each boy who lived on the slopes of Mt Pelion under the tutelage of Chiron and Chariklo left with greater knowledge than their families could have ever wished for.

CHAPTER 2

Phrixus, Helle and the Golden Fleece

One of the many highlights of Jason's life on Mt Pelion were the still, moonlit nights spent gathered around a large fire, listening to wonderous stories told by Chiron. These events were considered a treat by the boys who looked forward to each evening with great anticipation.

Once the decision was made by Chiron that there would be stories on a particular night, the boys knew exactly what to do in order to prepare for the evening. Young boys gathered small sticks to assist with the fire lighting while older boys amassed larger branches to make sure the fire would last until sunrise.

On these nights, Chiron also invited Chariklo and their daughters to sit and listen, as they also seemed to enjoy the stories. Over Jason's life, he must have heard the same tales many times, but with each telling, he was some years older, and more able to understand the purpose and subtle meaning of each narrative. To the younger lads, they were simply stories, but to the older ones who had heard them often, the valuable lifelong messages carefully woven were far more apparent. Each boy had a favourite. Some of the boys loved hearing about each of the gods, but for Jason, one specific story seemed far more important. It was the story regarding twins, an evil stepmother, a flying ram with golden fleece and a city at the end of the known world called Colchis.

Like me, Chiron would pad the story out with many side issues, interesting characters and intriguing plot lines, but I will only give you the bare necessities. The story goes something like this:

King Athamas of Boeotia, a land on the northern side of the Corinthian Gulf, married Nephele, a cloud nymph. Athamas was infatuated with the young, beautiful woman, and at first was not jealous of her direct links to the gods. As a cloud nymph, Nephele had the ability to bring water to rivers and streams and to nourish the earth.

In no time at all, Nephele gave birth to twins; Phrixus the male, then a female named Helle, born shortly after her older brother. Athamas loved his children, but soon grew tired and jealous of Nephele and made her life miserable. Nephele, although she was the mother of the prince and princess of Boeotia, grew apart from Athamas, but was totally devoted to her twins. She hated the idea of leaving them, but Nephele departed once she saw that Athamas had eyes for the Theban princess, Ino. Nephele's powers had little impact on changing the mind of King Athamas, so thought it would be better if she departed. However, she kept watch over her precious children by her ability to change into a cloud and hover overhead. The children would often be seen walking outside the palace walls, talking to the sky where their mother was cleverly disguised as a small cloud.

Once Ino was safely entrenched in the palace of King Athamas, she immediately took a disliking to the twins. On many occasions, she would follow the twins out of the palace and witnessed them talking with their mother. Following the birth of her own sons, Learchus and Melicertes, Ino hatched a plan to rid herself of the twins allowing one of her own children to become heir to the Boeotian kingdom. She hatched a cunning plan based upon the farmers genuine fear of an impending drought which had the capacity to destroy all crops and bring famine. Terrified of yet another drought, the farmers wanted to approach a nearby oracle for help, guidance, and assistance. Ino received word of this plan to seek the oracle's advice, and offered to go in their place. The farmers agreed, and sent Ino to visit the oracle.

However, her conversations with the oracle as to her reasons for the visitation were not made clear, and she manipulated the oracle into making a rather shocking prediction.

On her return, Ino asked local farmers to meet her outside the palace walls. It was here that she falsely claimed the oracle insisted on Phrixus and Helle be killed. This was not what the oracle had said. The oracle had suggested that the twins be

14

exiled, and only permitted to return if they were to renounce any claim to inherit the kingdom of Boeotia.

Somehow, Ino convinced her husband that the sacrifice of both twins was required, and a sacrificial altar was hastily constructed. She persuaded Athamas that unless the twins were sacrificed to the gods, the farmers would storm the palace and kill all who resided inside its walls. Nephele could not intervene directly, and knew what was to take place, so she sent a flying ram to rescue her children.

Phrixus and Helle were not told of the oracle's prediction, and went about their daily business as usual. Ino believed that Nephele could not save them, even if she wanted to, but underestimated a mother's love of her children.

On the day of the sacrifice, the twins were gathering vegetables from the palace garden, completely oblivious to the altar and its devastating purpose. Seemingly out of the clouds, a golden ram swooped down to the garden and implored the children to climb on its back.

"I have been sent by your mother Nephele the cloud nymph. Your father has been deceived and his wife is to have you both sacrificed at the altar when the sun is at its highest point today. If you want to live, do as I say. Hold on tight, and when we fly over water, do not look down under any circumstance."

Phrixus asked the ram where he was taking them, to which the ram replied that it was a land far away. A place where their father and stepmother could never find them. Phrixus would not look down and did dutifully as he was instructed by the ram through his mother. Helle was becoming less frightened and once they were over a narrow strait of water leading away *from the ocean they had just traversed, she took a moment to gaze down, noticing how low to the water they were flying. Helle was transfixed by some dolphins jumping out of the water below, and had forgotten the words of her mother "don't look down under any circumstance."*

Helle loosened her grip on the waist of her brother who was holding the ram's neck as tightly as he could. Phrixus noticed his sister's grip loosening around him, but was too late to stop her from falling to her death.

The ram knew Helle had fallen and begged Phrixus to hold on and not look for his sister as it was too late. Distraught by the loss of his sister, Phrixus held on even tighter. Though the tears in his eyes had dampened the fine golden fleece of the ram, he did not look down and only relinquished his grip when he was certain the ram had landed on dry ground.

The body of water over which his sister fell from the golden ram is today known as the Hellespont, in honour of Helle.

Phrixus survived all the way to the city known as Colchis. The golden ram informed Phrixus that he must sacrifice his rescuer to Zeus, and take the golden fleece directly to King Aeetes. Not wanting to harm the magnificent animal, the ram said it understood, but it was the will of the gods that this sacrifice be made.

Reluctantly, Phrixus did as the golden ram suggested, and took the magnificent golden fleece to the royal court of King Aeetes, ruler of Colchis.

Aeetes accepted the stunningly beautiful gift from the son of Athamas, and placed the fleece in his garden, the grove dedicated to the God Ares. So enamored with the gift, Aeetes offered Phrixus the hand of his daughter in marriage. Soon, the wedding of Phrixus and Chalciope took place, and they had four sons within quick succession – Argus, Cytisorus, Phrontis and Melas.

King Aeetes soon became known as one who had a truly wondrous item in his possession. At first, Aeetes thought strangers would come to see the fleece for themselves, if only to see that it was real, and not a myth. It quickly became apparent that these strangers had ulterior motives, and some even tried to steal the fleece. Aeetes had them put to death, and as a result, he became suspicious of any stranger coming to visit Colchis. Some quite innocent strangers, who did not even know about the fleece were killed on the king's instructions, despite pleading their innocence.

An oracle whispered to Aeetes that one day, a descendant of Aeolus, the founder of the kingdom of Boeotia, would kill him, so thinking Phrixus was that descendant, had him killed. Surprisingly, the oracle also predicted that if the fleece ever left Colchis, Aeetes would lose his kingdom.

However, there is one more part to this wondrous tale. Cretheus and Athamas were brothers!

Jason loved this story, and always looked forward to Chiron's telling of it so he could learn some other nuanced lesson not obvious in previous hearings. One thing that was not obvious to Jason was the meaning behind Chiron's last short comment.

The last part of Chiron's story at the time did not immediately have any apparent meaning for Jason.

CHAPTER 3

The Calydonian boar

There are stories by some of my contemporaries that the Calydonian boar was released into fields and crops by the goddess Artemis as punishment because the King of Calydon did not sufficiently make the correct libations, honouring Artemis and Dionysus correctly, nor make sacrifices and offerings for having such a bountiful harvest. After the boar was released, it caused substantial havoc and the peasant farmers were deeply worried and begged the king for help.

Here is what these myth makers said about the boar. Its eyes were a fiery red, and its hide hair was bristling shafts of palisade-like spears. From its incessant grunting, hot foam formed around its neck. Protruding from its brow were tusks the size of a grown man's leg. Leaves on the ground were scorched by its breath. It trampled young crops into the dirt, cutting short their longed-for ripeness by the farmers. It pulverised corn and brought down grapevines, low hanging fruit and green olives. Herdsman's dogs whimpered behind their masters and bulls could not defend their cows. People scattered and hid inside stone buildings. What a load of rubbish!

I can see that some of you are nodding. The truth of the story was not as fanciful as you have been led to believe. The boar hunt had a much simpler, and honest beginning.

King Oeneus of Calydon wanted a competition to showcase the hunting skills of his young, beard-less warriors. The idea of the hunt came to Oeneus as a means to offer something different to his ephebic warriors in their developmental military training other than the tried-and-true athletic games. Hunts of this kind are considered initiation rites and therefore especially important in normal society, so the king decided to introduce something new.

Fighting battles with neighbouring kingdoms had all but dried up, and his men were desperate to show their hunting and killing prowess. Apart from the traditional physical games of javelin, wrestling, running, archery, and discus, Oeneus decided to test his warriors' skills by releasing a purposefully bred wild boar to be tracked, hunted, and killed. When he announced this rather audacious plan, he was met with a degree of scepticism, but closer to the day of the first hunt, interest piqued. The warriors began sharpening their weapons and bragging to all and sundry that they would be the one to kill the animal, this gaining much favour with the king. What could possibly go wrong?

On the morning of the hunt, King Oeneus stood outside his

palace walls, and announced to the gathered warriors that the boar had been released in the forested area nearby, far away from any villages. On the drop of a red flag by the king, the eager warriors took to their heels in the direction of the forest, carrying weapons they honestly believed would present for them the desired kill. The king and his family awaited news of the successful warrior, and waited, and waited, until the sun had well and truly set for the day. Thinking the hunt might move into a second day, the king retired for the night, still hopeful that one of his warriors would soon bring to him the dead animal.

After three days, several warriors returned, with nothing to show for their time apart from many lacerations, cuts, deep wounds, and worse of all, their thoroughly battered egos. After five days, all warriors had returned without any success. Shortly after, news reached the king of a sighting of the boar from a village far, far away. This creature had managed to escape the forest and ended up in a corn field with at least six javelins protruding from all parts of its body, hurled at the boar from desperately worried farmers. The king was disappointed with his warriors and praised the farmers for killing the wild animal.

After the disaster of the first hunt, we move forward thirteen moons, and an even larger boar was ready to be sacrificed in the name of military training and entertainment. Villagers began taking wagers on how long the boar would take to escape, which of the king's personal guard would be injured in the hunt, and a whole manner of other less-than-complimentary, anatomically impossible situations involving wild boar and the king's guard. Local bards started to sing comedic songs lambasting the warriors lack of hunting ability, and one even suggested all girls under the age of thirteen should be permitted to enter. Why not? They could not do any worse!

On the night before the boar's release, there were two quite distinctly different groups of men gathered in Calydon. First, there were drinking halls filled with songs, laughter, mockery, and many libations to Dionysus. Second, there were the agitated and nervous warriors, soberly paying carefully measured libations to Artemis. Finally, the moment arrived when warriors could redeem their lost honour, but that was not to be. Once again, each warrior attempted to win the prize of killing the animal on their own and did not form alliances nor work in a cohesive hunting party. Once again, the boar escaped, more riotous songs were sung that evening, and in a repeat of the previous year, a different village nearby cornered and killed the wild beast, this time after attacking their sheep. The village strategy was simple: They worked together!

King Oeneus was furious and rightfully worried. Furious at his warriors for not capturing a simple boar, and worried that enemies might see this a sign of weakness and attack his kingdom at any moment. He need not have been too concerned, as no one attacked his palace or tried to take his lands during those unsuccessful boar hunting years. Maybe any potential enemy were afraid of the villagers, and not the king's warriors!

It was many years later that the king dispatched heralds to announce a hunting event, with yet another wild boar, but this time, the winner would be awarded the pelt and tusk once captured and killed. Previously, there was no prize offered for the capture, only the glory and honour of completing the task. For the first time, the event was to be open to any hunter from surrounding lands, and on the day of the hunt, over a hundred hunters gathered from far and wide to participate. They came from the north as far as Macedon, south as far as Sparta, and from many islands. King Oeneus was convinced his reputation would be restored when he saw the quality of hunters who had gathered.

Chiron heard about this special event and dispatched several of his senior boys to join in the hunt for the wild boar, including a sixteen-year-old Jason. Under the tutelage of Chiron, Jason had learned to stalk, track and kill wild game as well the most experienced of hunters. His accuracy with javelin and arrows over distance was excellent. Jason could move through forests, over twigs and light branches without making a sound. He had learned to hunt animals, not by recklessly making a noise, bounding through bush and bracken, but by silently stalking his prey, just like a wild animal would do. You could say he was a precocious talent, but he was very humble too. Humility was one of the principal lessons taught by his master, Chiron.

Jason and his friends arrived in Calydon the night prior to the hunt. Locating and securing a room to rest for the duration of the event, Jason decided to wander alone through the village and saw many of the men who would later join with him as argonauts. He also saw a young girl who he came to know as Atalanta, talking to a cafe owner regarding a room for the night when one of the rather inebriated guests thought he could lay his dirty, sweaty hands, on Atalanta. Within the blink of her eye, Atalanta had used her hidden knife to carve a rather large chunk from the forearm of her attacker, and now the blade was precariously close to his ugly bulging neck. Jason was instantly impressed with the ease shown in handling the attacker, and mightily happy with the use of her blade.

Also watching this incident was a young Meleager, the son of

King Oeneus. He immediately sprang to the defence of Atalanta and had the king's warriors take away the now heavily bleeding attacker.

"I did not ask for any assistance."

"You must be Atalanta" said the son of a king.

"And who are you" asked the female hunter.

"I am Meleager, son of King Oeneus."

"Please try to keep your imbecilic buffoons away from me, otherwise the next victim will not be so lucky."

"I will guarantee your safety, Atalanta."

"I do not need your guarantees prince. As you can see, I can look after my own safety."

With that brief conversation, Atalanta quickly departed to another establishment to seek a room for the night. Meleager carefully observed her departure and could not say a word. He was clearly in love!

Before I move on with the story, maybe I should give you some background to the prince. Meleager did not take part in the hunt on the first two disastrous occasions. Oeneus believed that his son was too young and forbade him. Also, the king only permitted his ephebic warriors to enter the competition, so keeping his son out of the hunt was easy. But not this time. With an open invitation, Meleager saw his chance to prove to his father, his ability, but most of all, he was seeking recognition that one day, he would be a worthy successor to his popular father as King.

The reason Meleager was able to watch the altercation between Atalanta and the attacker was simple. He was told by his father to enter the village with some of the king's personal guards and greet any man coming from lands far away. Meleager did not want to perform this task, because he too was intending to compete in the hunt. However, not wanting to antagonise his father, dutifully agreed to play his part in officially welcoming all participants equally.

Also watching the brief display of Atalanta's skills in dealing with an un-invited advance from a drunkard, Jason thought it was time to introduce himself to the prince.

Jason wore his long blonde hair tied at the nape of his neck with a leather strap and carried no weapons with him as he approached Meleager. Not dressed in anything but a rather dishevelled chiton, Jason most certainly did not look like one of the hunting guests, but more like a wine bar slave. Fearing a possible attack, one of the king's personal guards stepped in front of Jason, raised his short sword, and asked him to stop. Quickly surmising the situation, Jason put both his bare hands up in front of his face showing no evil intent, and clearly no weapon.

"Forgive my intrusion, but I am Jason, student of Chiron, I am here to compete in the hunt."

Instructing the guard to lower his weapon, Meleager asked Jason to approach.

"Forgive my guards. They are a little touchy with strangers in our village."

"I understand. I assure you, I come here only to compete in your boar hunt tomorrow."

To Meleager, Jason did not give the impression that he possessed any hunting skills at all. The guards were openly laughing at his appearance.

"I assure you good prince I do possess a little hunting ability."

"A little something I agree, but not hunting ability," said one guard chuckling to himself at his attempt at humour.

Meleager stopped his guards from laughing and asked one of them to hand over a javelin.

"If you can throw this, and strike that tree, I will believe you Jason."

"Which tree?"

One of the guards pointed to a large, shady mulberry tree about fifty paces from where they were standing. Each of the guards recommenced their laughing. One even said that the 'boy' could not possibly throw that far, let alone strike the tree.

Jason calmly turned to the guard who uttered the *'boy'* comment and issued a challenge.

"If I cannot strike the tree, I will leave Calydon immediately. If I can strike the tree, I keep the javelin."

The guard laughed even harder.

"Boy, if you can hit the target, you can keep all our javelins. But I will add one more thing. If you can't, we will each kick you in the arse and send you on your way."

Meleager pondered the wager and agreed to its outcome. He asked Jason if the terms of the bet were fair to him, to which Jason nodded, uttering not a word. Jason turned to the spot where he was to hurl the weapon and carefully looked in all directions, other than at the target. The laughing guard handed him his javelin and jogged back to be with his mates. Each of the other four guards were bending down to rub dirt into their sandals and toes, intending to give Jason a filthy kick up the bum.

A small crowd gathered lining the sides of the road, carefully positioned to avoid being struck by a wayward javelin throw. One of the guards bellowed to all the people watching to stand well back. Some of the bystanders were beginning to take side bets as to the outcome. Jason's hunting companions saw what was happening, and came along, not to watch, but to take a wager as well. They all knew their friend's ability with the javelin, and pretended to talk up how bad he was, thus increasing the chance of taking home a rather sizable wager.

"Jason is our worst hunter. He is not here to hunt, but to carry *our* weapons."

"He might look pretty, but he throws like my little sister, and she can't even throw a goat's fleece!"

"He is actually our cook. Makes a rather tasty lentil soup too!"

"But given all that, we will still bet on him because he is our friend, and that is what friends do for each other."

With that banter, many bystanders eagerly wagered small amounts of silver, and even kraters of wine at any nearby wine bar. The friends had set a wonderful trap. Chiron would have been proud of them. However, there was the possibility that Jason may not win, but each of the four friends were supremely confident in his ability!

Atalanta slipped un-noticed into the crowd, wanting to steal a glimpse of the unfolding side-show. She stood unmoved, staring intently at Jason. I wonder what she thought of him at that moment? She could not possibly have known that Jason would become one of the most important people in her life.

Jason grasped the javelin carefully in his right hand, and held it above his shoulder, pointing to the tree. Raising it higher, and further behind his head, with his left hand he licked his fingers, rubbed spit on to the point of the weapon, and carefully judged its weight.

Meleager ordered the crowd to hush, which by this time, had

swelled to over two hundred eager onlookers. Jason stood rock solid still, looking like he was a painting on the side of a large ceramic vase. His pose was classical – poised to throw at a target unseen. Trusting his own ability, Jason sensed the importance of the situation, and calmly drew a line on the dirt with his left sandal.

"From here is where I will throw the javelin. Is this acceptable to you, sire?"

"Of course," replied Meleager nervously.

Jason cautiously walked back a further five paces. He carefully felt the weight of the projectile for a second time, and taking his time, looked into the eyes of various members of the crowd. Wiping the sweat from his brow with the hem of his chiton, Jason now turned his attention to the one remaining laughing guard and mouthed the following words. "Nice javelin."

The crowd was hushed, and the prince's buffoon guards displayed signs of nervous perspiration. Comically, Jason sucked his right forefinger and raised it in the air to give the impression of judging the wind direction and force.

"Just checking the wind."

Much laughter erupted, and Jason's disposition immediately switched into that of a mature hunter.

Ambling slowly towards the line in the dirt, Jason took one purposeful step forward with his left leg and hurled the javelin at the target. All eyes in the crowd watched the quivering weapon arc towards the tree. Within only a few heart beats, it landed with a thud. A direct hit!

The crowd erupted. The guards stood silently, mouths agape, and at least half the crowd began to demand their winnings. Meleager stared too, not at the target, not at the crowd, but at Jason.

There was something special about this young man. Atalanta chuckled. She disappeared as quickly as she arrived. Jason's friends gathered their winnings, and Jason now found himself standing in front of the previously laughing guard.

"If you would be so kind, I will take your weapons now."

The guards wanted to kill Jason, but Meleager stepped in to say "If any harm comes to that man, each of you will suffer more than simply losing a weapon. Is that clear?"

Jason seized all five javelins, and walked over to his friends, who by this stage, had collected enough pieces of silver and promises of wine to celebrate long into the night, and perhaps the rest of the week. They were more chuffed at the quality of their new weapons. As Jason turned to leave, Meleager extended his arm in friendship and asked who he was, and where he was from.

"I am a humble student of Chiron, as we all are, from Mt Pelion. We are simply here to participate in the hunt. We do not want any trouble."

"I assure you all. There will be no trouble from my guards. If you don't mind me asking – where is Mt Pelion, and who is Chiron?"

Jason took Meleager aside and gave a brief account of how he and his friends had come to live with Chiron, and what skills they were taught, without giving too much away. Meleager was impressed and asked Jason to visit him once more after the hunt, and before they left for home. Jason agreed.

Meleager wished them all well in the hunt, but not too well, as he was also a competitor.

Like Atalanta, Jason was not to know, but standing in that crowd were nearly ten men who would later join him on the voyage of a lifetime.

Forgive me for rambling on about this meeting, but I think it is important. Where was I? Oh yes, I was going to tell you about Atalanta!

Don't believe a word of any stories claiming Atalanta was abandoned at birth only to be raised by she-bears, rescued by hunters and who hunted in the wild with Artemis. The truth is far more interesting than any mythological meanderings a wayward bard could possibly invent!

Atalanta was born and raised by her father Schoeneus in Tegea, a city from the Peloponnese region of Arcadia. Her early life was nothing spectacular, but she did show some ability at running as a young girl. So much so, she was a champion athlete by the age of ten, regularly beating boys as well as girls her own age and older on a regular basis. Not satisfied at simply being a fast runner, Atalanta wanted to learn to beat the boys at other, more important things, such as weapon usage and hunting. By the age of fourteen, Atalanta was as good a hunter and talented in the use of weapons as any boy, woman, or man in her village. Her reputation was growing, as people came to Tegea to witness firsthand, her ability to hunt, run and fight.

News of the Calydonian boar hunt reached Arcadia, and specifically Tegea. Begging her father Schoeneus to allow her to compete, Atalanta soon gained his approval, and was sent with her older brother to Calydon. Atalanta did not want her brother to travel with her, but her father insisted. Her brother Alexius was much more interested in catching butterflies and insects, constructing poetry, or wrestling his male friends, and was therefore the perfect travelling companion to his much more outgoing sister.

The fact that she had even heard about the boar hunt is

testament to King Oeneus' ability to publicise the event widely. Anyway, Atalanta was no ordinary female athlete. She was the fastest most agile runner, gifted warrior and expert hunter ever known in Arcadia. She appeared perfectly normal, but her looks were not only deceiving, but one of her greatest gifts. Apart from the polished brooch holding the neck of her chiton, she carried an ivory carved quiver over her left shoulder, and in her left hand, carefully clutched her bow. Her prized possession was the leather belt around her waist which contained two knives, able to be accessed in an instant. Meleager was clearly smitten with her looks, and it wasn't long before he was in awe of her hunting abilities.

Later that night, after a hearty meal, Jason and his four friends quietly accepted their wine winnings and celebrated long into the early hours of the next day. Jason was reported to have said to his friends "life does not get any better than this."

CHAPTER 4

The hunt

J ason and his friends arose early on the day of the hunt, but their heads were somewhat heavier than normal. A brief wash in the Evinos river was all that the five friends needed to freshen up for the exciting day ahead. After a few dried figs with honey and bread washed down by copious gulps of clear water, the boys chose their new javelins to bring with them and headed off to the king's palace, where the hunt was to begin.

Joining them along the road were about fifty other hopeful boar hunters. Atalanta walked with her butterfly catching brother, Meleager was accompanied by the same five guards, but this time, they were extremely circumspect and contrite when they spotted Jason and his friends. Jason didn't know any of the other participants but let me give you a brief list of who was there. Naming all of them is pointless, but as only time would tell, some of the hunters would later be invited to join Jason on the adventure of their lives. Apart from these future argonauts were fathers of, or actual heroes of the Trojan blockade. For example, Nestor, the King of Pylos was a hunter, as well as Peleus, father of Achilles, Telamon, brother of Peleus, and the King of Ithaca Laertes, father of Odysseus. Some of the future argonauts were Amphiarus, the twins Castor and Pollux, Ekhion, Iphicles, the twin of Hercules, Ancaeus, the prince from Samos, the future king of Athens Theseus, and the uncles of Meleager, Kometes and Prothous.

Making an appearance along the road was a youthful Orpheus, who was playing made-up songs on his lyre about what he saw and who he knew. Jason was instantly attracted to his exuberance and made a note to try to talk to him later.

On the appointed hour, King Oeneus delivered a short speech, and then wished the hunters well in their pursuits. He said that the person who takes down the boar will be awarded its hide and pelt. More importantly, the successful hunter will be referred to all over the known world as the best hunter in the land.

The weather on the day was not ideal. Having rained for most of the night, the ground was damp, puddles of water had pooled in all areas of the forest where the boar was released, and Jason thought some hunting methods would be rendered useless given the wet and muddy conditions. Tracking the boar would be best done using mature hunting techniques, and not the immature approach that many of the participants seemed to be taking.

With the drop of the traditional red rag, the hunt was underway. Jason and his group were still feeling the effects of the night before and decided to simply watch the proceedings up close and personal, instead of trying to catch the animal. One of the friends, Kristus suggested they split up to observe each of the other participants, and to report back to each other later that night, and to Chiron when they returned home. All agreed, and the five friends parted company. Jason made a point of following Meleager, as he had heard only positive reports of his hunting capabilities the previous night in the tavern between drinks. Kristus attempted to follow Theseus and the other three disappeared into the forest.

Although Meleager did not capture the boar, he played a part in its downfall, by assisting a group of equally young hunters, including the only female ever to stake a rightful claim to capturing the animal. Atalanta's appearance in the hunt caused quite a stir. Many of the older male hunters refused to allow her to join them and approached King Oeneus to complain bitterly regarding her admission in the competition. King Oeneus explained that his rules did not say anything about who could enter.

The hunt was over rather earlier than expected. Almost all the hunters took to the fields and forest in earnest to begin their search, but Meleager and Atalanta waited until the remainder of the hunting pack had vanished from sight, both walking separately in the direction the main group was not heading. They both rightly thought a wild boar would not be stupid, and could hear the baying pack approach, thus getting out of its way.

It was Atalanta that spotted the boar first. Carefully and quietly, she drew her bow and fired an arrow that caused the animal to lose footing and crash into a large rock while trying to escape. Fortunately for Meleager, he was near the rock and once he saw the wounded boar, drove his javelin through its neck, bringing the noble beast to its knees, and eventual death. His personal guards raised the successful capture alarm by blowing loudly on a bull's horn, and within a hundred heart beats, a crowd of hunters were standing around the dead animal congratulating Meleager with pats on his back and rubbing his hair.

Jason happened to be in the best possible place to witness the arrow of Atalanta strike its intended target, and then the final death blow by Meleager. Kristus and Theseus were close by, and saw the final blow just as Theseus was readying himself to heave his javelin, only to be beaten by Meleager.

The uncles Kometes and Prothous did not observe any of the crucial wounds inflicted but were quickly brought up to speed by Meleager's personal guards. Thinking of themselves as the senior royal officials, Kometes and Prothous announced to the now sizable group that Meleager would be awarded the pelt and tusks.

"I probably did cause this proud animal to breathe its final breath, but I cannot claim the prize. If it were not for the first arrow fired by Atalanta, I would not have been able to do what I did. She should be declared the winner."

Kometes was the first uncle to speak.

"Women do not belong out here hunting wild boar. It is an affront to every man here that they must work alongside women. Meleager killed the boar, so he must be the winner."

"I agree with my brother. Even though we allowed Atalanta to compete, she did not kill the animal. I say that the prize is rightfully Meleager's."

"No. I will not hear of it. All of you have heard of the skills of Atalanta. Her hunting ability is not in question. Although I did cause the animal to die, if I had not been there, it would have taken

Atalanta only one more arrow to finish the beast. I was lucky. I will not claim the prize. It is to be awarded to Atalanta, to do with it as she wants."

What happened next is subject to wild speculation. It has been said that the uncles were so incensed that they attempted to block the prize ceremony, only to be beaten off by their nephew. Some even say Meleager killed them both because they disagreed with his judgement. Some have the remaining hunters banding together to support Atalanta and her rightful claim.

The last comment was closest to the truth. Kometes and Prothous were such weak individuals, once they could see one hundred of the finest hunters and warriors in the land agreeing with the outcome, they backed down as quickly as they could, in the face of overwhelming odds. Nobody was killed, and certainly, Atalanta was clearly the winner. She was free to claim her prize.

That night, Jason, Kristus and the other Mt Pelion boys had much to drink and eat courtesy of their amazing good fortune a day or so earlier. All Jason could remember the next morning, waking from a drunken stupor, was the sound of the most beautiful voice and lyre playing somewhere nearby that put him to sleep. It was then that he noticed they were all sharing hay and shit with several donkeys!

CHAPTER 5

One sandal

J ason woke on the morning of his twentieth year with many competing thoughts running through his head. His time on Mt Pelion had come to an end, and he was soon to return to a family he did not know. When boys like Jason reached this important moment in their lives, they generally had two thoughts.

Their first thought was that of all the special memories of lessons learned and time spent with his extended family. The other troubling and uncertain thought was the worrying one. He now had to return to a life, long forgotten, or to a life unknown. When boys came to be on the mountain at such a young age, they had no memory of their previous existence. They could not remember their birth mothers, fathers, brothers or sisters, nor any other relatives. Some came from broken families, to be set on the right path under the tutelage of Chiron. But one thing was certain. They would all depart with the knowledge and skills necessary to live and thrive in a world outside the confines of this place. Each boy had to leave when this momentous day was over.

After a nervous and quiet breakfast with his friends, Jason prepared for his final talk with Chiron. Not so much a talk, but the final lesson. He had learned many things. There was so much more to learn, but not here. It was time to depart, but this last lesson would set him on a journey he could not have imagined in his wildest dreams.

Chariklo called for Jason to come to her table. She had grown quite fond of Jason. Afterall, she had raised him since he was too young to walk, feed himself or talk. Jason had come to accept Chariklo was not his mother, but to him, she was the principal matriarchal figure he had known all his life. Chiron was clearly not his father, but to Jason, he loved him as if he was his father. As for the daughters, Jason had come to love them as if they were his sisters. Pelionides, Okyro and Karysto had departed the mountain home long ago to start their own lives, but every year, returned to spend time with their parents. On one occasion, Pelionides brought along her own children, and both of her sisters had introduced their new husbands to Jason.

Jason sat in front of Chariklo with his hands resting gently in his lap. He loved this position, because nearly ten years before, the very chair he was now sitting on was nothing more than a stump from a recently felled tree. This was Jason's first lesson in wood carving. He loved that chair.

"Jason. You know what we must talk about today."

"Yes, I do. I don't know whether to be nervous, excited or frightened of what you are about to tell me."

"You should take what we say to you and use it for creating your life away from here."

Chiron walked past Jason, sitting on his carved wooden log, talking to Chariklo, and asked him to come for a short walk. Chariklo stood first, followed by a confused Jason. Chiron walked briskly out of the kitchen area and started to make his way towards the top of Mt Pelion, with his two surrogate parents leading the way. To reach this place, Jason could do so blindfolded. One of the lessons taught to Jason was to help negotiate movement through forested areas when vision is impeded, relying on memory, and a complete reliance and trust on the other senses.

The top of Mt Pelion used to be covered in rocks, bushes, and trees, but these days, all vegetation and rocky areas had been totally cleared to reveal a slightly level field of soft grass. From the centre of this field, it was possible to view the horizon in every direction. Visible from this very spot was the city of Iolchus, far away in the distance, but not too far. Chariklo spoke first.

"Jason, your parents are still alive, and live in Iolchus. As you know, we were never going to tell you this until today. Your parents know you are here. In fact, they are the ones who are responsible for you being here."

Chiron sensed Jason's next question but beat him to the answer.

"Your parents asked me to look after you. If we had not taken you in, you would surely have died at the hands of your uncle, the king. Your father should have been king, but that was not what transpired."

Chiron, his wife, and their prized and favourite pupil sat together on the soft grass while Jason's parentage was fully laid bare. Chiron did not hold back and told Jason everything. Jason listened as if it was a story about someone else. He was emotionless yet completely engrossed in what he was hearing. Over the previous few years, Jason had been sent to Iolchus by either Chiron or Chariklo for simple errands. Mostly, these errands were to purchase necessary items that would not bring attention on the purchaser and not raise any suspicion. Jason learned that these items were not necessary at all, but each trip was designed to assist Jason study the layout and culture of his native city. Each trip into Iolchus was different, with a purpose only known by Chiron and Chariklo.

Looking back, Jason understood the true reason for these excursions, and smiled at their cunningly designed strategically significant purpose.

"And here was I thinking that you really needed imported olive oil, fish sauce or what was the last visit for – cucumber and tomato seeds."

"Your parents will not be expecting you. We have had no contact with them since you arrived here. King Pelias does not know you are alive. Remember, he thinks you died soon after birth. Be careful with the king Jason. Never forget what you have learned with us. Never stray from your path to honour. Never forget that a flight of virtue will take you higher than wings of evil. We would rather see that you are defeated than be dishonorably victorious."

Jason was not entirely sure what those words truly meant, but he was confident that one day, he would discover their meaning.

All three descended from the peak of Mt Pelion and made their way to the food preparation area, where the other boys were now taking their morning comestibles. Jason could also have walked this trip blindfolded as the smells of freshly cooked bread and the sounds of chatty boys was enough to guide him. Once in the bosom of the group, it was time for him to say farewell. Every boy expected this day, and each one approached Jason like a brother would wishing his sibling on a good and prosperous journey. Chiron and his wife were used to these farewells and did not shed any tears. Once Jason had finally left them, they simply returned their complete focus to the day's lessons for the remaining boys.

Packing his meagre possessions into his leather bag, another useful item Jason made from the skins of hunted animals, he left his home of twenty years to commence the next part of his lifelong learning.

Wandering alone down the mountain, through the familiar forest of his life, Jason was not sure what to think. He did not really have any specific plan, other than to go to Iolchus and confront King Pelias. Explain to him who he was and see what would happen. Not much of a plan really, don't you think?

At the base of Mt Pelion, the Anavros river flows gently by for most of the year, but on this particular day, the torrent had risen rapidly due to recent rain. What would normally be a simple crossing required some degree of careful planning and thought. Jason had visited this spot many times throughout his life, and knew of places where even at peak flow, the river could be forded effectively, although not without a degree of difficulty.

The precise point where Jason decided to cross was a place he had done so before, but not when the river levels were up to his chest. Using the two spears he had, Jason tied the leather bag to them and held his few belongings above his head, then carefully entered the fast-flowing stream, ever cautious of the slippery rocks lurking dangerously below. At about the halfway point of the crossing, he slipped on one such rock, but managed to keep his belongings dry. After the final rock was used as a stepping point, Jason felt soft sand under his feet. The sand made him sink almost to his knees, but he was close to the other side. After a final push forward, and he collapsed on the dry riverbank. Carefully checking the contents of his leather bag, he noticed something odd.

All objects were safe, but one item of clothing was sadly absent. Looking at his feet, Jason saw that he had lost one of his sandals. Not quite sure where it went missing, the quick flow of the river, slippery rocks and deep, soft sand meant that it could be anywhere, so he took the only course of action available to him. Remove the other one and travel the remainder of the journey in bare feet.

Carefully watching from a distance was an old woman, washing her clothes in the river. Jason did not see her at first, but once she started laughing at him, he too burst out laughing.

"Can you come back again tomorrow and do that again? It was the funniest thing I have seen in a long time."

"I am not sure I will be here tomorrow, but I am so glad to have given you some joy."

"Are you one of Chiron's boys?"

"How do you know that?"

"Why else would you be coming from that side of the river carrying your possessions above your head, considering how high it is these days? Let me guess. You must be twenty years old today, and it is time to leave. Am I right?"

"You are right. How do you know this?"

"Let me say that I have seen many boys like you come down

from that mountain, cross this river, and leave down that track, travelling towards Iolchus. But you are the first to lose a sandal!"

"You seem to know a lot about us. What happens to the boys after they come by this way?"

"I have never seen any of them again. But you look different. What is your name?"

Jason told her his name, and she suddenly fell to her knees on the soft sand. She put her hands out as if to ask for help in getting up, and Jason obliged and offered her a helping hand. She stood looking up into his eyes and said something to him that made Jason take a step back.

"You have your father's eyes and your mother's hair. I would recognise you anywhere. I am a friend of your parents, and an enemy of the king, although he does not know the extent of my involvement in your life. My name is Julia, and I was the nurse to your mother when you were born Jason."

Jason was by now most interested in her and her fantastic story. Remember, but he had only just recently learned who *he* was.

The two talked for a long time. Julia sat and stroked Jason's hair, and he listened intently to all she had to say. She told him how King Pelias had thought she was a perfect person to spy on Polymede, but not realising Julia had been a friend of Polymede's since birth. Jason asked many questions and Julia did her best to respond.

Armed with this new information, Jason decided the best course of action was to try to make Iolchus by night fall, and rose from the sandy river beach to make his way.

"Wait a little while for me please Jason. I would like to walk with you some of the way. I do not live far from here and you can walk me to my home. I live alone. That is not quite true. I have four goats and three sheep. They keep me company, my skin warm and my belly full."

"There is one more thing I want to tell you. It is a kind of confession. I have been waiting at the river for you to cross for many days now. I know that Chiron's boys leave after their twentieth birthday, and, well, you know that I was present at your birth, so I knew how old you were. And I knew you were living with Chiron and Chariklo, so it wasn't too hard to guess the time of your arrival at the river crossing."

"Do my parents know I am coming?"

"In a way yes, but they do not know when. I will not tell them. That is news for you to share."

Jason and Julia walked along the track to her house. Along this part of the journey, Julia spoke of Jason's parents, how she knew his mother, and when she met his father and knew that they were meant to be with each other. She also told Jason of his grandparents Cretheus and Tyro, but when she tried to explain further the failed marriages, number of siblings and family troubles, Jason asked her to stop. It was getting too much to bear in such a short space of time.

"Julia. Stop! I can't remember all of this. It is too much for one day."

Julia stopped, and pointed ahead to the gate to her quaint house. The two parted company, promising to meet again one day, when Jason had decided what to do with his life.

Once inside, Julia immediately picked up her krater of her best wine, poured a drink into a favourite cup, sat by the now smoldering fire, re-lit the ashes with dry sticks of recently gathered kindling wood, curled up on a fleece of one of her long since departed sheep and took a healthy gulp of wine. This was the happiest day of her life.

Jason by now was well on his way, bare-footed, walking along the dirt road to Iolchus. He too had a smile. The city was still a distance away, and Jason was beginning to feel the cold. Ahead to his right on the now deserted track, he saw a rooming house, and inquired if he could spend the night. All they had remaining was a stable with some confused animals, but that didn't bother him at all. Considering the many nights he and his friends had made shelter out of whatever they could find before it became dark on Mt Pelion, a dry, warm stable with fresh straw was luxury. Before sleep took its hold, Jason dreamed of meeting Atalanta again. Not in any romantic way, but in a purely friendly way. He wondered how her life had been in the past four years, and how many other boars she managed to slay.

Sleep did not come quickly. At an inn nearby, a crowd had gathered to listen to a musician, and Jason could hear the gentle, sweet melodies of a lyre, and the honeyed voice of a man singing. Given the lack of any wind, the night air was still and cold, so these beautiful sounds wafted gently into the barn where Jason was as snug as a bug in a woollen rug. Sleep eventually arrived, and Jason soon completed his first night away from the safe confines of life under Chiron's guidance.

On waking, Jason could not get the ear worm of the beautiful sounds from the previous night out of his head. Who was that singer? Why did he sound so familiar? How could someone play the lyre so well? Jason had learned music with Chiron, but not like that. He had to find out.

After a quick wash in the same water troughs as the animals, which didn't worry Jason one bit, he gathered his possessions in his leather bag, tied his one sandal to the belt around his waist, and headed out into the brisk morning air. However, he had one piece of clothing very different to those of the people he noticed along the road that morning.

The last animal Jason killed on Mt Pelion was a leopard. Chiron had discovered the wild animal terrorising lambs and offered the pelt to Jason if he could hunt and kill the beast. Not one for backing out of a hunt, Jason successfully stalked the animal and killed it as soon as it attempted to take a new-born lamb away to eat. So pleased with this kill, Jason gutted the leopard and fashioned its fur into a cloak.

A little way along the road, Jason came across a man selling freshly baked bread. On Mt Pelion, baking bread was only undertaken one day each week. In his early years, Jason thought the taste of fresh bread was such a delight, he had to try some. Bread was not the only item for sale. A tasty supply of olives and honey rounded out his first morning meal. Barely twenty paces along the road, another seller offered some highly watered-down wine. Jason could not have wished for a heartier breakfast.

Closer to the city of Iolchus, houses were becoming more prevalent, and the number of people on the road increased. So too did the gawking. Jason thought it may have been his lack of suitable footwear, but when one person commented to him on his fine fur, he realised that he was the only person wearing an animal fur, no one was bare foot and everyone else wore sandals.

A sandal maker even offered to sell him a new pair, specially made for his sized feet, but Jason was extremely comfortable without footwear. In fact, growing up, he rarely wore any kind of sandal. By not wearing them, the soles of his feet became harder and more able to withstand the terrain of any part of Mt Pelion. Jason had always thought any sandal as a luxury item, not essential clothing. Being bare foot was normal for him. However, he did wonder if strapping the one good sandal on his belt was the cause of all these stares!

He soon came to realise that the sight of a stranger walking with two spears, a leopard fur over his shoulders was a cause for concern for some. People walking towards him on the road into Iolchus moved out of the way, fearing he may have been some kind of bandit. To offset these constant stares and sideways movements of wary road users, Jason took to smiling more, and offering a "good morning" and "lovely day" to any person he saw.

Arriving short of the main entrance to the city, Jason spotted a young boy climbing a stone wall in a clumsy attempt to reach some eggs in a bird's nest high above. In a last-ditch effort to strain an outstretched palm to gather in the eggs, the boy fell, and Jason heard the all-too familiar sound of a bone breaking. The boy was in agony and people came from all over to offer assistance, but mostly to simply stare at the poor unfortunate lad.

People stood around the boy, not offering any help until one old woman came out with a cup of water. Another older woman gave the boy a blanket to place under his head, but no one else offered any help. Unable to resist any more, Jason quickly approached the boy, asking the gathering crowd to step back. Seeing this leopard skinned, bare footed, long hair, disheveled individual coming close, some young men tried to block Jason's path. With a simple manoeuvre of his arms, Jason managed to pass through without any fuss and bent down to cradle the obviously broken leg and place the blanket under it to help protect the boy from damaging his limb any further.

Chiron had taught all his boys to mend broken limbs, and use whatever equipment was close and necessary to help in the healing process.

"Can someone please get me two sticks, an old chiton, and a cup of strong wine – immediately?"

Nothing happened, and the boy let out a terrible groan.

"Now, you sheep shaggers! Get me what I asked for and bring it here now."

One of the young men pushed aside a moment earlier raced off to find sticks, and a shopkeeper selling baskets handed over an old chiton used to wipe sweat away from her brow on a hot day. A cup of strong wine also emerged.

Now he had the items needed, Jason took a quick swig of wine, tore the chiton into long strips, and he broke the sticks into lengths necessary for the boy's leg. At this stage, the boy had stopped wailing, but was still deeply hurt. The shopkeeper was cradling his head in her lap, and Jason was ready to set the leg.

Speaking to the shopkeeper and asking the young men to help hold the boy steady, Jason carefully and quickly stretched the boy's leg and reset the bone in a straight line. The boy screamed at the intense pain, and then soon stopped.

"Give him a drink, and make sure he takes the rest of this sheep's piss."

By now, a considerable crowd of onlookers were praising the strange, leopard skinned, bare footed, broken leg mender. A woman, obviously the boy's mother arrived and bent down to care for her little boy.

"Thank you, sir. Thank you."

Jason stood back from the mother and son, slightly bemused by all this sudden attention, when only a few short moments before the accident, people were avoiding him. Suddenly, another cup of strong, unadulterated wine emerged, and was thrust into the dusty hands of Jason. It took one quick gulp, and Jason was now feeling the effects of the rather potent, and highly pungent grape juice.

"Do you people not make wine from grapes? This surely is from a sheep or goat, or perhaps a unique blend of both?"

At this stage, a strange feeling came over all the crowd. After Jason drank his wine, all eyes in the crowd were trained on a man riding a chariot approaching from inside the city gates. Once they noticed who the person was, eyes quickly dropped to the ground, with no-one wanting to make eye contact with him.

Seeing a crowd standing around a little boy who appeared to be crying, the chariot rider stopped his horses, jumped off onto the dusty road and asked what was going on.

"This little boy broke his leg and this man helped to fix it" came one reply.

"This man here was the only one who knew what to do to help the little boy."

In a hushed tone, Jason asked the nearest women standing near him who the chariot rider was, and he was told that it was King Pelias.

"Is that so? He doesn't look much of a man."

"Looks are deceiving my friend. This king is the most deceptive, nasty, insensitive person I know. Beware of him."

King Pelias casually walked over to where the boy was lying, and asked in a rather harsh voice "Can someone please remove this urchin from my road? My horses need to pass." With that, King Pelias mounted his chariot, and rode off down the road leaving a cloud of dust in his wake.

"See what I mean friend?"

"I'm not afraid of him. Maybe I will visit him when he returns."

The mother of the little boy approached Jason and offered him anything he wanted. Clearly seeing that this family were poor, Jason simply said that all he wanted was for her son to get well.

"Keep him off that leg for at least ten days, and slowly let him stand for a little while each day. Encourage him to do that for another thirty days, and he will slowly regain his strength. The leg will mend itself, but don't rush it."

"By the way, there is one thing you can do for me."

"Just name it," said the mother.

I am looking for the house of Aeson and Polymede. Do you know where they live?"

"Anyone here can help you find them. They do not live far from here. They are good people. Everyone likes them."

The mother asked a child who was a friend of her sons to show the stranger to the house of Aeson. With that, Jason said his goodbyes, gathered his possessions and walked to the house of the parents he did not know.

CHAPTER 6

Aeson and Polymede

Jason's parents had never given up hope of being reunited with their son. They had also never given up any hope that one day, Jason would take his rightful place on the throne of Iolchus. Since the fateful day that their baby was taken by Julia to live with Chiron and Chariklo, they had heard nothing of their son. They were under no illusion that he would survive at all, just hoping that he would not perish.

Aeson and Polymede lived a simple life as farmers, like most of the people around them in Iolchus. Living in the city and working on farmland a mere walk or donkey ride away was considered normal, and honest. They did have two more children after Jason, two girls, Daira and Sophia, who still lived with their parents. For fear of King Pelias discovering the truth, Aeson and Polymede had never told the girls they had an older brother.

So scared that they might have another male child, Aeson and Polymede were strangely happy that they did not produce another boy, and were totally devoted to the girls. There were times when Aeson wondered what it would be like to live with his son, but he had to suppress those feelings, and put them far away in the deep recesses of his mind. But once a year, on the celebration of the birth of their first-born child, Aeson and Polymede walked every street Iolchus, looking into the eyes of any boy who would be the same age as Jason, and smiling at them.

The day started out like any other. Aeson loaded his donkeys for the short walk to his farm, and Polymede, together with the girls, commenced preparations for the day's meals. It was mid-morning, and Aeson had returned with yet more vegetables to sell and for their own consumption. Along with the loaded sacks on his beast of burden, Aeson had a lamb trailing along behind tied to his saddle by a rope. This little animal was to be slaughtered later that day, have its blood drained, and then butchered. Aeson often gave most of the meat away to those less fortunate than themselves. For people who had little income, or anything to trade, Aeson always felt that he should look after these people. Knowing that he could have been king, giving this meat away was his way of sharing what he had with those who had precious little. He behaved like a king. He felt like a king.

The timing could not have been better, but the moment Aeson arrived home with the lamb and vegetables, Jason and the small boy arrived.

"See that man there? That is Aeson. Goodbye."

Waving his goodbyes to the boy as the urchin ran off at such a pace, dust was being kicked up behind his feet, Jason turned around to look directly into the eyes of his father. Aeson thought to himself what a handsome young man the stranger was and asked him to help him with the sacks still tied to the donkey. Jason had a strange feeling he had been at this place before. On his many trips into the city for Chiron, he was sure he had passed this way on several occasions. Past this very house, and even past these very people.

Carefully laying down his down his spears and leather bag, and cautiously removing his leopard pelt, Jason approached Aeson, still gazing into the eyes of the man who was his father. Now, they were only a body length apart.

"Are you Aeson, husband to Polymede, brother to the king, and father of Jason?"

Clearly taken aback by the brashness of this stranger, Aeson said 'yes,' but that his son had died many years ago.

"Do you know the nurse, Julia?"

By now, Aeson was becoming agitated, and angry. He thought this man might have been sent by King Pelias to create yet more trouble. Jason quickly noticed a change in his father's demeanor and said the words Aeson had been hoping to hear for twenty years.

"I am Jason, your son!"

His mother screamed in delight and rushed to embrace her long-lost son. Once Polymede had released Jason from the tight grip any pankration teacher would be proud of, and Aeson had stopped crying, Sophia and Daira wandered outside to see what all the fuss was about. Within a few more heartbeats, a small crowd had gathered around Polymede, Aeson and Jason. The girls felt that the occasion was important, but had no idea who this young man was, why their parents were hugging and crying, and why a crowd milled around them.

Aeson and son Jason stood with their hands on each other's shoulders, looking into each other's eyes, trying to make sense of what they were feeling. Polymede stood back a few paces and said to the girls "I think we need to go inside the house. Your father and I have something to tell you both."

For the remainder of that day, wine flowed, freshly baked bread arrived, honey and olives from clay jars appeared from nowhere, but most importantly, a family was finally talking and eating together for the first time. Sophia and Daira could not leave Jason alone. So excited they were to have a big brother, the smothered him with questions and did not even listen for his responses. Sophia was fascinated with Jason's hair, and kept stroking it, weaving it around her fingers and even pressing her nose to his long, blonde locks.

As sure as night follows day, it was not long before news of this recent arrival reached the king. Pelias was reported to be very calm on hearing this news. After all, he had heard from the oracle at Delphi to expect something soon from a man wearing one sandal.

Pelias had installed many spies all over the city. He typically chose vulnerable people who could not say no to a king's demands. People who dared not challenge the king or refuse to gather evidence for fear of losing their freedom, or even their lives. Stories were spread about such people who dared to say no, and who were never heard of again. Whether or not this happened is difficult to know, but there had to be some degree of truth in the stories.

One of Pelias' spies was a neighbour of Aeson, and observed

the crowds gathering all afternoon. Not being on speaking terms with Aeson, who most likely knew the man to be a lickspittle of the king, the man hurriedly raced to the palace to inform on his neighbour. Safely grasping a piece of silver for his troubles, the man departed and slunk back home to share his new-found wealth with his long-suffering wife.

Once the adoring crowds had quietened down, and the only people remaining in the house were direct family, Aeson and Polymede explained fully their story about how Jason came into the world, and how he went to live with Chiron on Mt Pelion. The girls stopped talking long enough to listen intently while Jason attempted to condense two decades of his life into those few hours.

By morning, after the barest of sleep, a bleary eyed Polymede answered the door when a loud knock woke them all. Knocking on the door, waking all inhabitants inside the humble home, was one of the King's personal guards.

"Open up. Open up in the name of the King."

"What is it?" yelled a clearly not-yet-awake Polymede.

"Open up this door immediately, or I will be forced to..."

"What is it?"

The guard did not enter the house as the door opened, but instead stood rather menacingly in the doorway bellowing his instructions.

"King Pelias demands to know who the stranger is who has entered this house."

"Why does the king want to know this?" asked Polymede.

Clearly the guard was a few sheep short of a flock, and simply restated his instructions. I don't think king's guards were employed for their intelligence.

"The stranger is from out of town, and he has lost a sandal. We are making a new one for him. Tell our beloved King Pelias that the stranger will be leaving as soon as we have made his new footwear."

Obviously confused by this enigmatic, yet mysterious response, the guard departed and took the message to his employer. When Pelias heard the reason for this stranger's appearance in the city, he remembered the dire warning from the Oracle and slumped back into his chair. All colour drained from his face. His palms became sweaty. Once composed enough, Pelias rose from his chair, walked to the window, and let the cool breeze wash his face and thoughts. "Get my chariot. Now, you idiot!"

"Who was that?" asked Aeson as he rose from his slumber.

"Pelias knows Jason is here. We must be careful," explained Polymede.

Jason knew what he needed to do to have the king forfeit his crown and install the right and true king. Ever since Chiron had informed him of his parentage, Jason had thought of how he could attempt to claim what was rightfully his, if his own father agreed.

"Father. I have a plan. I cannot visit Pelias on my own. He would no doubt invite me in, but I cannot be sure he will not have me killed immediately, by one of his moronic guards hiding behind a tapestry. I have friends who might be able to help me."

What Jason was referring to, were a few of his former Mt Pelion friends who had since departed the care of Chiron and who were now living a normal life somewhere nearby.

"Father, Chiron taught me many things, but most of all, he taught me how to use weapons if I am in trouble. Can you help me locate some of my friends who will come to my aid and accompany me when we visit Pelias? Do you have anyone who can slip away from the city and find my friends?"

"Jason. I do. I can call on a dear friend immediately."

The friends Jason wanted to find were all at some time, students of Chiron, and therefore in Jason's eyes, his brothers. People he could depend on and trust. People he really knew. His father's helper soon arrived, and Jason gave him the names and possible locations of the young men he needed to find quickly.

The helper was a man a few years older than Aeson. Jason took one look at his father's friend and wondered if he could carry out this rather important task. The man was very thin, hunched over, and walked with a limp.

"Are you sure this man can find my friends? I doubt he could even find one of your missing goats!"

"Son. Never judge a man by his appearance."

At this last comment, the hunched over elderly man suddenly stood upright, and walked over to Jason to look him firmly and confidently in the eyes.

"Jason. My name is Aegeus. I too was a student of Chiron. I do believe that I was one of the first intake of boys given over to his care."

"One minute you were hunched over. Now you stand perfectly. Why?"

"As you father said. Never judge a man by his appearance. My story can wait for another day. But I promise you this. If I cannot find your friends, they do not want to be found. When you were young, did Chiron teach you how to find boys that ran away and hid? Did he teach you how to walk over the forest floor without making a sound? Did he teach you the secret calls of animals and birds? Did he teach you the special calls you made to locate your friends when hunting? Those noises that helped you to communicate with each other, without frightening your prey?"

"I am sorry to have judged you. Forgive my impudence."

"No need Jason. My current appearance is a ploy to fool people into misjudging me. Clearly, I am good at it. Now then, tell me who you want found, and where I might find them. One thing you will learn is that we students of Chiron stick together. You will come to understand this in the coming years. I won't be searching on my own. If you understand my point."

With that simple lesson in humility, Jason gave Aegeus the details of the people he wanted to help him. One of the friends was Hippomenes, who had joined Jason on the boar hunt four years prior. Hippomenes was a small man and had the cunning of a fox and rat rolled into one. Jason and Hippomenes spent many nights trapping and capturing animals alive to bring back to Chiron so that they could be used to teach young boys about how the animals lived, ate, hunted, and looked after their young.

Remember the boar hunt? I need to ask you this, just so that I know you are following this story.

On the hunt, Jason met Telamon and Peleus. I mentioned them briefly before, but I left out one important piece of information. Soon after the hunt ended, Jason and his Pelion friends were sharing stories about hunting with these brothers, and they were intrigued to learn that a person such as Chiron existed. They wanted to meet the teacher, and immediately after the post-hunt activities concluded, the two brothers agreed to visit Jason and the others on the mountain.

Normally, Chiron would not have been amenable to this, but

once Jason explained that these boys were eager to learn, Chiron agreed to let them visit. The brothers did more than visit. They stayed for two years!

The final person Jason wanted found was one of his oldest friends, Kristus. The two were inseparable when Kristus first joined the extended family of lost boys on Mt Pelion as a nine-year-old. Although Jason was two years younger, he took the new boy under his wing and soon became best friends, learning the skills imparted by Chiron. Kristus was fascinated by all things to do with wood, such as making fires, designing furniture, carving bowls, making weapons, and creating objects such as children's toys.

With limited instructions of where he might find these four friends of Jason, the man given the rather impossible task of locating four men and bringing them back in the short space of seven days departed. Aeson assured Jason that if his friend could not find his four friends, then they could not be found.

"He will be back with your friends before you know it. I am sure of it."

"How can you be so sure?"

"Son, there are many things you do not know yet. You may not have known about me, but I have been following your life secretly, through Aegeus and his contact with Chiron ever since you were given to him to care for you. I had to keep this a secret even from your mother and sisters. Remember, the king wanted you dead, and if he discovered you were still alive, we would have been killed, and all the people we know would have also been in mortal danger. Aegeus is a masterful tracker. Chiron has used his skills, the same skills you now have, to keep an eye on many of his past pupils. Not for any nefarious reasons, but simply to see how the boys have fared out in the real world. When travelling the length and breadth of our country, Aegeus can blend in perfectly. He is a human chameleon. When tracking his prey, he is invisible."

"I have never given a second thought to what may have happened to any of the boys after they left. It was never anything we talked about. I guess there was always a new boy coming in as one departed. No time to dwell on it. To know that Chiron cared for us so much is wonderful news to me."

In the days that followed, Aeson and Polymede did not receive any more home visits from royal guards, but the king was obviously nervous. Rumours began to spread that he was accepting no visitors for any reason. Delegations which had previously made appointments to meet with him were suddenly and abruptly turned away, without explanation. One of the king's suppliers of wine amphorae told Aeson that he had not delivered any wine in recent days. This was most unusual because the king was a notable wine drinker and loved to lavish his guests with an array of wine from many regions of the country. Guards were more noticeable at all gates, stopping anyone who wanted to enter the grounds of King Pelias' palace.

Jason enjoyed this valuable time, getting to know his parents and sisters, discovering all the little things about them that made them who they were. What did they like to eat? What clothes did they like to wear? Who were their friends? What flowers did they like to grow? Who were their neighbours? He spent much time with his father, talking about his own childhood, but one topic kept coming up? Why was Aeson not the King?

Aeson tried to explain to Jason, but Jason did not initially accept the explanation.

"I am going to visit King Pelias and demand our birthright. That is why I wanted to find my friends with me. I do not trust the king!"

"You cannot just walk in and demand to replace him. I know my stepbrother. He is evil, cunning, and not to be trusted under any circumstance. He will try to silence you."

"I am well aware of his personality and character. Chiron has kept me informed for many years of his traits, but I had no idea until only recently that I was related."

Conversations continued for days like this, only ever interrupted by eating, drinking, helping with work on the farm, sleeping and simply being with his family. On the fifth day, just as Aeson and Jason were about to leave the farm for their short walk home, they noticed five men approaching. Jason immediately, and without thinking, attempted to arm himself with his javelins, but before completing this simple task, done many times on Mt Pelion, Aeson told him to put them down.

"But they could be armed!"

"Jason. Look carefully at the man leading the other five."

Behind Aegeus were Hippomenes, Kristus, Oileus, Telamon and Peleus. The friends were singing a song taught to them many years before by Chariklo, while throwing small rocks at trees lining the path to Aeson's farm. Once Jason heard the song, his mind raced off to a time when he had sung this song, surrounded by boys circling a fire, about to eat their evening meal. All his senses were immediately overloaded by the memories of the song, the heat of the fire, the taste of roasting meat, and the sight of his friends.

You would probably expect me to say that Jason ran to his friends and embraced them. But that did not happen. Jason let out a long low, whistling sound. His five friends, and Aegeus too, stopped singing and without thinking, immediately whistled the same sound. After a brief period of silence, Aegeus then made another bird noise, and then there was more silence. By now, Aegeus and the travelers adopted a position that could only be described as lying flat on the ground, with their head slightly raised, eyes scanning the land to the left and right. The only man standing was Aeson.

"What is going on?"

With that, Aegeus and his new friends, along with Jason, jumped up and ran towards each other.

"What was all that about?"

Aegeus was the one to break the silence.

"My old friend. The bird sounds you heard were taught to us by Chiron. They are part of a multitude of bird calls we all learned on Mt Pelion. These sounds helped us locate each other, especially in the dark when hunting for food. I learned them when I was on the mountain, and these young men also learned them. Maybe one day I will teach you Aeson."

The walk back into the city was full of laughter and song. Jason was so happy his friends had been located, and that he was once again reunited with them, his plan of what to do next was forming quickly. Before he could lay out his ideas of seeking his birthright, one more night of feasting and wine was necessary. Aegeus joined in along with Aeson's family and the four friends of Jason. It was a miracle anyone could wake in the morning without a thumping head and dry mouth. But wake they did, and a plan was hatched.

Jason now had his most trusted friends at his side. Not only the five of them, but Aegeus was now also determined to help Jason and his father Aeson claim their birthright and demand King Pelias abandon his throne and make a peaceful transition to Jason.

For the remainder of that day, a plan was discussed, debated, changed, altered, and pondered until the final arrangement was settled upon. It was blissfully simple in its form. King Pelias knew Jason would come eventually. He had been warned of this, and indeed he had fully expected it once he received the oracle's prophecy. Jason was rightfully concerned that he could not simply walk up to the king and ask him for the crown. He was fearful of the king's personal guard stepping out from hidden places and striking him down at the mere drop of a stone.

CHAPTER 7

King Pelias

There were many entrances to the palace. Each one of them now heavily guarded by Pelias' thugs. On any normal day, these gates were completely free and open to the people to enter at any time during daylight hours. Jason, Hippomenes, Peleus, Aegeus and Kristus carefully surveyed the perimeter of the palace to note each entrance early in the morning, taking particular interest in the physical state of each guard. They were especially keen to note how tired or bored they looked. Aegeus knew some of the guards and gave Jason some valuable insights into each of their personalities.

"I know their families. I know much about them. Fortunately, they do not know anything about me. They think I am harmless. Lucky for us."

Selecting one group of guards to approach, Aegeus said "leave this to me."

Turning to Jason, Aegeus spoke in a hushed voice "Trust me. Bring Telamon and Oileus. Meet here at this tavern" pointing to a rather dishevelled establishment adjacent to this particular palace entrance.

By the time Jason located his other friends, Oileus and Telamon, the group were now standing outside the tavern, but Aegeus was nowhere to be found. Immediately, Jason was concerned for the safety of Aegeus, thinking the worst had happened, and that Pelias had discovered their plans.

As he pondered this situation, Aegeus exited the tavern, carrying with him two large pieces of cooked lamb, cold from the previous night's meal, and two exceptionally large kraters of wine.

"I didn't know you were that hungry old man" said Telamon.

"Not for me, but for the two guards at that entrance. They are hungry and thirsty. They have not had a break all night and are starving."

The first part of the plan had fallen into place. Aegeus was to give the two guards something to eat and drink. It would be more than their entire pay for that week. The tavern was operated by a cousin of Aegeus, and the wine was top quality.

As expected, the two guards were presented with food and wine, and the tavern owner even brought two seats for them to sit at. They were most thankful for the food and wine, but to be able to sit was a bonus gesture from Aegeus. The guards did not suspect anything other than Aegeus and the five young men were going to visit the king with a proposition.

Aegeus had visited the palace many times. Ever since he came off the mountain, Aegeus has been helping deliver food and wine on occasion to the king, his family, but mostly to the many kitchens located inside the palace. During these working visits, he had befriended many of the servants and slaves working in the palace. These people saw Aegeus as a friend. One who was like them. They talked to him. Joked with him. Told him about any rumours circulating. One of the many faults of people like King Pelias was to assume that all his servants and slaves were stupid, ignorant peasants blindly loyal to him and his family. Nothing could be further from the truth.

Aegeus knew that one day, Jason would leave the care of Chiron and enter the palace to reclaim his birthright. He had been planning such an event for twenty years. He knew the king better than anyone. He knew his wife and daughters. He knew the palace better than the architects and builders who constructed it. He also knew that Aeson would not approve of such a plan, so he kept that tasty morsel a secret. He knew where the armoury was located, where weapons were kept in secret hiding places throughout the palace. He knew of secret passages and a tunnel through which he, Jason and the five friends could escape if necessary.

The only weapons each of the men carried were small hunting knives, inconspicuously strapped to their bodies by a leather belt under their chitons. Jason did not want to use them, but, if necessary, would have no hesitation in defending his friends if attacked.

Following the lead of Aegeus, the group made their way directly to where he knew the king would be taking his breakfast. The area was adjacent to the normal room where Pelias received guests and dignitaries, and often dined each morning with his wife Anaxibia, son Acastus and his eight daughters. Aegeus went directly to the kitchen and spoke to the head slave and asked if he and the others could take in the food for Pelias and his family. The slave agreed and gave each man a clean white chiton to wear, so that they would not look out of place.

With the palace guarded at all entrance points, Pelias did not think to have any personal guards present and was most surprised when six men entered with plates of food and watered-down wine to serve to his family. Not wanting to show any fear, he calmly asked "what happened to the regular slaves?"

"You will find that they will return tomorrow morning. I gave them the day off," said Jason.

"You are the young man I saw attending to that poor unfortunate urchin who broke his leg."

"That is right. And I would like to thank you for showing your concern as well" said Jason sarcastically.

"Who are you really? Who are the rest of your thugs?"

At this time, Aegeus thought it wise to speak.

"King Pelias. I think it would be in your best interest if you listened to what this young man has to say. If things go in a way that I believe they should, we will quietly leave you and your large family to dine in peace. If they don't.....or should I say, if you don't decide to do the right thing, things could get a little ugly. That is entirely up to you, King Pelias."

At this moment, Jason and his friends all placed their right hand inside their chitons in a move that was to imply they had weapons, but Pelias was not to know that they each left their knives in the capable hands of the slaves in the kitchen. They had all exchanged their knives with wooden spatulas!

Each of Pelias' family were now suitably terrified that their lives could end any time soon. Acastus, who was the same age as Jason, felt completely defenceless. He was visibly shaking in his chair. Each of his sisters were frantically trying to not look anyone in the eyes, and Anaxibia sat with her hands folded on the table looking directly at Jason.

"I am Jason. Son of Aeson and Polymede. You thought I was dead, but as you can clearly see, I am not."

Pelias was now surprisingly calm. He spoke.

"You look like your father. But your hair is like your mother's. Beautiful."

Jason was not about to let a casual insult like this go without comment.

"Thank you for the compliment, King Pelias. I quite like my hair too. It keeps my head warm on cold nights."

"I wondered if this day would ever happen. I did think you had died, but as years progressed, I was not so sure. But let us cut to the chase. No doubt you have something to ask me. Well? Ask. Get to the point quickly as I have business to attend to today."

"My Grandfather, King Cretheus of Iolchus, wanted my father to be king on his death. But you made sure that would never happen. You had my father sent to prison. You killed for this. You are not the rightful king of this city. I am here to claim what is rightfully mine. Is that succinct enough for you uncle?"

"Then why the need to have your own bodyguards with you Jason?"

"I will answer that question with one of my own. Why the need to have guards at every entrance to the palace?"

"I have been expecting this day for many years Jason. I will make my offer to you very simply. The kingship position is yours. Truly. It will be yours. I must know that you have got what it takes to rule a kingdom before I let you have any of this. Are you capable of handling any situation that arises? I'll give you an example. How would you get rid of someone who was giving you problems?"

Jason thought about this for a moment. "I would send him on a quest to locate the impossible?"

"Excellent idea Jason. Have you heard of the fabled 'Golden Fleece' of Colchis?"

"Yes uncle, I have."

"Do you think it is real Jason?"

"Yes uncle, I do."

At this response, Pelias chuckled. He strongly believed Jason was an idiot and was about to fall for an improbable quest to find the impossible, mythological golden lamb's fleece, from a place no-one had ever been to and returned. Pelias believed all the stories about the fleece were just that – stories.

Pelias continued…

"Imagine if you were the one to find the 'fleece' Jason. This is the kind of quest that any hero would jump at. Your name would be remembered and spoken for generations to come. In fact, you would be remembered for all eternity."

Aegeus placed his hand on Jason's shoulder and whispered, "Do you know what you are doing?"

"Aegeus. Chiron has told us of this fleece for many years. It is real. He has spoken to people who have seen it. Now it is time for you to trust me."

"Alright Jason. I trust you."

Hippomenes, Oileus, Kristus and the brothers Telamon and

Peleus all agreed with Jason. Kristus also whispered to Aegeus "We have heard these stories all our lives too. We trust Chiron completely. If he says it exists, then it exists."

"Uncle, I accept your challenge. I will find the fleece and bring it to you. Then you can take your fleece, your wife, and children, and leave the palace. But I may have some specific needs you can provide to assist with this quest."

Pelias could not believe his luck, insofar as Jason was actually going to attempt the quest. He thought that the very notion of the fleece was nothing more than a myth, and therefore, he would not have to find alternative accommodation, because he was destined to remain king for many years to come. The fleece could not be found because it was not real!

In a cynical voice, Pelias asked "What do you need Jason? Anything I can do to assist? Just name it."

"Give me one day, and I will present you with my requests."

With that, Jason, Aegeus, Oileus, Telamon, Peleus, Hippomenes and Kristus departed the king's morning feast returning to the kitchen to replace the spatulas with their knives. Leaving the palace by the same route, the two guards were now sound asleep on their chairs, with nothing but scattered lamb bones on the ground and two empty wine kraters neatly cradled in their laps. It was a wonder that their snoring didn't wake each other! Little children were standing around laughing at the sleeping, happy, drunk guards. It was a good day.

When Jason told his father what had transpired, Aeson was furious.

"Father, the 'fleece' is real. I know it. King Pelias is foolish enough to believe that it isn't. He is convinced I am the stupid one.

All we must do is find it and bring it home, then we will be back in the palace where we belong. The simplest plans are always the best."

When I am telling stories, I have always wanted to say this next bit. So here it is.

Meanwhile, back at the palace......

Pelias jumped up out of his chair as soon as Jason and his entourage departed. He grabbed Anaxibia and danced around the table. His daughters were getting stuck into the wine more than they normally would, and Acastus was still sitting at the table, worried.

"What is it boy? Why are you not rejoicing in the fact that we will be in this palace forever? I could not be happier. We are about to rid ourselves of the one true threat facing our family. Jason will never find the fleece because it does not exist! This is a good day."

"What if the fleece is real father?"

"Do not worry my boy. Believe me when I say that the fleece is nothing more than a myth, and he will come home with nothing. Then we will be rid of him forever. He will fail."

At the home of Aeson and Polymede, Jason and the friends were eagerly planning their requests for King Pelias and discussing the journey that lay ahead of them. Kristus was totally convinced the fleece existed.

"Remember when Chiron first told us of the story? He said that the fleece was seen by travellers passing through the city of Colchis. All we need to do is to visit Colchis, find the fleece and bring it home. How hard can it be?"

"Where is Colchis exactly?" asked Peleus.

Aegeus had been quiet until now and decided to add his thoughts to the discussion. "Colchis is at the far eastern corner of the Black Sea, in the land ruled by King Aeetes. I too have spoken to someone who has been there. The king will not give up his prized possession very easily Jason."

"Then it is agreed. We will go to Colchis, but first, we need a boat. Do you know where we can obtain a boat Aegeus?"

"I know of a master boat builder by the name of Argos, who lives and works here in Iolchus. He has built several boats for King Pelias in the past and would be favoured by the king to build this. We can go to see him if you like?"

The brisk walk to the port did not take long at all. Argos was in his usual place, constructing a fishing boat for a well-to-do client with deep pockets filled with gold pieces. Aegeus asked him if they could spend a few minutes to discuss a matter. Argos laid down his tools, sat in the shade of a fig tree, and offered his guests some figs and wine.

"What can I do for you boys, and you too Aegeus?" You see, Argos was also a friend of Aegeus.

"Are there any people in Iolchus you don't know Aegeus?" asked Jason.

"See that man working over there pulling fishing nets from that boat? I do not know him!"

"Argos. We want you to build a boat for us."

"Jason, is it? I am a boat builder you know. It is what I do."

"What I mean to say is this. King Pelias wants you to build a boat to my specifications, to travel to Colchis and back."

"You want me to build a boat to travel further than any one has ever travelled by sea before? Is that what you want me to do?"

"Yes, sir. That about sums it up."

"And King Pelias is paying for this, you say?"

"That is true Argos. I can vouch for it," said Aegeus.

"Just say that you will do it. That is all we need to tell the king."

"Oh. One more thing Argos! I want it to be capable of taking about forty-eight rowers, so twenty-four oars each side."

"Not only do you want me to build a boat that will go further than any boat, but you also want it to have twenty-four oars on each side. No problems. I suppose you would like it to have a sail as well?"

"Now that you mention it, that would be a good idea."

"I was joking."

"I am not. We will see you soon with more details. Until then."

Although somewhat perplexed, the brief encounter with Jason saw Argos return home to tell his wife the good news relating to his new project, despite having serious misgivings about the challenges of building the largest boat in existence!

Jason and the others returned to Aeson's house to solve the minor puzzle of where and how they would attract so many rowers. Before these important discussions took place, Jason said he needed to clear his mind and took a walk around the city of Iolchus. After all, he had not really seen much of the city.

Not far from his parents' home was a tavern where travelling musicians often plied their trade for food, wine, and a bed for the night. Sometimes, musicians had to share a bed, but none of them seemed to mind! Walking towards the tavern, Jason heard the most beautiful sounds of a lyre, and a man singing. He could hear it so clearly because the normally rowdy crowd were silent, listening intently and extremely respectful of the man's musical talent and ability. But something struck him as familiar. He thought he had heard that voice and sound before. Racking his mind, he was taken back to the night of the Calydonian boar hunt, when he woke remembering the sounds from the night before. This music sounded to Jason like it was the same person.

Entering the tavern, he noticed a rather thin man, his hair tied back by a strap of leather sitting on a stool, gently caressing his instrument and talking to the audience. He was not singing but seemed to be talking to them. It was like he used the lyre as background sound to his questions and answers. Jason heard the singer ask a patron for his name, and then asked him what he did for work. The response came back immediately.

"Leon works with sheep, to make milk and cheese."

"Are you married Leon?"

"Yes," yelled his enthusiastic wife.

The singer immediately worked these pieces of information into a song about Leon, and how he loved to make people happy by making cheese so tasty it would be fit for a king. Jason was intrigued. Was this the same man he heard in Calydon all those years ago? Was this the same music he heard over a night of heavy drinking and eating?

"He makes great milk and cheese, with his hairy little sheep.

He does this every day.

It sure beats cutting hay.

And he milks her every night when she's asleep."

After the singer finished his performance, a krater of wine was thrust into his hands. He drunk it like a thirsty man who had not had any refreshments for days on end. The krater was emptied in one long, continuous gulp, and another was soon asked for. Jason saw his chance to speak, and approached him asking his name.

"Orpheus", came the reply.

"Were you by any chance, in Calydon several years ago after the boar hunt, performing at a tavern just like you are doing now?"

"Let me think. Oh yes. I do remember that night. Some young men like you had many pieces of silver and plied me with wine and food. I seem to remember a fierce looking, yet gentle woman who simply vanished into the night. Yes, I do remember some aspects of that night. Why do you ask?"

Jason offered to buy him another krater of wine along with some cold meat and figs and attempted to explain his quest to find a golden fleece aboard a boat made by a local builder, manned by forty-eight rowers gathered from all over the known world to help.

"And you want to give me a seat on your vessel – with all those strong men, rowing to the ends of the world. Will you pay me?"

"Yes. If we are successful, your name will become immortal."

"Wait a moment. Only people who have died become immortalised?"

"What I mean to say is that if we...*when* we are successful, I will be king of this city, and you will have guaranteed work for life here."

"Let me think about it. It is a promising idea, but I do really need to think it over."

"What is there to think about?"

"I hardly know you, and yet you are offering me a job to do what exactly? Row?"

"No. I see you as the travelling bard. Making up stories. Setting them to music, just like you did with Leon the cheese maker, immortalising our group through song. Entertaining us both in difficult and pleasant times ahead."

"Jason. I will give you an answer tomorrow morning. I have one more session to perform here tonight. Bring your friends if you like."

Jason did invite his Mt Pelion friends along that night. Initially, they most likely thought Jason was completely nuts, but listening to Orpheus changed their minds. The night of music and stories went as usual, and then Orpheus asked Kristus what his name was, and what he did for work. Kristus told him his name, and then said that he had no work, but was preparing for a long trip by boat with his friends.

"Kristus....the adventurer......I think I can work with that."

What Orpheus sang next convinced all Jason's friends that he had to go with them. Kristus was a tough man, who had a hard life. Growing up on Mt Pelion taught him to be wary of others, and to fend for himself in the world. He could hunt, track, prepare food, repair clothing, mend broken bones and prepare poultices for any ailment. He rarely showed any emotion, apart from anger. Orpheus made him cry like a newborn baby with the song sung in his honour.

Wiping away tears of joy, Kristus said "Jason. I never thought I'd ever say this, but you have to convince that man to be with us. We are going to need him."

By the time Orpheus laid his head down on a bed of straw that night, he had become a friend of Jason's, and more importantly, a passenger on the yet to be built boat, in the quest for a sight unseen object, with a group of yet to be finalised members. Jason, Kristus, Hippomenes, Oileus, Peleus and Telamon, and of course the wily Aegeus staggered back to Aeson's house where they too would spend the night on a different bed of straw. Jason lay down dreaming of many things that night, but one thing stuck in his mind more than anything else.

Early next morning, Jason arose before the others and decided to visit Argos again. With the morning sun barely nudging the horizon, Argos was busy in his workshop measuring and carefully cutting pieces of wood for a new boat.

"Jason. What are you doing up at this time?"

"I could ask you the same question Argos."

"For me it is easy. The wood behaves differently at various times of the day due to the temperature, humidity, and wind. This morning is a perfect time for me to get some of the finer work done on this new boat."

"Argos. I have been thinking. You said that you had never built a boat as big as the one I need."

"That is right. Never even seen one that big."

"What are the potential problems with building a big boat?"

Argos loved boats, and everything to do with them. He was surprised Jason wanted to know, so he spent a great deal of time discussing leakage and storage on such a long trip, strength of the wood, different effects water has on the wood under the waterline, effects of sun and salt on the wood, but most of all, leakage.

"Would a water-proof, or nearly water-proof wood, strong and durable be of any benefit to you?"

"Yes, it would. But I do not know of any around here."

"Argos. I grew up on Mt Pelion. On the north-western side of the mountain grows an oak tree different to any other. We used it for water storage, and it never rotted or leaked. Some of the other boys and I spent countless days carving and using this wood for a range of things. Do you know of it?"

"I have heard of it, but never seen any of the trees."

While Jason and Argos were discussing this wonderful water-proof wood, Aegeus appeared and asked what they were talking about.

"I know of this wood Argos. Believe me, it is good. I have some items at my home that are made from this tree. Would you like to see them?"

Like Jason on Mt Pelion for twenty years, Aegeus was taught how to cut, shape, and make objects with the materials at hand available on the mountain. He took Argos to his house and showed him some of the objects he was referencing. Argos was particularly interested in a rather large urn used to hold water. It wasn't ceramic, but made of various pieces of oak from the slopes of Pelion. It was not carved from one massive piece of the tree, but rather made from carved and bent pieces of the wood seamlessly moulded together. Argos was most impressed when Aegeus told him that it was nearly ten years old and had never leaked in that time. Argos was now convinced.

"Can you take me to the mountain to show me where you find this marvellous wood. Of course, I will be using it to build a boat, rather than a container, but the wood is beautiful. This will be my best work so far Aegeus."

Argos was most excited at the prospect of building a boat made from this wondrous wood from trees that were so close to where he had lived his whole life but had never seen. Before any boat could be built though, there was one very important meeting that had to take place.

"Will you come with me to see King Pelias, Argos? If he hears this from your mouth, and you hear from his that he will finance the project, all I must do then is find enough strong rowers, and I already have some."

Argos dropped his tools, gathered his thoughts and walked hurriedly to the palace with Jason and Aegeus to see the king.

Strangely enough, the guards at the main palace entrance permitted them to enter immediately.

Pelias was by now, fully convinced the journey to Colchis was so far-fetched, he was positively joyous at the thought of Jason attempting the impossible. He did not at any stage entertain the possibility that the boat would be built, that it would be sturdy enough to complete the journey, and that Jason could bring back the fleece. All he could see was a lifetime ahead as the king, where one of his daughters would take over the role of monarch. Pelias was drunk with anticipation. Of course, he told Argos to build the boat and to spare no expense. Pelias had so much wealth that he could afford to make one boat! What could go wrong?

Pelias never had much regard for his son Acastus. He thought him a dolt, incapable of ever truly being a King, which is why he thought one of his many daughters would replace him one day, or if he lived long enough, he could choose one of his daughters' husbands to take over the throne. Thinking that the journey to Colchis would end in disaster, Pelias decided it would be a good idea if Jason took Acastus on as a rower.

"I have one more request Jason. You said that you needed many rowers for the boat. I have a strong young man in the palace who I would like to go on this journey with you – my son Acastus."

Jason could not refuse this rather awkward offer, and reluctantly agreed to take Acastus on as one of the rowers.

"Is he afraid of hard work Pelias?"

"Not at all. He will do as I require and he will be more than capable of tugging on an oar in your boat."

Acastus was furious with this offer, but had no comeback to

his father, the king. Swallowing his annoyance and frustration, Acastus dutifully agreed.

Jason, Argos and Aegeus quickly departed and decided to take some wine in a tavern on the way to the port. It was here that Jason outlined to Argos the finer details in terms of the brief for the project. The boat would now be built, and in the meantime, Jason could address the need to urgently find more rowers.

CHAPTER 8

Finding rowers

Argos decided not to return to his boat building after leaving the tavern. Not because he'd had a few wines, but that he desperately wanted Aegeus to show him where this wonderful wood could be found. Once he could smell and caress the special oak trees, see how large they were, how many he could use, and how he could have them transported to a wood cutter near the port, he could then start to plan the build. Argos had never before been this excited at building a boat. Normally, his boats were standard designs and although perfectly built, it was his trade after all. He knew what he was doing, he enjoyed it, and his customers paid handsomely which was the best part!

Jason located his friends working at his father's farm. Aeson could not let the opportunity of having so many able bodied, young men at his disposal slip by. Joining his father and the new farm labourers for a piece of bread and honey in the shade of a staggeringly old olive tree, Jason spoke.

"We need to find a lot of rowers. Before you all run off, I have a few things to say. Firstly, I want that woman from the boar hunt to join us. I know what you are probably thinking but hear me out. I do not know what to expect from our journey to Colchis, but we need the best archers on our side just in case of trouble. Kristus, you saw what she did with her bow. Peleus, you saw it too. I saw how well she handled her weapons, but more importantly, how she handled the unwanted advances from Meleager's men. I was most impressed."

"Will you want any other women on the boat Jason?" asked Kristus with a hint of cheekiness.

"I am sure we will find women on our journey, and who knows, you may find a toothless old crag for yourself Kristus!"

Jason and the farm labourers worked assiduously all day on his father's farm, repairing stone fences, fixing gates for animal enclosures, pruning vines and other fruit trees, and anything Aeson asked them to do. It was a busy day, and normally, Jason would empty his mind and focus on the task at hand. Not this day. Occupying all his thinking, Jason was imagining where he could find forty additional strong and able young men for rowing. He did not want them to be married in case they would not return. He only wanted single men.

However, his single man policy was soon to be put to the test. Peleus thought it might be time to let Jason know his marital status.

"Jason. I do not know how to tell you this, but I am to be

married soon to a wonderful woman, and we have a child. I do want to go with you, and I know of your desire to take only single men, but can't you make me the exception?"

"That is great news Peleus, about your future wife and child. My single man policy is not that set in clay, but you do realise our journey may encounter difficulties on the way?"

"I am fully aware of that. Like you, I am prepared to take that risk. After all, what is life all about?"

"My point exactly. I know there may be troubles ahead, but that is what makes it more exciting. Tell me about your betrothed and child. What are their names?"

"Her name is Thetis, and we named our little boy Achilles. He is nearly a hundred days old, and has a mass of blonde hair like you Jason. He is certainly destined for big things. I can feel it. May I say though, he is much better looking than you. We are to be married on Mt Pelion soon with Chiron and Chariklo at their home. I hope you can attend."

Jason did attend the wedding, and what became of Achilles and Thetis is a story for another day. In the meantime, Jason still had to work out how to attract the necessary rowers to power the new boat.

After a hearty and well-deserved evening meal, Kristus had an idea. "Why don't we put out the word through our existing contacts to young men to join us."

"Just how do you *put out the word* Kristus?" asked Jason.

"Easy. How did we find out about the boar hunt? How do you think so many men attended that event? It cannot be that difficult. If my memory is any good, I remember men from all over the land. By the time we gather enough men, Argos will have built the boat.

I say we ask Meleager how he did it. What do you think?"

Jason liked the idea. The boar hunt was a success simply because news of that event reached all parts of the land, and many men attended. Surely he could implement the same strategy.

It was decided that early in the morning of the next day, Kristus was to travel to Calydon to visit Meleager to ask for his assistance. His message to Meleager was simple – can you help in attracting fit, strong young men to travel on an adventure by boat to the furthest point of the known world, to locate and find a special object and then return?

Hippomenes agreed to go by horse to the Peloponnese to find Atalanta, and Aegeus agreed to do the same to the north of the country. Oileus offered to find Locrians to row. Having just returned to his homeland after ten years with Chiron, Oileus had made a considerable impact on his people, and offered to find as many potential rowers as he could. "But who can we ask in the west?"

Peleus responded.

"I know the perfect man for this. I met him a few years ago near the island of Ithaca. His name is Laertes, and he has contacts all over the western islands, and the western coastline of our country."

"What about your wedding Peleus? Shouldn't you be preparing for that?"

"This will only take me ten days to find him and convince his sense of adventure to come with us. Trust me, Jason. I will be back in time for my wedding."

"We will travel together brother," said Telamon.

"And one more thing Jason. Like my brother, I too am to be married soon and I too have a son. We have called him Ajax."

"I give up. Maybe we should ask Argos to build a bigger boat to bring our wives and children."

Seeing Jason's attempt at humour, the friends laughed, and Peleus said he would ask his mother to come as well.

The next day, Kristus, Hippomenes, Oileus, Telamon, Peleus and Aegeus departed Iolchus for all parts of the country on their quest to convince men to join Jason's quest. Jason sought out Argos to see how far progressed he was with the boat.

I know I could depart from the main story and tell you of the trials and tribulations of these men and their ordeals to find rowers, but I will leave that for another day. The shortened version of these events is that within ten days, each of the men had returned, and by the time thirty days had passed, over forty men were sitting on Aeson's farm listening to Jason and Argos talk about the newly built boat, the plan to find the fleece, the future claim to the kingship of Iolchus and life beyond for each of them should they return victorious. In short, the group consisted of future kings, strong men, expert horse men, archers, blacksmiths, warriors, cooks, boat builders, a musician, healers, navigators and most importantly a leader – Jason!

As it turned out, Argos did not have to travel to Mt Pelion to see the trees. A local wood turner and carpenter had access to sufficient supply of the special oak, but Argos paid nearly double for the material in his desire to commence construction immediately. The carpenter was ecstatic to be paid handsomely for the wood, and for Argos, he could begin to carve, bend, cut, burn and splice the wood into planks as soon as the precious resource was delivered to his workshop. Jason was completely surprised to see that Argos had already begun.

"That was quick. Did the gods spirit you away and bring all this back with you?"

"No. Nothing like that. I simply asked a carpenter friend of mine about working with the oak from Mt Pelion, and he told me of a friend of his who had been working with that wood for many years, and who had one year's supply already in the city. I visited him, talked for some time, and paid him for all that I required. When I say I'd paid him, of course King Pelias will pay eventually, but the carpenter was very happy with the transaction."

Argos sketched Jason a quick, yet detailed design of the new boat. With nearly forty-eight rowers, there was to be twelve oars on each side. Taking the helmsman and musician Orpheus who was to beat drumming rowing rhythms as well as entertain with lyre, the rowers who were not engaged in rowing were to rest and be on standby to take over when needed.

To accommodate so many people, the new boat was to be longer than anything Argo had ever built. He was adept in building smaller, curved hull boats for coastal fishing, short trips, and trading, but had never built a large boat for lengthy travel. His boats were designed for rowing or sailing close to the coast line, rather than the high seas. His largest boat to date was one that had only eight oars, being four each side. Boats such as this were not strong enough to be rowed in the open sea attempting to withstand strong winds and large waves. Trading vessels were much wider, to allow for increased room for storage, such as pottery and other tradable commodities.

Argos was fascinated by Phoenician boat builders who were beginning to construct much larger boats for trade and possibly for potential hostilities. Once he accepted the task of building the new vessel, he wanted it to be a low draught, flatter boat, capable of landing on any sandy beach with ease. It did not need a port or wharf. A low draught boat also meant that it could be hauled up onto a beach with ropes.

The new boat was to have a large mast in the forward section set back from the bow. A rope from the top of the mast would be securely fastened to the bow, and the second rope fastened at the stern, allowing for a sail to be hoisted at any time when a favourable wind was blowing. Two more ropes each side firmly secured the mast for stability. On top of the mast, Argos allowed for one of the crew to stand as high as possible, whether the sail was in use or not. This crew member was a lookout for any dangers lurking in the water below, or for locating landing sites on beaches.

Argos wanted to always have rowers on hand to take over if sickness, fatigue or other unforeseen circumstances were to take hold. Under the main deck was to be storage area for the food, wine and water amphorae, spare oars, rope, fastenings, weapons, body armour, replacement sail, ballast and some room for personal possessions.

If the boat was to spend a night on the water, there was just enough room above and below deck for sleeping, but conditions would be cramped. At the rear of the boat, the helmsman would stand working his oar, and in front of him was to be the seat for Orpheus. Not knowing if they would meet hostile natives, the musician's job was to drum a faster beat for getting into and out of trouble.

Argos and Jason talked about what might happen should they come under arrow attack.

"I have thought of that Jason. You see that the rowing seats are to be situated below the top sides of the boat, so no rowers head will be visible from a distance. Should it be necessary, we will be able to use our spare rowers for attacking enemies while the full contingent of rowers can remain at their seats. No boat will be able to match our rowing pace with twenty-four rowers."

As Jason knew nothing about rowing, boat building or leading a group of men all the way across the seas to the end of the known world, he was eager to learn. He would have to bite his tongue lest he ask a stupid question showing his ignorance, and show complete faith in Argos' craftsmanship and knowledge.

"You will have to trust me, Jason. I am going to be one of your rowers, so if anything goes wrong along the way with my boat, I will be on hand to resolve the issue it immediately."

"What do you mean when you say 'goes wrong'?"

"I mean if anything needs to be repaired, either on water or on land, I can make those repairs. These boats do not last forever Jason. Parts of it will require replacing from time to time."

Jason stood by and watched Argos and his trusted apprentice Markos begin to lay out various sections of wood on the ground. Within a matter of moments, six more men appeared out of nowhere to assist with the skeletal plan on the ground. Tools appeared, along with wineskins, tables, chairs and a very large krater of wine, courtesy of the king!

By now, Argos had a crew of boat builders working with him. News soon spread throughout the other boat builders in Iolchus about this new, super boat being made from Mt Pelion oak at the boat yards of Argos. Before the middle of the day, nearly twenty other builders had abandoned their employers and agreed to work for Argos, thinking that this new boat would somehow curry favour with the king. Argos didn't mind at all. He knew all the men. His reputation as a builder of quality was renowned throughout the land, and he could sense that this vessel was to be special.

Keen to assuage the other builders from whom he'd co-opted a complete workforce, Argos promise his vessel would be completed soon and within a matter of only about twenty days, they would all be ready to return to their regular employer with vastly new skills!

Argos was not wrong about learning new skills. He found while building his boat with this special oak that had never been used before for this purpose, it behaved differently to previous raw material used. Only time would tell if the new timber was successful or not.

Crowds of keen onlookers surrounded the men cutting, bending, scraping, boring, and hitting varying sizes of wood. Two of the workers were cutting a large piece of course linen into two large sails. Two sails were necessary to be made at this time as one was to be kept as a spare in case of damage to the one in use. Argos gave the carpenter, from whom he'd purchased the required timber, the important job to carve a bow figurine. Argos told Vassilis the carpenter to carve the bow, but to also carve two eyes, one for each side of the bow. Argos didn't have any particular reason for the eyes, but he liked the idea of a boat capable of watching for potential danger that might be lurking under the waves.

The finishing touch to the bow was to be a large, carved wooden figure-head of Athena. At Jason's insistence, Athena had always been his patron goddess and he expected her to protect him at all times on the journey. Once the figure-head had been completed and placed in position, Jason could only stare and wonder at the adventures about to unfold in his life, with the protection of this marvellous goddess.

Within ten days, the new boat was beginning to resemble the finished product. Each day, onlookers brought food and wine to share, as well as their own stools to sit and watch patiently. On one day, King Pelias himself visited with his wife Anaxibia, son Acastus and a retinue of guards, to see what progress was being made. Argos was most excited to show Pelias all the features of the new boat including the specially carved bow spit, the two carved eyes, holds for amphorae of various liquids and foodstuffs and the oars also made from Mt Pelion oak. All the while, King Pelias was outwardly pleased, but internally worried that the boat was looking very good. He began to entertain the distinct possibility that Jason might indeed succeed.

Pelias reminded Jason of his request that his son Acastus was to be one of the rowers, and was ready for Jason to refuse him.

"Of course. I hope you like hard work Acastus. Welcome aboard. We leave soon."

Secretly, Acastus welcomed the opportunity to make the king proud. All Jason thought at that stage was 'one more rower to add to the team.'

In addition to the eating and drinking by onlookers, the musician Orpheus contributed to the spectacle with his lyre and songs to keep people entertained. He saw it as a way to both entertain and be paid, in food and wine, preferably wine! Some of the onlookers paid extra for Orpheus to sing a song about them, and they were not disappointed. Many food vendors arrived with enough food fit for a royal banquet. Great cheers went up every time planks of wood were added to the skeleton of the boat. One of the biggest roars was when the sail was first attached to the mast. A heavy sigh sounded soon after as the sail was quickly taken down for some minor adjustments. When it was raised a second time, the cheering was deafening. A truly festive event was taking place at the port of Iolchus, never seen before, and never seen since for the building of a boat.

Over the many times I have told this story, I have always been asked if these onlookers knew why the boat was being made. My answer has never changed. Yes. The people of Iolchus hated Pelias with a passion, but dared not to show it in public, lest any of the king's spies were milling about. The city folk knew Aeson, his family, and now they were beginning to know Jason. Some had heard of the fleece, and rumours abounded as to the existence or otherwise of this great mythical object.

Joining the crowds of people milling about were the eventual rowers, who by this stage were arriving daily. One rower's arrival had an impact like no other. Hercules! Standing head and shoulders above any man there, bystanders and festive onlookers could not fail to see this man mountain. With his muscles glistening in the midday sun, and a fair degree of sweat, Hercules made a grand entrance. Even Orpheus stopped playing to simply stare at this marvellous specimen of a man.

With Hercules was his squire, Hylas. In his own right, Hylas was not a small man, but standing next to the noble Hercules, it was easy to look past his own wonderful physique. Knowing that people wanted to meet and speak with his friend, Hylas preferred to hide in plain sight.

Soon after the great Hercules toured the new boat with Argos, Atalanta slipped quietly in behind Orpheus and stood motionless, carefully studying the faces of everyone around her. Hippomenes was successful in enticing her to become part of this adventure. That in itself was a struggle worthy of another story. All I can say here without going into too much detail was that Atalanta was reluctant at first, but when she remembered Jason and his friends at Calydon, she relented and agreed to join the adventure.

One of the strangest arrivals came in the form of a young, slightly built young man from a city only a few days walk north of Iolchus. The young man had heard about the new boat being built and decided to see it for himself. Packing only his bow and quiver of arrows, his trusty short sword and a few silver pieces to buy food, King Poeas of Melivia wished his son well and instructed him to come home soon. Philoktetes agreed, and in two days found himself standing at the port of Iolchus joining the festivities.

Approaching an older man sitting in the shade of a fig tree near the port, Philoktetes asked if this was the boat he had heard about.

"Yes, it is. Nearly finished too."

The two talked for a while when Philoktetes asked the man to point out the apparent leader called Jason.

"That is him, standing talking to the musician over there. You cannot miss him. He is the one with the golden hair, but do not let looks fool you. He must be something special if he could persuade the king to build this boat."

"So that is Jason? I must go and meet him. Thank you for your time."

Jason was busy discussing something important when Philoktetes approached.

"I heard that you are the one responsible for building this boat."

"I am, and who are you?"

"I am Philoktetes, son of Poeas, King of Melivia."

"Ah. Royalty. What is it that you do, son of Poeas?"

"I can use this bow rather well. Apart from that, nothing much really."

"Have you ever been to sea in a boat like this?"

"No. Have you?"

Jason liked the response immediately, appreciating the young man's quick wit.

"You said that you can use a bow. Care to show me?"

With the challenge of a bow contest in range of all to hear, Atalanta edged closer to Jason and Philoktetes. She simply nodded to Jason, who acknowledged her with a gentle nod. He was very happy to see her, and already familiar with her ability and reputation. He was hoping Philoktetes had not known of either.

Atalanta, Jason and Philoktetes drifted carefully away to the rear of the crowded area to arrange a little competition, with a small group of about a hundred eager spectators. Jason knew what to do. He chose a tree in the distance, drew a line in the dirt and asked both archers to strike the tree at a particular spot. On the main trunk of the tree sprouted a smaller branch, with a slightly bulky base as it protruded out of the main trunk.

"See that branch, try to hit that."

Philoktetes was insulted at such an easy target, and consequently aimed his first arrow to purposefully miss the mark by a hand's width. Atalanta silently chuckled to herself thinking that the contest was hers for the taking with just one arrow. She pulled back her bow string and let fly with a sizzling twang of her weapon, and it struck exactly in the middle of the target. The crowd were cheering, but before she could claim victory, Philoktetes asked if he could try one more time. Atalanta agreed, thinking she would remain victorious, even if her opponent was to be given one more attempt.

Sensing the theatre of the situation, Philoktetes joked that he would soon be conceding defeat, but it was worth another attempt. He half-heartedly selected his final arrow, raised it to his bow, took aim, and let it fly. Without even looking after the arrow departed his weapon, he turned around to look directly at Atalanta.

"Did I miss? Did it strike anything?"

Atalanta, Jason and the stunned, silent crowd stared at the tree in disbelief. Philoktetes continued his feigned defeat and said it "... was worth a try. Better luck next time I suppose?"

Atalanta burst into a smile. She had been beaten by a man for the first time. Philoktetes arrow had struck Atalanta's arrow, and split it in half! She instantly liked this man. He had won this contest, but there would be more. She still had a few tricks of her own to show him, but they were to be saved for another time.

For several more days, a steady stream of rowers enlisted by Jason's friends grew. With Jason, Orpheus, Markos and Argos, the optimum number had almost been reached. Only two more were needed.

Hercules mentioned to Jason that he had a brother Iphicles, and that he would be arriving any time soon.

"Is he like you Hercules?"

"We are identical twins, so yes, he is like me."

"That's it. When Iphicles arrives, we'll have enough rowers."

Iphicles walked into the port later that day, and like his twin, all eyes were on him. The two men were used to the adoring smiles, gentle touches, and offers of beds to spend the night. Hercules greeted his brother, and introduced him to Jason. Jason explained the purpose of the boat, the intended journey to Colchis and return, the king's challenge, and anything Iphicles asked, he answered.

That night, Aeson's farm had over forty men sleeping on hay, under trees, and in barns. Atalanta spent the night with Jason's family in the city, and Jason spent his first night aboard the boat, which was close to being completed. He wanted to see and experience it for himself, to see what was still needed, but also just to be there on his own.

Next morning, Jason despatched a boy to run to his father's farm and ask all the rowers to assemble at the port. Jason himself fetched Atalanta, and Orpheus even managed to make an appearance at such an early time of the day.

This was no simple walk from a farm to the port, and certainly no everyday occurrence. Nearly fifty perfectly sculptured, fit, healthy men walking with each other, chatting, getting to know each other, laughing, and carrying their meagre possessions, the walk turned into something of a procession. Following behind was a growing group of young children, parents, farm workers, city people and the odd donkey or two. On arrival at the port, the crowd sat quietly on the ground and observed the god-like figure of Jason addressing his new crew.

Amazed at the level of community support and interest shown by the citizens of Iolchus, Jason scanned the crowd and smiled when he spotted his parents and sisters. But he was not thinking of them at this moment. His thoughts were elsewhere. He addressed his men.

"You all know why we are here. You all know that our trip to Colchis is not going to be easy. No one has ever taken a boat like this so far and returned alive! But we will. The boat is ready to prepare for our voyage. I do not know how long it will take, or if we will all make it back alive, but I promise you this. It is my intention for us all to return, for the fleece to be handed over to Pelias, for me to take my rightful place in the palace in this beautiful city and for all of you to be immortalised for all time."

At the point in Jason's speech where he said he would return with the fleece and claim the role of king, a great roar went up. Jason continued.

"You have all noticed that we have some truly remarkable people joining us, and for those especially keen, we have one woman. Atalanta is here at my request, and if you doubt her particular skill set, you had better say good bye to your precious jewels."

"Why do we have a musician with us? Wouldn't he be much happier staying here and playing with his instrument?"

This raised a chuckle. But before Jason could respond, Orpheus stepped in to ask a question.

"What is your name?"

"I am Theseus, and one day soon, I will be king of Athens."

"Well now, not yet but future king of Athens, let me see what I can do with your name and future occupation."

With that, Orpheus launched into a wonderful, improvised song about how a sheep herder from the village of Athens would be much more comfortable pulling sheep teats instead of pulling on an oar. As the rest of the rowers were laughing, Orpheus suggested lyrically that maybe he would be even more adept at pulling on another object. It went something like this.

"Theseus of Athens loves pulling on sheep's teats.

He'll need to pull on oars, while sitting in his seat.

As kings often do, when sitting on their throne.

To pull on an appendage, the slug he calls his own."

Sheepishly, Theseus laughed at himself, and promised never to question Jason's reasoning again. I am sure Jason said more, but he was not one for big, long speeches. However, there was one more thing he wanted to say.

"In three days, we leave. There is much to do in preparing the readiness of this boat for our journey."

Hippomenes, Kristus, Peleus, and Telamon were given eleven others to look after in what could only be described as a family situation. With forty-nine people eventually on the boat, his four friends were responsible for their own family, which left Jason to assume overall responsibility.

On the much-anticipated day of departure, Argos assured Jason the boat was sea worthy, Hippomenes assured Jason that all food supplies were in place and Kristus assured them that barrels of both wine and water were stored safely below deck. Argos performed a final check on ropes and sails and as he was about to step onto his creation to take his place, Jason stopped him and asked him to wait just a moment.

"I am not one for making long speeches, but this speech needs to be made. Argos. To show you our gratitude, this boat will be given a name. Never have we named boats, but never before has one been built quite like this. From this day forward, this boat is to be called the 'Argo,' in honour of the master craftsman who built it."

Jason and Argos embraced, and the boat builder was filled with excitement and a fair degree of dread. What a responsibility he had been given. The entire crowd cheered.

"Does that mean that we are now 'Argonauts' Jason?" asked Hercules.

"I like that. Why not. We, no you are all to be known as 'Argonauts.' From here on until eternity, we will be known as 'Jason and the Argonauts."

Orpheus took up the theme immediately and began to strum and sing "Jason and the Ar-go-nauts. Jason and the Ar-go-nauts."

With that, another cheer erupted not only from the newly named Argonauts, but from the gathered crowd who had arrived to see the boat commence its journey. But there was one final, important task for Jason to perform. The dedication to the god of the sea.

"I dedicate the mighty Argo to Poseidon, who will guide and comfort us as we journey into the unknown. May he protect us from dangers, and give us the courage and strength to overcome any obstacles."

Stepping out from the crowd, an old man appeared as proud as any man could. It was Chiron. He wanted to see his former student and graduate of Mt Pelion take his rightful place in the world. Chiron and Jason embraced, a few quiet and personal words were spoken and all Argonauts, except for Hercules, Iphicles and Argos boarded the Argo. The reason why these three did not board immediately was that they supervised the crowd of onlookers to help push the Argo away from the port. Once it was safely away from the wharf, the last three Argonauts boarded. The search for the fabled fleece had begun.

CHAPTER 9

Island hopping

The wharves and jetties of Iolchus together with a multitude of smaller boats were crammed full of well-wishers. Any boat that could float was taken out into the bay. Most of these people wanted Jason to succeed for the simple reason that it would mean an end to the reign of the hated King Pelias. With the barest of breeze, the sail was not raised, and twenty-four oars heaved in time with the commands of Typhus, Argos' choice of helmsman.

Typhus was one of the only argonauts to have any experience in a vessel such as the Argo. Not only was he an experienced helmsman, he possessed an excellent knowledge of navigation. With his two hands firmly on the steering oar, Typhus stood proudly above the novice rowers below, who were following his every command. Never having rowed together, it took a few attempts for all argonauts to be working in unison.

His major skill in navigation was the ability to predict wind directions on the basis of rising waves and changes in the colours of the sea around them. He also used the sun by day and stars at night to find his way on the open seas. At this moment however, he used none of those skills. Brute strength was all that was needed, and he was in charge of twenty-four rowers, propelling the mighty Argo for the first time.

The oars were designed by Argos so that either one or two rowers could work on each oar simultaneously. Jason thought it would be beneficial if all Argonauts started together so they could learn faster. Even Orpheus rowed! Effortlessly, the Argo gently made its way along the eastern coastline of the Pagasaean Gulf, turned westwards to exit the enclosed body of water, and once clear of the gulf, turned east to follow the southern tip of Magnesia and toward their first scheduled rest at the island of Skiathos.

Skiathos is a small island. It is equal in distance between the larger island of Peparithos and the mainland. Jason thought it might be a good idea to beach the Argo on Skiathos, eat some food, find and replenish fresh water reserves, and perhaps rest for the night depending on the weather. Approaching land, moans from muscle weary rowers started to take over the conversations that had been a feature of that first day. Not knowing the depth of the water where Typhus chose to beach the Argo, twelve rowers jumped from the bow into the water to help drag the heavy boat onto dry sand. Luckily, the water was only as deep as the tallest man, and in several heartbeats, each of them were on dry sand, pulling on the special ropes designed for this purpose. Once safely beached, it was not long before each rower was lying on their backs on dry sand.

Jason noticed that almost all of them were complaining about their hands, many of which were already forming bulging blisters. Jason instructed some of the argonauts to start searching for a particular plant. He did not know the name of the plant, but described it carefully.

"We will need this plant, and a lot of it, to make into a paste so that we may relieve our aching hands."

Chiron had taught this remedy to Jason many years ago on Mt Pelion. Kristus volunteered to lead the search party as he also knew what to look for. In his group was Eurydamas from Thessaly and Eurytus from Alope. Both grew up nearby but knew this island very well.

Hippomenes took his group in search of precious water to refill the almost depleted amphorae while Atalanta and Philoktetes disappeared into the nearby trees in search of animals to shoot and butcher. After a brief rest, Argos, Markos and Typhus inspected the Argo to examine anything that needed repairing. Luckily, they did not find any major problems, although there were some minor leakages that were skilfully attended to by Markos.

Jason did not know how much water to allow each Argonaut to drink each day, and didn't have any restrictions on this at all during that first full day of rowing. At some stage later that night, he met with the four group leaders to discuss a rationing system in case they remained at sea for longer than one day. Key points for discussion included the following: what to do once the Argo was beached day, the need to locate suitable drinking water, build a fire, search for food, arrange for shelter, post sentries to guard against possible attack, and if appropriate, contact local people to negotiate for any items they may need. Both Argos and Markus knew which wood to search for in case urgent boat repairs were necessary. Everyone had a job to do. Being the first night together, Jason wanted to see how each man, and Atalanta, worked together for the common good.

Argos believed it important that his boat was to have a brazier holding embers on board. This would allow for fires to be lit once on land. The brazier was situated on the stern side of the main mast directly in front of Typhus, and in the days leading up to the departure, two Argonauts were tasked with keeping the embers alive. Being farmers, Butes and Canthus were knowledgeable in making fire and keeping the coals alight. With a good supply of flint and dried leaves in case the embers died, it was hoped that lighting a fire would not become a problem. Using the coals from the brazier on the first night, Butes was the first Argonaut to light their nightly fire. It would not be his last.

Around the fire that night, Jason made a short speech.

"Tomorrow, we will rest. Our hands and arm muscles need to recover. The day after, if the gods allow, we will leave for the island of Limnos. Depending on the breeze, this part of our long journey could take a day if the gods favour us, or it could take many more. We are fortunate to have with us two expert brothers in all matters pertaining to the prevailing air flows. Please listen to Calais and Zetes, and they will teach us all how to read and predict wind directions."

Jason allowed Calais and Zetes to give a brief lesson to everyone. They talked about how to determine shifting patterns in overhead clouds, changing colours of the water, distant clouds moving in different directions, and subtle changes in temperature. Even Argos and Typhus learned something. Orpheus even concocted his first song that night in dedication to Calais and Zetes, soon to be known as the *'wind'* brothers.

Two days later, with hands healed, muscles soothed and amphorae filled to the brim with precious drinking water, the Argo set sail for Limnos at sunrise. Calais and Zetes predicted no wind for a day, and they were not wrong. Water rations were adhered to with little or no dissent. Rowers took their turns at the oars, and Orpheus began his daily improvisations of songs about each argonaut. Having them all laugh at his witty ditties seemed to make the aching muscles less of an issue. Atalanta and Philoktetes managed to catch fish and some sea birds with an ingenious method of tying fine rope to an arrow, and the other end to their legs, then shooting arrows at fish and birds. Most of the time, they were unsuccessful, but from time to time, a decent size fish was hauled up and cooked on the brazier directly in front of Typhus. Some of the argonauts were skilled in gutting and cooking fish, so it was never a problem finding someone to perform cooking duties, as it meant relief from rowing. No wind blew that first day, and Limnos was nowhere to be seen.

Typhus knew his navigating skills would be needed that night, and set about reading the stars. He was certain he knew where he wanted the Argo to be by morning, and predicted, with Zetes' help, they would be able to sight land by morning. It was a long and tiring night.

Morning came, and land was in sight. Renewed efforts to reach dry land meant that when it was your turn to row, it was done with enthusiasm. Hercules and Iphicles took control of the rowing tempo and with inspired vigour, seemed to lift the other rowers.

"I don't think this island is Limnos" said Meleager to Jason.

"Why do you say that?"

"It has no trees!"

As the Argo gently glided into a picturesque bay to the backdrop of fine hills and crops of all sorts, a local fishing boat hastily rowed out to meet them.

"What island is this" asked Jason to the fisherman standing in his small boat, rowed by two fine young men.

"Alonnisos."

"May we come ashore and stay for a night? We mean no harm, and will be gone by sunup in the morning."

"By all means."

With that brief conversation, Jason and the Argonauts landed on an island a full day away from Limnos. Much to their surprise, this island was not known to Typhus or any of the Argonauts. The village was very small with only about a hundred inhabitants. Apart from some olive and fig trees, hills of vines and various small patches of vegetables, the main fare for these villagers appeared to be fish. The introduction of nearly fifty more mouths to feed was a stretch, but the Argonauts were welcomed to stay the night, re-supply the boat, and with full bellies, row out in the morning. Getting to sleep that night was effortless. The beach was littered with extremely tired rowers, who after some fish, green beans and very strong local wine, scared off any wildlife with the noise of their snoring and farting. Hercules decided to sleep on the Argo, to keep a guard over their supplies, but especially their weapons. By morning, there was still no breeze.

Jason spoke to one of the locals and asked about the wind direction this time of year.

"Here in our village, we are protected from the strong north wind, the meltemia as we call them, but as soon as our fishing boats are safe from the protection offered by these hills, the wind can be quite strong all day."

"Are you saying that when we leave this port, we are likely to be facing a head wind?"

"Yes. It blows every day, all day, at this time of year."

Jason knew the next day or two would be a significant test. If there was to be a head wind, the journey to Limnos could take two days, which would mean another night on the water.

Hercules spoke to the argonauts as they made their straggling way on board.

"If we could have harnessed the power of your farts last night, we would be in Limnos by midday."

Laughing at his attempt at humour, Orpheus managed to work his magic into a song about the argonauts baring their backsides to the sail and letting go with community farting fuelled by beans, fish and wine.

With much laughing and ribald jokes, the Argo rowed out beyond the harbour, turned right, and made its way north. Once leaving the safety of land to their right, Phlias spotted an island to the north.

"That must be Limnos."

At that moment, the wind rose, but it was not helpful. The Argo was facing directly into a head wind. Limnos in sight did make it easier, but rowing nonetheless was difficult. Many rotations of positions at the oars were necessary. Even Orpheus put his lyre down to lend a hand with an oar.

Soon enough, smoke could be seen wafting skywards in one location, and Jason reckoned that it must be the main village on the island. Phlias now took to leaning over Athena's head straining his eyes for a safe place to beach the Argo. The first thing he could make out was a large rocky hill, behind which was the source of the smoke. Not far to row now. Rounding the promontory, a small sandy beach was spotted in the distance.

"Head for that beach" suggested Phlias. Jason agreed.

Waves became smaller, and the Argo gently floated towards the shore, but it seemed they were to be met with some resistance. Standing on the beach, Phlias noted the existence of warriors wearing breast plates, carrying spears, and standing to face the incoming vessel. Thinking that it would be wise to send a messenger before beaching the Argo, Jason instructed Orpheus to dive in, swim to shore, and make peace with the King.

Let me tell you a little about the appearance of Orpheus a moment prior to him diving overboard and swimming to shore. He was only twenty-one years old with piercing blue eyes, and after some serious rowing, his muscles were well defined. His normally flowing blonde hair was tied at the base of his neck with a small piece of leather, and he was wearing enough to cover his manhood.

Three women approached him while he was still climbing his way through the soft, wet sand.

"Stop right there" yelled one of the women.

"Who are you, and what are you selling? Your boat does not look like anything I have ever seen, but whatever it is you have, we have probably already got it."

"We are not selling anything, but if you take me to your king, I can explain who we are and why we are here."

"Do not come one step closer. My archers are itching for some live practice."

Orpheus turned to wave at Jason, in a pre-determined hand gesture indicating that he was safe. But one thing was now puzzling Orpheus. All the archers aiming their arrows directly at him appeared to be women, and the three people who approached him in the water were female. He could not see any men, but had no way of relaying this message to Jason. Maybe this was a trick, and at any minute, men would come out from behind trees. Something else didn't seem quite normal to Orpheus. Looking at the archers, he noticed that many of them appeared to be smiling, and looking him up and down. It was at this moment that Orpheus remembered what he was wearing, or to be more accurate, what he was not wearing!

The three women standing closest to him asked Orpheus to follow them to the palace. Finally, he thought he would be taken to see the king, but after walking through an ornate courtyard with statues of men and women in fighting poses glistening in the sunlight, he was led into the throne room.

On the Argo, Jason and his four leaders hastily discussed what they might do next if Orpheus did not return to the beach. All eyes on board the boat were trained directly at the archers. Atalanta, Philoktetes and about ten others gathered their weapons, while Hercules and his old friend Theseus started to bring all shields and javelins to the Argo's deck. Two argonauts, Ekhion and Mopsus, slipped quietly into the water behind the Argo and swam out to sea before turning to their right. They were instructed to make way to a headland nearby, to attempt to swim behind the low, rocky hill. Once on dry ground, to make a sound of a bird to let Jason know they had made it safely, but most of all, to remain out of sight.

Ancaeus and Admetus did the same a moment later, but swam without making any splashes, to their left to where a very high rocky hill was situated. They were also instructed to keep out of sight, move as close as possible to a cover of trees, and to make a similar bird sound to indicate their position.

Each of these four swimmers could go for long periods of time underwater without taking a breath. Jason hoped they would not be caught. At this moment in time, Jason and his four leaders did not know there were no men on the island. From their distance at sea, the archers still looked menacing.

Orpheus was stunned when he noticed one of the three women take a seat on the throne.

"I am Queen Hypsipyle. This is Katerina and Polyxo, my two senior advisers. Now, who are you and what are you doing here?"

"My name is Orpheus. With our leader Jason of Iolchus, we are travelling to Colchis, to search for, find, and bring back a special golden ram's fleece. We are forty-nine, forty-eight men and one woman"

"A ram's fleece you say? What is so special about this sheep?"

"We are not sure, but some say, those who have seen it, is that it is made from gold. The current King of Iolchus wants to own it, and we are going to get it for him."

"We have plenty of rams here. Take one, and be on your way. Consider it our gift."

"Orpheus, can you please say that again."

"Which part?"

"About the forty-eight men and one woman. Why only one woman?"

"Where do I start Queen Hypsipyle? May I ask our leader Jason to explain all this to you?"

"All in good time. Why one woman? Is she your cook? Does she perform other tasks for you men?"

"Her name is Atalanta, and she is the best archer in the whole of Greece."

"Tell me about the other forty-eight. You know, the non-women!"

"Our leader Jason will be made King of Iolchus on our successful return with the fleece. We have fighters, archers, farmers, hunters, cooks, navigators, boat builders, athletes, strong men, healers and perhaps the best musician in the whole world!"

"We mean you no harm Queen Hypsipyle. But I would like to ask you this one question. I do not see any men."

"Ok. Just one question."

"Where are your men?"

"Our men left some time ago to fight pirates on Samothraki. My father, the king, was one of those men."

"When will they return?"

"I am sorry Orpheus. You only asked for one question, and I have answered."

"Forgive me. But I will say this on behalf of Jason and our crew. We have been rowing for several days now. We are hungry and tired. May we rest here for two days, repair our leaking boat, and then move on?"

The queen conferred with her two senior advisors. While this was taking place, several more unarmed women entered the throne room and stood silently in the background. One of the women asked Hypsipyle if she could speak.

"Yes Komi. You may speak."

"I need some work done at my house, and it seems this boat has plenty of strong, healthy young men who could lend some assistance. Would that be a problem?"

The Queen made a rapid decision without any additional consultation.

"Swim back to your boat and inform your friends that they are to leave all weapons on the sand. Also tell your leader that you are permitted to stay for two days. If you do not follow my instructions, I will have no hesitation in asking the archers to start practicing on live targets. Is that clear?"

Jason was becoming nervous at how long Orpheus was taking. Was he alive? Had he been killed? But as soon as these thoughts entered his mind, they soon evaporated with the afternoon heat. Orpheus was alive, and swimming back to the Argo.

Meleager and Acastus hoisted the drenched Orpheus out of the water and onto the deck. Smiling like a young child with a new carved wooden toy, the swimming musician gave a brief report.

"We will be permitted to stay for two days. But there is something you all should know."

"What is it? What can possibly make you smile like that?"

By now all ears were listening to Orpheus speak, all except the four swimming spies, who by now had given their bird sounds to indicate safety. Little did Jason know, but the swimming spies had been captured, and were being led to the beach.

"Like I said. We can stay for two days, but there are no men in this city."

"What do you mean, no men?"

"No men? None at all. Not even boys or old men. They all left for Samothraki to fight pirates, and have not returned. There is one more thing. We must leave our weapons on the sand just over there."

Hercules, Atalanta and Philoktetes were not at all happy with this last comment.

"I'm not leaving my weapons on that beach", said a clearly annoyed Hercules.

"Jason. Look. There on the beach."

Kristus noticed the four spy swimmers were now four captured spy walkers."

"We will do as they ask. Hercules – keep some of your weapons in the secret compartment so if they search the Argo, they won't find them."

When Argos constructed the boat, he thought it might be a good idea to build a surreptitious, hidden cupboard under the helmsman's seat. It was large enough to secrete weapons in case of a situation such as this.

Instructions were given to Telamon, Peleus and Hippomenes for their groups to jump into the shallow water, take ropes and haul the Argo closer to the beach. Kristus' group was to sit at the rear of the boat, which made the bow sit slightly higher in the water, making it easier to haul ashore.

The sight of over thirty men leaping into the water, dressed only in the barest minimum of clothing must have seemed a strange sight to the gawking onlookers gathered on the beach. All archers remained in their 'ready' position, in case an instruction to shoot was ordered. Fortunately, it was not necessary.

CHAPTER 10

Limnos

Queen Hypsipyle positioned herself on the beach, observing all around her. Immediately behind her stood two trusted advisors, and fanning out along the long, narrow strip of sand, women were gathering in groups to witness this unfolding event.

"You must be Jason, leader of this group" asked Queen Hypsipyle as Jason steadily made his way out of the soft, wet sand onto dry land.

"I am. You must be Queen Hypsipyle."

Jason followed the Queen to the palace. The Argo was dragged safely up onto the beach, all Argonaut weapons placed in a pile under a tree, and the four drenched spies were released. Archers surrounded the rowers, who by this stage, were now resting comfortably on sand, under shade, and drinking much needed water from some shared cups, passed around to each weary rower by eager young girls.

Atalanta sat with Philoktetes, Peleus and Hercules and discussed the situation. After satisfying their thirst, Atalanta spoke.

"I don't think any of these archers knows which end of the bow to hold."

"What do you mean?" asked Peleus.

"Look at that one there," pointing to a nervous looking woman who was shaking ever so gently.

"She is gripping the bow all wrong. Look at her hand! Too soft. She is holding it like she is about to prepare some food, not fire an arrow at us!"

Philoktetes noticed more of them holding their bows as if it was the first time they had done so.

"Apart from that one there, they look like this is their first day of weapon training!"

One tall slender woman stood apart from the rest. She held her bow correctly, had the look of a hunter, and her hands were steady.

More young girls moved between each weary rower offering not only water, but figs, bread, and something else. Wine! By now, each of the argonauts were feeling completely relaxed. The hours spent rowing into a head wind with blisters, sore bums and strained muscles were now becoming a distant memory. Orpheus approached a rather officious looking older woman, who he noticed was one of Queen Hypsipyle's advisors.

"May I retrieve my lyre from our boat" asked a sheepish musician.

"What do you want that for?" replied the stubborn old woman.

"To play music" responded the cheeky but beautiful looking young man.

By now, all the beached Argonauts were sitting with their backs to the city of Myrina, where shops, taverns, houses, and a group of resting donkeys were basking in the late afternoon sun. Many of the milling women had not really seen any of their new island guests up close, but that was about to change.

Iphicles, the less muscular brother of Hercules was one of the first to stand and stretch his arms and legs. As he rose, a collective gasp erupted from some women close by. Iphicles took all his clothing off and washed it in the sea. As he turned to face the city, the faces of the women of Limnos were staring directly at his naked body. Purposely ignoring the ogling stares, Iphicles simply sat back down on some grass, squeezing his chiton as dry as he could. Not to be outdone, most of the seated argonauts did the same. But when the man-mountain Hercules took his clothing to rinse in the shallow salt water, a brave Komi quickly rushed to his side, took the chiton gently out of his hands and offered to wash it for him properly.

Seeing Komi's laundering actions, it didn't take long for all Argonauts wet clothing to be taken away for some much-needed cleansing by an eager Limnian woman. The only ones not undressing were Philoktetes and Atalanta, who remained vigilant, observing the archers' movements.

Near the water's edge, a short walk away from where the Argo was beached, was a stone circular well, which usually had about three or four people at a maximum attempting to take water from a bucket on a long rope dangling over a tripod of lashed wooden posts. Next to the well were four carved, hollowed out stone blocks where women and their daughters would perform daily washing rituals. The scene now was one of complete chaos. Women were jostling each other to take their turn at the bucket. While I say it was chaotic, it was also a joyful occasion. Normally, the conversation between women at the well was centred on what to eat that day, what was fresh in their gardens and how fast the girls were growing. Today, the conversation was completely different.

Wooden stakes, tree branches, and hastily constructed clothes lines of rope were springing up all over the beach. The argonauts watched in awe of the industrious women. Jason still had not emerged from the palace, and Orpheus was tuning his instrument under the shade of a plane tree.

The closest tavern to this unfolding event began supplying more wine. Shuffling between the tavern and thirsty argonauts were a bevy of girls carrying kraters of wine and tasty morsels of a mixture of bread and figs. Even the girls were now used to the sight of naked men lying on the beach, resting on one arm, and discussing any mundane topics they could imagine.

While many of the tired men of the Argo were now resting with a belly full of wine and food, Jason appeared and took up a position near Philoktetes and Atalanta. He noticed most of the men were now asleep, snoring like an old donkey. He took off his clothes and almost immediately, a woman emerged to whisk them away for washing. Atalanta decided it was time to approach the archers.

Sitting on the beach, observing the archers, Atalanta thought of a way to talk to the woman who looked like, and acted like the leader. Clearly not looking as though she posed a threat, Atalanta asked the name of the woman.

"My name is Aspasia. Who are you?"

"I am known as Atalanta. If you don't mind me asking, but can you see that tree down at the end of the beach?"

Atalanta was pointing to a tree, about a javelin's throw away.

"Of course, I can see it. So what?"

"Can you see the knot about half way up the tree, on its right-hand side. It seems to be the size of a lemon. Can you see it?"

"Yes. Again, so what?"

"I doubt if your best archer could strike that knot, firing from here."

Aspasia was falling into the trap set by the wily Atalanta. She didn't know what was to happen, but Atalanta, the skilled and talented hunter was preparing her ambush.

"No one but a god could strike that target. It is impossible for mere mortals like us."

"Are you sure? It isn't very far. I could possibly hit it......I think."

At this stage, very few argonauts knew of her ability with the bow. Although they had heard snippets of her reputation, almost all of them did not really appreciate her unique talent. After all, she was just a woman! Jason most certainly knew of her skills, which is why she was chosen as part of this voyage.

Aspasia said that she was the best archer on the whole of Limnos, but Atalanta was not finished with her deceptive ruse.

"How about you fire ten arrows at the target. I predict you will miss with all of them. Then, give me one shot, and I promise you, I *won't* miss."

The Limnian archers laughed the kind of laugh when someone else knocks their elbow on something hard, but Atalanta and

Aspasia were not laughing.

"Ten arrows you say," quizzed Aspasia.

"Yes, ten. Start whenever you feel ready."

Aspasia took her bow and fired the first shot. It missed. Not even close. She fired another eight and they all missed, but she was getting closer to the target. At least some of the arrows struck the tree. Her hands were trembling. She was the best archer on Limnos and she had just missed nine shots. One arrow to go. She waited for her hands to settle, wiped her brow free of stinging sweat somehow finding a way into her right eye, raised the bow, loaded her arrow, aimed, released and missed everything yet again.

A collective groan was heard from the group of eager onlookers.

"Are you happy? I am the best here and I missed all ten shots. The target is much too difficult to hit from this spot. No women or man could strike it. It is impossible."

With drooping shoulders, Aspasia trudged her way back to the rest of the group, gently placed her bow on the sand, folded her arms defiantly and stared at Atalanta, who by this stage was showing no emotion of any kind.

Seeking reassurance from the rest of the group, and speaking to no one in particular, Aspasia pleaded "no one can hit that target – right?"

"Now that I think of it, it is a long way from here. You may be right. It might be impossible, but may I now take one shot at it anyway?"

Aspasia, feeling quite proud of herself for getting close to this impossible target, was convinced that this woman from the Argo would have no chance, and even with weapon in hand, would present no danger to her or her company.

"Go ahead. One shot."

"Before I take my one shot, I have one small request. May I please use my own bow that was taken from our boat? It is in the pile of weapons over there."

Not for one moment thinking that any bow belonged to a woman, Aspasia said "Sure, but I will get it. Wait here."

Atalanta described the bow to Aspasia, who then strode confidently to the weapons, discovered the bow, and brought it back, admiring its characteristics and feel. It felt strong. Now she was completely convinced that it must have belonged to one of the men aboard.

"Here it is. You have one shot," she said as the weapon was handed to Atalanta. "Here is one arrow."

Atalanta gently held the arrow, found its centre of balance, and appreciated its feel and superb craftmanship.

Carefully watching from the beach amongst the sleeping crew was Philoktetes. He knew Atalanta's ability, and apart from himself and Hercules, she was the next best archer on the Argo. He knew she could strike this target ten times out of ten, but he was not about to spoil her demonstration.

Aspasia and the other archers were watching Atalanta and nervously chuckling amongst themselves.

"No one can hit that."

"Impossible."

"Not even a man could strike that target."

Imagining what was about to transpire, Philoktetes casually strolled over to the archers and joined in the chuckling.

"Forgive me for this interruption, but you are right. No one could strike that target. I might be able to get close in ten arrows, but Atalanta is our cook. She does not know the first thing about archery. An expert in the fine art of food preparation, but she would not know the first thing about archery. There is no chance that she will come close to that target."

Philoktetes was rather pleased with his story about Atalanta being the cook, as she hated cooking. Atalanta joined in the ruse by saying that she was a cook, but also loved a challenge. She knew what Philoktetes was doing and added to the charade.

"Let me introduce to you, the best archer in all of mainland Greece, Philoktetes. If he says he would have trouble making this target, maybe you should listen to him. But I still think I can do it with but one of your arrows."

"Go ahead Atalanta. There is no way you can strike that target from here. Not even if you were twenty paces closer. Not even if you were ten paces from the target" mocked Philoktetes.

Feeling confident after hearing Philoktetes' fabricated story, Aspasia said "yes, go ahead. One arrow. Impossible."

Before Atalanta could pick up her weapon, Philoktetes snatched her bow, selected an arrow, and asked "May I shoot first?"

"Why not? If you are who she says you are, maybe you could get close to it? But I still think it is impossible."

Philoktetes nodded in the direction of Aspasia, and then carefully studied the target ahead of him on the beach. He carefully scrutinised his immediate environment to gauge the wind's direction and strength, and estimated the distance to the tree. Placing the arrow in its correct position, he took stance, aimed, and released.

The bowstring fizzed and the arrow flew in a graceful arc

towards the target, missing the knot just to the left by the width of a little finger.

"That was close" said Aspasia, who had never seen such a display of archery before. Not even her late husband, who had been Limnos' best archer, could have gotten so close.

Philoktetes had intentionally aimed at this very spot but did not dare admit it to the admiring band of part-time archers. Atalanta silently snickered, as she knew Philoktetes had aimed to miss. She was quietly impressed with how close he could be without striking the intended target.

Appearing disappointed with his one and only shot, Philoktetes walked backwards a few steps, turned, and handed the bow to Atalanta.

While this was taking place, Aspasia said under her breath to the other women that she had never seen such accuracy. They all nodded. None of them had ever seen it either.

Now it was Atalanta's turn to display her skills. In one fluid motion, she took the arrow, placed it in its correct position, gently pulled back the bow string, and released.

Bullseye!

All eyes were on the target. Atalanta was suppressing a smile. She said "That must have been a lucky shot. May I have one more to show you that it was pure luck?"

Without taking her eyes from the arrow quivering in the knot of the tree, Aspasia handed over another arrow.

Same result. Bullseye.

"All right. How about I go further away, say twenty paces."

Aspasia handed over another arrow, reluctantly. By this time, she was rubbing her eyes in amazement. Collectively, all the archers were standing with mouths wide open and eyes even wider.

Same result, now the target had three arrows firmly wedged together.

Philoktetes could see the Limnian archers were now completely confused. He asked if he could go back thirty paces more and have another shot.

Atalanta handed him the bow, and Aspasia gave him another arrow.

Bullseye! Now there was no room on the target for any more arrows, but not to be outdone, Atalanta requested one final shot. She retreated further along the beach to almost double the original distance.

Everyone was shaking their heads. Not Atalanta.

"Let me try one final time."

Now at twice the distance from when they commenced, Atalanta fired her last shot, splitting the arrow Philoktetes just fired, and striking the target.

Aspasia asked "Who are you?"

Looking directly into the eyes of Philoktetes, she asked inquisitively "are you Apollo" and then turning to Atalanta, she asked "and are you Artemis?"

Philoktetes stepped in to respond. "We are very sorry to have deceived you. We mean no harm. Atalanta is not our cook. She and I are the best archers in the whole of Greece. That is why we are on this voyage with Jason. If you like, we are his personal bodyguards. We are most certainly not gods. We happen to be mere mortals who are very good at this. Nothing more."

Aspasia knew that she and the other women were in the presence of archery gods, regardless of what Philoktetes said.

She was not upset or annoyed at being deceived but thrilled at the possibilities of what could be learned from these two experts. Without asking the other women, she spoke quickly.

"While you are here, can you please tutor us? As you can see, we need help. Just a few lessons. Please."

"I am sure we can do that tomorrow at first light," said Atalanta. "But first, I believe a feast is in order."

Aspasia and the other archers had never imagined there could be this degree of accuracy over such a long distance. When Philoktetes and Atalanta finally returned to their crew, Aspasia and the archers could not believe their good fortune. They were about to learn archery skills from the best possible teachers in the modern Greek world. With a high level of nervous excitement and anticipation normally associated with children immediately before receiving a gift, they could not wait until the following morning.

Some of the Argonauts were now waking up after a brief rest and could be seen sitting on the beach talking to each other. Orpheus climbed onto the Argo to retrieve one of his instruments. On the voyage from Iolchus, he did not row a great deal, causing many of the others to wonder why he was on the voyage at all. Jason responded by saying each of the crew members had been chosen for their specific and different skills. Orpheus was a musician, which elicited great consternation and some resentment amongst the rowers, straining their muscles on the oars.

Typhus the helmsman was most annoyed at first, because Orpheus sat directly beneath him, and he thought that having a musician at his feet was not conducive to a well-run ship. He was heard to ask early on in their voyage "Why do we need an effeminate musician?"

About half way between Iolchus and Limnos, Orpheus had gently picked up his lyre and started strumming, making up songs as he went along. Playing in rhythm with the stroke of an oar, each rower began to forget the pain in their arms and backs, and became mesmerised by his music and sweet voice. Orpheus' voice seemed to transcend the sounds of the sea and enter the minds of each rower to act as a soothing balm for aching muscles. In line with his well-rehearsed formulae for creating songs, Orpheus soon had each rower singing along with the words and music. It was not uncommon for the rowers to attempt to out sing each other.

At one stage during an Orpheus song with a competition to see who could sing the loudest, Jason turned his head sharply and was heard to have said rather abruptly to Typhus "Now you know why he is here."

Sitting on the beach at Myrina, Orpheus again picked up the lyre and played once more, creating yet more new songs as he went. This time, it wasn't the Argonauts who were listening, but Limnian women and children coming to the beach to offer succour to the waking argonauts.

I am not going to try to sing any of his songs because they were improvised at the time, and quickly forgotten, but in doing so, Orpheus established his credentials as a talented musician, capable of taking everyday events, people and situations, and turning them into lyrical poetry set to music.

In his repertoire, Orpheus sang on his own, encouraged his audience to join in, sang sad, happy and romantic songs, but most of all, accurately reflected the mood of the occasion as he deemed necessary with his music.

From the palace gardens, Queen Hypsipyle heard the music on the beach, and quickly ventured to hear its source. On her arrival, she soon came under the musician's spell and could not comprehend how someone could make music so effortlessly, as if it had been sung hundreds of times before.

"Orpheus, please bring your instruments tonight to the feast. That was beautiful. We have never heard such melodic and interesting music before."

"It would be an honour, Queen Hypsipyle. I look forward to it."

"As do all of us."

Watching from the bow of the Argo was Hercules. Keeping an anxious eye on the weapons, and making sure the boat did not drift back into the sea on a high tide, he sensed that his fellow crew were not in any present danger, and eventually allowed himself a short rest. Like all the other Argonauts, it was the first real respite he had had since leaving Iolchus.

Constantly trying to live up to his image as a strong man all the time must have been tiring, and Hercules soon fell into a deep sleep. His pulsating rhythmic snoring could be heard all over the beach, and it was not long before Orpheus picked up on it and started to sing songs about the noise emanating from Hercules' throat and nose. For a gifted and talented musician like Orpheus, he had no trouble using the rhythm of Hercules' snoring to make an instant tune. His method of song writing was to first hear a rhythm, then hum and strum the lyre. When he was satisfied with the sound and melody, he experimented with key words and phrases. To the untrained ear, it seemed like he was a musical genius, but to Orpheus, it was little more than a well-rehearsed method of song writing and performance.

Enough of how to write songs. Bring me another wine.

Myrina was a beehive of activity in preparation for the welcome feast. Wine amphorae came in from neighbouring vineyards by the score, and fruits and vegetables were being ripped off tress and pulled from the Limnian soil. Women were busily preparing food all afternoon. Every farm had something to offer, and a number of sheep had already been slaughtered and prepared as soon as the feast was announced. There was a heavy smell of garlic and onion in the air, indicating the Limnians really enjoyed these ingredients.

Hypsipyle, Katerina and the young girls of Myrina began decorating the palace in preparation for the feast. Seats were adorned with colourful cushions, flowers arranged in vases, pottery strategically placed where it could be seen and garlands of olives and oregano were hung from any vantage point available. It was not well thought out, but Hypsipyle was happy with the outcome given such short notice. After the palace decorations were completed, the girls seamlessly moved on to running deliveries between their laundering mothers and the naked Argonauts.

Dressed in freshly laundered clothing, the Argonauts wandered away from the beach to explore the surrounding environment such as the port area and castle hill situated within walking distance from the palace. Some could be seen strolling through farm land and talking to the women working on the land.

Sunset came, and all roads led to the palace. Women from their farms, women from village homes, Argonauts from their meanderings and young girls, well, from everywhere, made their way to the palace. The anticipatory mood was joyous and light hearted.

Hypsipyle invited Jason to start the evening by making a small speech.

"All of you know that we are on a very important quest to find a most valuable fleece in Colchis. We also have another part to this quest, that we have not told you about yet. You may have noticed the boat we arrived in. Its builder, Argos is here with us on the journey, to see how the vessel fares, and to make the necessary adjustments and repairs as and when they are needed. This is the finest boat ever built, and it is manned by the finest and strongest athletes and artisans ever assembled. In honour of Argos, the boat builder, we named this boat, the *Argo*, and we are Argonauts. We believe that all boats should have names, because to us, we feel part of it and it is part of us. It is alive, and we are its very beating heart."

"Tonight, we are honoured to be your guests. We intend to stay with you for as long as necessary to help with any jobs you feel that we are capable of, since your own men have been called away; absent for so long. We appreciate how difficult this past year has been for you all. We are your humble servants. We are here to help."

Many argonauts looked puzzled at this speech, thinking this was to be only a brief layover until the Argo was repaired, and supplies filled in preparation for the next leg of the journey. But the Limnian woman were hoping for something more than a one-night feast. You can imagine the roar of approval from all women at Jason's' final words. Now it was Queen Hypsipyle's turn to speak.

"As Queen of Limnos, I welcome you all to this special feast tonight, to honour Jason and his Argonauts, who are at the beginning of a very significant journey of discovery. We trust you enjoy the hospitality offered and that you stay for as long as you feel is necessary to prepare for what lies ahead. We have been without male company for quite a while now as has been explained to you, so forgive us if we seem overjoyed and just a little bit excited. I will not speak any longer, so eat, drink and be merry and enjoy the feast."

Before any ritual throat cutting of sacrificial animals, or any food or wine was consumed, Polyxo rose to speak.

"You can see that we are without men. Tragically, they were taken from us some years ago, leaving this island vulnerable to attack."

Jason noticed Hypsipyle looking directly at Polyxo with a confused expression on her face but allowed her to continue.

"In the intervening time we have become strong. However, we also know that this life for us cannot go on much longer unless our young women produce sons. We are ready for a new beginning, and if you or any of your crew would like to remain here on Limnos, we welcome you. This is the new beginning the god Phoebus promised me in my dreams. She promised new marriages for all and that life would begin again."

Jason too was confused by the comments regarding a new beginning and was not quite sure what it meant, but given his lack of context regarding the situation, decided not to comment at that moment.

Rising together, Hypsipyle and Jason undertook the usual feast rituals of animal sacrifice and wine libations and the celebration officially commenced. All argonauts, with the exception of Hercules, leapt into the spirit of the night immediately. Orpheus played his lyre, invented new songs, and sang about anyone and everything. Although he was performing in front of a captive audience, he was a sight for sore eyes and a sound for sad ears.

Limnian women had not heard music since their men departed but tonight most certainly made them feel happy once again. Orpheus clearly had a gift, and that night, he shared his gift with the women of Limnos and with the Argonauts.

After consuming glorious food and not-so watered-down wine, mixed with music and dancing, conversation and laughter, and then more wine, the long-suppressed urges of women bubbled to the surface, and couples started to depart together.

Orpheus was playing to a dwindling crowd, but he didn't seem to mind at all. Soon, the only people remaining were some older women, children, Hypsipyle and Katerina, Jason, Atalanta and of course Hercules who had stayed all night on the Argo. Hercules did have some food and wine brought to him by Komi, who then left him in peace and returned to serve food to others.

Atalanta lost sight of her fellow archer Philoktetes early in the night. She assumed he had wandered off with a local woman, but that was not the case. Philoktetes did wander off, but he was alone. He enjoyed his own company, and many times on the Argonauts journey after Limnos, he would be seen walking on his own and exploring the surrounding lands. Philoktetes had no idea at the time, but he was destined to spend ten years on Limnos in the future. Perhaps he developed a deep affection for the island on this short visit as an Argonaut, but that is another story for another time.

Philoktetes returned to the feast before the night was over, and made a point of speaking to Atalanta about archery training planned for the morning. The two archers chatted well into the night, talking about their lives, how and when they became interested in weapons, and who their mentors and teachers had been. Although from different geographical and cultural backgrounds, their lives had many similarities. There was a deep respect each had for the other, and before sleep took over, they bid a good night and settled down on the Argo for a well-earned night's sleep – separately!

Hypsipyle and Jason also sat together for a long time talking about many things. Hypsipyle felt that she could talk easily with him, and thought that the feelings were reciprocated. She calmly explained to Jason about the island's history and probably did love him from that moment, but it would take her some time to win him over. She didn't allow love or passion to cloud her judgement. She was calm, eloquent, and relied on persuasion to gain his trust.

No one can tell with any confidence where each of the Argonauts slept that night, or if they did actually sleep. All we know is that Atalanta, Philoktetes and Hercules spent the night aboard the Argo and Jason curled up next to the weapons on the beach.

Sunrise the next morning saw some unusual activity in and around the village. All women archers were ready with their bows and arrow, firing at the same target Atalanta and Philoktetes had hit the day before. Aspasia was as excited as a cat playing with a field mouse.

Philoktetes and Atalanta arrived with their bows and arrows and set up several targets, well away from the main beach, and closer to the castle at the top of the nearby hill. For the remainder of the day, a master class was given and both Argonauts enjoyed giving and sharing their advice. In years to come, these lessons helped the Limnian archers repel a few small pirate raids and certainly added to their perceived and no doubt actual prowess.

Orpheus was sitting in the plateia outside Ambrosia's wine bar first thing in the morning, waiting for it to open. He wanted to let Ambrosia know that the wine from the previous night was the sweetest wine he had ever tasted. He probably was angling for a free drink first thing in the morning, but there he was, strumming his lyre and sitting quietly. Ambrosia opened her doors, and heard the music coming from outside.

Ambrosia always wanted to learn how to play a musical instrument and asked him if he could teach her something. Orpheus agreed, but said in quick response, that a wine would help him with the lesson. Before ten heart beats, he was quietly sipping his first wine for the day!

Orpheus could not have imagined, but that first lesson given by him to Ambrosia sparked her interest in music, and more importantly, having musicians regularly play in her wine bar. Ambrosia told him about a dream she had many years ago about travelling to many places she did not recognise, and immediately Orpheus began to try some words to accompany his strumming. He added to Ambrosia's idea slightly and ended up with a girl travelling to new and wondrous places. He called the song 'Somewhere I've Never Travelled,' which was about a girl dreaming of travelling the world, and wondering what life would be like in these other places. Long after the Argonauts left Limnos, Ambrosia set up a music school in Myrina, called 'Orpheus.'

Down at the water's edge, Hercules was still a lone sentry guarding the Argo. During one of his visual scans along the beach, he saw Argos return with one of the Limnian women, Anna. During the feast, Anna spoke to Argos and asked him many questions about his boat, and how much she liked the look of it. He promised to take her aboard the next morning to see more closely. But that night, she asked him back to her house to check for 'spiders'!

For many years, Anna had always liked fishing, boats, and all things to do with the water. Her husband, now gone for more than a year, would often take Anna with him on fishing trips. Becoming quite the fisherwoman, Anna was also rather adept with a knife for gutting and cleaning any fish caught. Since her husband had gone, so too was their boat, and she longed for the day when she could travel beyond the shores of the port at Myrina.

Always wanting to return to spending time on the water, Anna was resigned to being a farmer for the rest of her life, due to the lack of a boat. Now, her secret passion had been rekindled with this arrival of new life and new possibilities. She soon became interested in how the Argo was constructed, and on the morning after the feast, was seen with Argos inspecting the boat and asking a lot of questions. Argos could see that she had some knowledge and was pleased to explain anything he could to her.

Hercules also seemed at ease with the stranger on board, because Anna had bought a plate of fine food. Argos knew Hercules would be hungry, so he asked Anna to help win over the giant warrior with a plate of Limnos' finest fare. It worked.

Anna spent a lot of time with Argos over the next few days. So much so, that she asked him to build a smaller boat, in a similar construction style to the Argo, for use in fishing. Argos was thrilled to be creating a second, smaller version of his boat, and agreed to build it for her. He enlisted the help of 10 members of the crew with carpentry skills, showed them what wood to find, and then set about creating a new, smaller fishing boat for Anna.

So studious was Anna's observations of the skill of Argos and his builders, that she remembered every detail of its construction with precision. From that point on, Anna and Argos spent day and night with each other. Long after the Argonauts left Limnos, the boat Argos built for Anna which still survives and can be seen in the port.

Unlike the story that has been promoted for many years and told by people who were never there nor spoke to anyone involved, the women of Limnos did not only want to mate with these men. They wanted so much more, and this new beginning was a way to achieve it. Yes, mating with the Argonauts would guarantee a continuance of life on Limnos, but that was not to be achieved overnight. Time spent without men had allowed their thoughts to ruminate on what would make them happy, and what was important to them. For some, it was as simple as wanting to stay at home and raise many children. For others, that was a part of their dreams, but they also wanted something else. The arrival of so many men aboard the Argo allowed each woman to find a man to help them learn new skills.

Stella was a woman who did everything her husband said. She stayed at home and raised children, but lost a husband and two sons. Since then, she and her two daughters struggled initially, but the sudden change in life circumstances had given women like Stella a new resolve.

On the night of the feast, Stella was in her element. She had always loved cooking and food preparation, and with her daughters, served their own food to many of the Argonauts. During the evening, Theseus asked if he could speak to the person responsible for food preparation. Stella spoke up and said that it was she together with her daughters and several of the other women.

At this time, very few Argonauts, and certainly none of the Limnians knew that Theseus was the future King of Athens. Obviously, Stella did not know this when she and Theseus started talking about food. Theseus was genuinely interested in the food quality, and the recipes Stella used. He had never tasted food like this.

Of course, Stella took Theseus back to her house that night, but all they did was to talk about food. Stella was not interested in Theseus as a man for sexual purposes, but was extremely interested in what he had to say about food.

The next morning saw a continuance of the previous night's food discussion, without any undue influence of wine consumption. Stella said that her dream now was to start a business whereby travellers could come to her shop and sit down to eat a meal, prepared by her, but a meal that reminded them of home. She knew this was a different idea, but it was something she always thought could be done. Many captains and crew from boats visited Limnos for trade, but all they could get at Ambrosia's tavern was wine, and fresh bread if lucky.

In her café, Stella asked Theseus if he could arrange for some of the Argonauts to help her and her daughters clear their land, and plant some seedlings. Theseus agreed and with the help of Laertes and five Argonauts, spent the next week clearing, planting, preparing, pruning, and general maintenance of their farm. The additional workers also repaired the dry-stone walls around the farm, and the wall surrounding the animal enclosures.

By the time the Argo departed Limnos, Stella had established her cafe next to Ambrosia's bar, in the port area. The two businesses complemented each other perfectly. One sold locally grown and produced wine with bread, honey and olives to weary travellers in the early mornings to mid-afternoon, and the other sold freshly prepared food in the evenings that reminded each traveller of home.

Laertes was the father of Odysseus, who years later would rise to fame in helping to bring about a solution to the Trojan blockade. During the week of hard work on the farm, Stella and Laertes were beginning to develop a very close and personal friendship. They were falling in love. It was not too long before he stayed at her home one night, and it would be fair to say, they were not discussing the next day's work schedule!

Allow me to digress here and jump ahead many years in time. Laertes was made king of Ithaca upon his return from the voyage of the Argo. He had not been married at this stage and had met his future wife Anticlea only days before the voyage departed.

Towards the end of the Trojan blockade when neither side was winning, Odysseus visited Limnos to ask for Philoktetes' help in bringing about a swift end to the problem. Philoktetes had returned to Limnos to live a life of solitude after the Argo's voyage ended. Odysseus sought the help of local people in Myrina to find the missing and enigmatic master of arrow and bow construction, Philoktetes. Visiting Ambrosia's bar on arrival in the port, Odysseus asked Ambrosia where he could find Philoktetes.

Overhearing the conversation was Stella who entered the bar and said that she could help in the search for the missing reclusive Argonaut. Stella told Odysseus that her son knew where he lived and would take him there in the morning.

Before the night ended, Stella and Ambrosia, who were now very advanced in their years, could not help but notice the resemblance between Odysseus and Stella's son Sophocles, who had just arrived after a long day in the field tending their sheep and goats.

After washing away the grime of the day's agricultural activities, Sophocles sat down with his young children and asked for a krater of Ambrosia's finest, while his mother prepared a meal. Sitting on the next table was Odysseus, who politely asked him if he could take him to where Philoktetes was.

"Sure. First thing in the morning, I'll meet you here, but when I say first thing, I mean before the sun comes up. We will have to travel for most of the day by donkey, and we won't get back until much later in the day."

Odysseus agreed. As the two men were discussing the logistics of the next day's travel, Stella and Ambrosia sat listening intently.

"If you don't mind Odysseus, could you tell me a little about yourself?" asked Stella.

The Greek army blockade of Troy was well known throughout the northern Aegean islands. To satisfy an entire army with its caravan of followers, Limnos had been selling wine and some food for many years.

"I am Odysseus. Son of Laertes and Anticlea. I am King of Ithaca."

Before he finished his rather short speech, Stella appeared to choke on some bread and honey.

"Are you alright Aunty", enquired the polite Odysseus. "Here, have some of this fine wine."

"Did you say Laertes, from Ithaca?"

"Yes. He is my father. Why do you ask?"

At this stage, Sophocles was busy devouring his meal, washing it down with Ambrosia's fine wine. He was not paying any attention to the visitor. He was more intent on discussing what his children had done that day while he was out in the field.

"Was your father, by any chance, one of the famed crew with Jason from the Argo?"

"Yes, he was. How did you know that?"

"The Argo visited these shores many years ago, and I met your father then. Did he ever mention Limnos to you Odysseus?"

"My father talked about many things from that voyage. I seem to recall that he said he came here, but it was only for a few days. He said that they were very well looked after and cared for, and after a few days restocking the boat, left for the rest of their journey."

Clearly, Laertes had not told his son about how long they remained on the island. Clearly, he had not mentioned to Odysseus he had a half-brother, who was about to take him on another journey the next day to find Philoktetes.

Sophocles finished his food and wine and bid Odysseus a good night, blissfully unaware he was talking to his brother. Odysseus did the same and retired to the beach to sleep for the night.

Stella and Ambrosia were by now chuckling and smiling. After Odysseus had left, and just before Sophocles retired, he asked his mother why she was laughing.

"Sophocles, the visit from Odysseus reminded Aunty Ambrosia and me of the days the Argonauts visited here, that's all. We were young then and his visit today has jolted our memories. Our marvellous memories. Good night son."

"Good night mother, good night, Aunty. See you in the morning."

Sophocles had no idea of the real story. He had no idea that he was the brother of perhaps one of Greece's most famous warriors. For the rest of his mother's life, she never revealed the truth.

Sophocles and Odysseus were physically alike in so many ways, and neither of them ever suspected anything, even though they spent a day travelling together on the backs of donkeys to find Philoktetes.

Let me return now to the present tale.

There were numerous stories such as these where a Limnian widow together with an Argonaut spent intimate nights together, but the tryst later developed into something more substantial. To Polyxo's surprise, this new beginning went in a far better direction than she could have possibly imagined. Every crew member of the Argo helped at least one Limnian woman with a task, other than making them pregnant, that was to have far reaching and positive ramifications for many years to come.

Even Hercules, the self-proclaimed Argo and weapons watcher had weakened a little and allowed himself to be taken away from the beach. One day while she was helping Anna prepare food to take on board to the hungry Hercules, Komi said she would take it herself. At this stage, Anna did not mind, as she and Argos were busy constructing a new boat.

Komi came to the Argo each day to offer Hercules a plate of food, which he dutifully accepted. Komi didn't say anything for the first few days but gathered enough courage to speak to him on about the fifth day.

Komi had asked him politely to help with some house re-building, and Hercules surprisingly said yes. I say surprisingly because he had been so rigid and strict in his guarding of the boat, that he had not abandoned its deck, apart for personal exercise or a quick swim in the sea to wash since their arrival. He would sit on the port rail, watching Philoktetes and Atalanta teach the archers each day, listen to Orpheus sing and make up songs at Ambrosia's bar, and observe the activity immediately adjacent to the Argo on the beach where Argos and Anna were busily designing and constructing a new boat.

Seeing his comrades going about what appeared to be normal daily activities, he agreed instantly to Komi's request for him to assist in domestic duties.

Over the next few weeks, Hercules would be seen working on her house lifting large rocks into place to strengthen the walls and the roof. Komi knew they had no future together, and Hercules did not promise anything he could not deliver. He never promised to return after the voyage of the Argo, and Komi understood, but those few weeks had an impact on Limnos more than we can possibly imagine. But it is true that Hercules did more with Komi than merely help with house construction.

Eight months after the Argo departed Limnos, Komi gave birth to a healthy baby girl, who she named Atsiki. As with all the women who gave birth, everyone knew who the fathers were, and no one was judged.

If it wasn't for Komi and her pursuit of Hercules, they would not have had a child, and I may not have known my life of storytelling. See what I mean? The impact of these long-ago events are still being felt today. Now, after a slight detour I return to the story once again.

After her husband disappeared, Magda was eager and keen to find an Argonaut who shared her passion for butchery. On the first night's feast at the palace, Magda bought along several lambs and goats to be slaughtered and prepared for eating. Several of the Argonauts offered to help in the slaughter, but were surprised when Magda quietly declined their offers, and proceeded to carefully and methodically kill, bleed, skin and carve each animal into portions ready for the ovens.

One Argonaut who volunteered to help was originally offended when his offer for assistance was rejected, but his feelings soon dissipated as he watched a master butcher apply her trade. Butes, an Athenian shepherd and warrior, was fascinated by Magda's skill and dexterity with a knife.

He introduced himself to her and asked if he could at least kill the last lamb. Magda reluctantly agreed and handed over her knives. It was the turn of Butes now to politely reject her offer and took out his own knives. Before Magda could say anything, the lamb was dead with its throat cut, and she sat back to watch Butes apply his talent. She too was amazed, and for the rest of the night, the two butchers talked all things knives, sharpening techniques, the slaughtering of different animals, and surprisingly, of cooking tips with succulent ingredients.

Over the following days and weeks, Butes and Magda were seen together constantly. After their first night, subsequent evenings conversations shifted to milking, cheese making and what to do with the fleeces of lambs and goats. It did not take long for Magda to ask Butes to come back to her house so that she could show him her woollen blankets and woven rugs.

Sophia was one of the women who made constant trips to the beach on the first day to investigate the Argonauts clothing needs. She was particularly taken by one member of the crew, Eribotes, who appeared to be different to the others.

On running back to the beach to return Eribotes his chiton, Sophia slipped and cut her leg on a branch that was hidden just below the surface of the sand. She fell quite awkwardly, and sprained her ankle in the tumble. Eribotes saw the accident and immediately went to offer her his assistance.

Sophia was most embarrassed, not at falling over on a hidden branch, but because she had ripped Eribotes' chiton during her fall.

"Let me take a look at that for you" said Eribotes.

"I am so sorry that I have ripped your chiton. Let me return home to repair it immediately."

"I want to look at your wounds, not my clothing."

Sophia was further embarrassed even more, as she was being cared for on the beach by a stranger, a naked stranger who was now carefully washing and cleaning her wound while resting her ankle on his knee.

"Give me that chiton. It will make the perfect bandage."

He took the chiton from Sophia and began ripping it into long strips to be wrapped around the ankle to give support. Some additional strips were used in cleaning the gash that had now almost stopped bleeding.

Sophia forgot about her naked medical assistant, and was feeling less embarrassed about her clumsiness, and his lack of clothing.

Surprised as his tenderness, Sophia enquired as to his past. Eribotes told her that he was a member of the crew because of his surgical skills. He then asked about her past and she told him she had a passion for making jewellery.

"My mother had the same passion, and she taught me many of her skills," said Eribotes.

For the rest of that first night at the feast, and long after Eribotes found some fresh clothing, they talked about rings, bracelets, necklaces, earrings, pendants, arm bands, diadems, and hair ornaments. Sophia told him about her own clothing she was designing, and the next day Eribotes paid her a visit. By the end of ten days, Eribotes was the best dressed Argonaut in Myrina!

While all these liaisons were taking place, Hypsipyle and Jason were just as active. A surprising announcement was made thirty days after the Argo's arrival. Jason was so taken with Hypsipyle and living in Myrina, that he asked her to marry him. Hypsipyle said 'yes.'

The wedding was a different ceremony to the normal weddings of the day. With no mother, Hypsipyle spent the final few days in the company of Polyxo standing in as her maternal guide. Hypsipyle, Katerina and some of their closest friends took Hypsipyle's childhood toys to the temple of Aphrodite, to symbolically announce the formal end of childhood, and the start of life as a wife. Hypsipyle cut her hair, and on the day of the wedding, she and Jason bathed in holy water. Jason did not have his parents present, so no dowry could be offered, only promised.

A feast was held in the palace, attended by almost all Limnians. This was the first of several weddings between women and the Argonauts. Jason promised to return to Limnos immediately after his quest was completed, and Hypsipyle had no reason to doubt him. At this stage, Hypsipyle was most certainly pregnant.

Over the next thirty days, many more weddings occurred. All grooms made promises to their brides that they would return on completion of the quest.

On reflection now, it was highly likely that most of the women who married, and even those who did not marry but still coupled with an Argonaut, expected their new partners never to return. They were fully aware of potential dangers with the long voyage ahead and resigned themselves to not just the possibility, but the reality of a life with no man at home, and a new beginning through children born soon enough.

It had been seventy days since Jason and the Argonauts landed in Myrina, and now it was time to leave. Hercules was the one who forcefully reminded Jason and the others of their true purpose and mission. After helping the people of Limnos with rebuilding their lives, it was time to move on to the next stage of their journey. Many storytellers over the years have tried to paint the visual picture of hundreds of crying women on the beach, as the Argo was re-floated. Nothing could be further from the truth. All women knew that one day soon these men would have to depart. In their brief time together, normal life had returned, and seeds were sown for new life to germinate and prosper, and a new beginning for the women of Limnos could be seen on the horizon.

Before the Argo finally slipped effortlessly into the sea, Hypsipyle asked Jason to wait just a moment longer, as she had something to give him. Jason agreed.

Running back from the palace, Hypsipyle had a sword in her right hand which caught Jason's eye, and a cloak in her left. He did not notice the cloak because his attention was firmly and squarely on the sword.

"Jason, this sword belonged to my father. Please take it on your journey, and I hope it will be useful for you one day."

Jason was delighted with this gesture from his wife. He knew the value of such a gift and thanked her for it. Hypsipyle gave something else to Jason. She handed him a special woollen cloak, made from local cloth, and dyed purple. She told him to remember her each time he wore it.

With that gesture of gift giving from a wife to her husband, the Argo drifted slowly out to sea before all oars on the port side were engaged to turn the mighty boat around in readiness for the next part of their journey. Typhus shouted instructions and in no time, the freshly victualled vessel clicked into a slow rhythmic beat with Orpheus once again playing his lyre.

During their stay on the island of Limnos, the Argo was repaired and hopefully, all leaks and creaks were patched, plugged, and greased. A set of new sails were brought onboard, and many of the oars were replaced. All storage spaces were filled with amphorae of wine, water, salted meat, olives, oil, and dried figs.

Jason called on Typhus to set course for the next island.

CHAPTER 11

Theseus

As a storyteller of many old and some new tales of heroes and wild animals, I have always had a soft spot for other storytellers. Jason's Argonauts were full of current and future heroes, whose stories would be told and re-told for generations to come. But there were some stories so twisted after these re-tellings that it became impossible to separate the myths from the truth, if there is such thing as story truth. My narrative of Jason's life most certainly has some incorrect and possibly outright false stories. I may choose to generalise, delete or distort some of these events, but let me tell you, not on purpose.

One of Jason's Argonauts was an old friend he met while chasing a wild boar. After the voyage with Jason, Theseus would go on to become the king of Athens, and marry the lovely Phaedra, but parts of his story have become so twisted and shredded, whether on purpose, or by inexperienced story tellers that I want to set the record straight by focusing on one such legend – that of Theseus and the Minotaur!

During the voyage, there were times when the Argo was so becalmed by wind, it was necessary for the rowers to work in shifts to propel the vessel on to its next destination. Other moments when the wind was favourable, the oars were taken out of use, and gusts filled the sail such that human exertion was not necessary. Apart from Typhus and Orpheus, who worked tirelessly at navigation and music, there were considerable down-times on deck when the wind was strong.

On one such occasion, Jason asked Theseus to set the record straight about his 'Minotaur' experience. Theseus agreed, and positioned himself at the bow, high enough on a pile of ropes where his voice could be heard be all. Even Orpheus stopped to listen to his tale. Before I begin, at the time of me chronicling this tale, there was already an outrageous myth surrounding Theseus. I have heard that some story tellers say there was such a Minotaur, which is believed to be half man and half bull, which lived in a labyrinth beneath the palace of King Minos.

Here is the tale, according to Theseus, as told to the Argonauts travelling with wind in their sail between Limnos and Imbros.

As all of you know, I have met some of you several years ago when we were hunting the Calydonian boar. Let me be the one here and now to tell you that my hunting skills are not as good as the legend has, because I did not slay that beast.

After the boar hunt, I returned to Athens, where my father King Aegeus of Athens and King Minos of Crete were locked in heated battles debating who had the best navy. Minos was a greedy man, and saw the land around Athens as land he could simply take from us, due to the superior nature and sheer size of his navy and soldiers. At the time, we were a growing city state, and Crete was large and powerful, blessed with many fine natural qualities, but Minos wanted much more.

He had threatened Athens on several occasions when I was younger, and my father was fearful our defences were not strong enough to withhold an invasion from Crete, so an agreement was made and agreed to by Kings Minos and Aegeus. The agreement was to last for nine years, where we would be forced to sell our grain and many products to Crete for well below market value. In addition, each year, seven males and seven females were to be sent to Knossos from Athens to work as slaves for twelve months. While this may seem a trivial contractual point, it had the effect of forcing us to adhere to Minos' wishes, and in the process, humiliating us. Each person sent to Crete had just turned eighteen.

Each of the seven males and females were treated poorly for the entirety of their twelve month enforced labours. Cretan palace slaves looked forward to the new Athenians each year because it meant they did not have to perform their normal, disgusting duties, such as cleaning animal enclosures, clearing human waste from the palace slop buckets, being groped by fat, smelly diplomats from countries and places of which none of us had ever heard. Each returning Athenian took years to shake off the humiliation and degradation of their time under the laws according to King

Minos. Some never got over the degradation suffered at the hands of these Cretans.

One of the duties each year was to see if one of our males would fight a bull, one that Minos had trained carefully to charge at any individual. The bull had a sixth sense and could smell fear. He told the participants that if any of them could last one minute in the bull ring with the beast, the whole deal between my father and Minos would be torn up. For the first three years, a brave male stepped forward to see if he could be the one to bring our shame to an end. Each time, the bull tore each volunteer to shreds.

The bull ring was no ordinary stadium. It was a specially contrived and constructed labyrinth where each frightened hunter was lead in blind folded from one entrance directly to the middle. The construction was made from stones and wood, and it was just high enough for the hunter not to be able to see over the walls. However, the watching crowd of eager, blood thirsty onlookers were high enough for them to see the sickening events unfold below them. If they couldn't see, then they could hear the blood curdling cries from a dying hunter. If any member of the crowd was heard shouting which way to escape, they would immediately be forced into the labyrinth by Minos' guards as the next participant in this deathly entertainment.

Each year, the labyrinth would be re-configured with only a handful of palace builders knowing the path out. However, one slave by the name of Daedalus, who built the labyrinth, would make last minute changes to his design, which only he knew of by the time a hunter was forced into the centre.

I had reached the age of eighteen, and I informed my father that I wanted to be one of the seven males to go to Crete. Of course, he told me that it would not be permitted, but I insisted, and after a few moments of heated discussions, he agreed with my decision. How could I look Athenians in the eye after I became of age and not volunteer for this? Jason, it was after meeting you the previous year on the boar hunt, that I became interested in hunting wild animals. I met one of the men who returned from Crete a year prior, and it was he who told me about the wild bull. He and all the others who were slaves for that year were too afraid to take Minos' challenge.

It was at that moment on my seventeenth birthday that I started to take secret lessons from some of my grandfather's best, and obviously retired hunters, in how to kill a charging bull. One of the old men told me about how young men of Crete had learned to jump over the bulls using their hands and flipping in the air when charged by the enraged beast. He said he had seen it for himself in Crete many years before.

I became adept in this manoeuvre, and after working on my strength and short weapons training, I felt it was time to see once and for all if I could end this conflict between Crete and Athens.

So off I went to Crete with the other thirteen terrified young citizens of Athens to be slaves for a year. Each of them knew I was the son of the king, but they had little inkling of my intentions to challenge the bull.

We arrived in Heracleion by boat from Athens and were taken directly to the palace at Knossos, some twenty stadia from the port where we disembarked. I say directly, but what I really mean is that we were forced to walk every step of the way. People on the side of the road threw rotten fruit at us. They knew who we were. We could not say anything or do anything. I felt completely powerless for the first time in my life. On arrival, the men were sent directly to the slave quarters and the women were taken to King Minos. I won't bore you with what happened at the palace between the women and Minos, but let me say that if he were here now, I would kill him.

One by one, we were taken to work for various members of the royal family and their entourage. Knowing that I was Aegeus' son, I was sent to work with the pigs and cows, where I shovelled shit. I slept alone in the male slave quarters because the others couldn't stand the smell of me. I kept to myself for about fifty days. Some of the other men were starting to lose hope, due to the constant humiliation each day. Their confidence was eroding before my eyes. My strength and resolve to end our suffering and cease the senseless embarrassment to the citizens of Athens was growing stronger by the day.

Three of the other men were sent to fish markets every morning and cleaned and gutted fish all day. The other three were given the task of cleaning latrines all around the palace. Now I look back on this, I laugh at the memory that they all said I was the one who stank the worst!

Knowing that our path out of this was for me to face the beast, I asked if I may speak to King Minos. "Why do you want to speak to the king, slave?" 'Because I want to face the beast' was my reply. My handler immediately began laughing, and rushed off to find some of the kings' servants. Within a matter of one more barrel of shovelled shit, I looked up from my grime and stench to be standing face to face with the king for the first time. I sensed it was him before I could see him, because the smell of scent and oils was not a smell akin to anyone or anything in this barn.

"What do you want, Prince Theseus?"

I told him I wanted to face the bull. I did not change expression, but I noticed a smile appear on his face. Little did he know what I was capable of, but I tried to appear slightly scared. Funnily enough, a piece of shit dribbled down under my filthy chiton, and onto the floor of the barn. King Minos noticed this and must have thought I had shit myself at the prospect of facing his bull. The timing of that piece of disgusting excrement sliding down my leg could not have been any better timed.

Within two days, I was able to sleep inside the palace, and not in the slave quarters where I had spent the past fifty days. I was bathed, oiled, and cleaned by our own Athenian women, who I had not seen since our arrival. Their expressions said it all. They had been asked to perform the most horrible of duties, and none of them could look me in the eye. These were women I had known since I was a baby, and they could not speak to me. I only found out much later what they had endured.

One of the women told me a strange story, of one of the King's daughters befriending the women and bringing food and water. If not for this woman, we would surely have suffered miseries of the worst kind, she said. She appeared to be making sure we were looked after, even though it could cost her dearly if the king ever found out. I didn't know what to make of this story, but it wasn't long before it became clear to me.

Let me tell you about the morning of my battle. Not long after I was cleaned to within a whisker of my life by the Athenian women, I was left alone in one of the palace rooms normally occupied by visiting dignitaries. A young woman who I had never seen before, entered alone, with the confidence of a member of the royal family. She told me her name was Phaedra, a daughter of King Minos. Being reluctant to talk to any member of that family, I was initially very hesitant, but she did not take no for an answer.

Not being in a position to argue with her, seeing as though she was a princess and I was a slave, she talked quickly with me in a hushed tone. I had the impression she was not meant to be talking with me, and she was trying to avoid any possible eavesdroppers.

"Theseus. No one has escaped with their life once inside the labyrinth. I know how you can escape with your life."

My initial reaction was that this must surely be a trap. But she convinced me it was not. How did she do that you may ask? She told me that she was making sure the Athenian women were not being mistreated, and she was looking out for them.

"You are the one who has been helping our women. Thank you, but why are you doing this?"

We only talked for a few moments after my question was answered.

"I want to leave Crete. My father is a tyrant, and this madness must stop."

Very cryptic I know, but within a heartbeat, she had departed. But not before telling me the secret to coming out alive. I thanked her for sharing this with me, but then I said to her that I would not be using this.

"Why not Theseus? No one has ever emerged with their life after entering the arena."

"Simple dear Phaedra. I intend to kill the beast!"

While this unnecessary conversation was taking place, King Minos and his slaves were preparing the labyrinth for my grand entry. I would only find out later, but the bull had not been fed for two days. Once it saw me, it would think that dinner was now being served!

Four slaves arrived at my room to lead me down to the arena, which was by now filled with baying spectators. It was difficult to know if they were expecting to see my blood or that of the bull. Most of the spectators did not want to be there, but the king's guard made sure every slave in the palace and all lowly citizens of Knossos were actively encouraged to attend. Anybody who did not accept a guard's polite request to attend the arena would be met with the sharp end of the guard's javelin.

All available seats were filled. Now for the grand entry of the poor unsuspecting meal – me! I was led through a heavy wooden gate and out into the arena. My beautifully prepared chiton was removed, and I was given one weapon – my personal hunting knife. I had not seen or felt this for fifty days, and it was like meeting an old friend. The crowd cheered, and a mixture of wild pig shit and offal was now being thrown at me – not because I like that particular aroma, but apparently, the bull loves this garnish with his food.

I felt calm, and strangely confident. My mind was going back to Athens, and thinking of the fields in which I grew up, the smells and the sounds. By closing my eyes for an instant, I managed to block out all around me, and was able to focus on the task at hand. I was not imagining victory. I was imagining doing my duty. Doing what I had been trained for a full year to do.

A blast from a bull's horn forced me to open my eyes and signified the entrance of the main attraction – the bull. It looked pissed. It looked hungry, and it looked at me. Moving away from the edges of the arena, I began to circle the bull, not taking my eyes from its massive head, the slobber and snot dripping from its nostrils and mouth. I was hoping for one of those bulls where its horns were sticking directly sideways from its enormous head, and not sticking up. I was in luck.

With its nostrils now flaring, it smelled me, took a few tentative steps in my direction, and charged. I took up a fighting stance, like standing on a boat where my right foot was slightly back and left foot forward, and my right hand gripping the handle of my weapon. The knife was not facing the bull, but tucked back along my arm, being held in place with two of my fingers.

It charged at me and I ran forward. At the appropriate moment, my training for this very situation kicked into motion, and I put both arms out and cartwheeled over the bull. This specific manoeuvre is easy once you get the first hand to land on the bull's head while your legs simply are kicked up in the air. When the bull meets your first hand, it knocks you around, and your legs follow. My right hand came down somewhere near the back of its head, and I completed a full circle in the air, landing safely on my feet.

I could hear the blood pump through my body as the entire crowd cheered. I do not know who or what they were cheering for, but it felt good. My spirits lifted. The crowd was on my side, or so it seemed to me. The bull stopped its charge as its massive hooves skidded to a halt, and soon realised I was nowhere to be seen. It turned its giant head around to see me standing, waiting in the middle of the arena. Now it was even more pissed!

Gesturing for it to try that one more time, I braced for another impact. This time, I was the first to start the slow jog towards the beast. It joined in the theatre and took off charging me again. This time, my knife was now ready to make the first cut. Leaping into the air towards the fast-moving bull, I once again placed my left hand on its head taking a clump of its hair to steady myself. As I spun around in the air, my now free right hand brought the knife down at the back of its neck. The penetration stunned the bull, stunned me, and stunned the whole crowd. They went completely silent for a moment, and then let out a mighty, collective roar.

After performing this action twice more, thick red blood began to stream from the wounds in the bulls' neck. Its energy was being sapped, as was mine because in all my training, I had never done this leap more than four times. My blood was pumping, but thankfully, not out onto the arena floor. I managed a glance at the royal box and King Minos was most obviously annoyed and displeased with the situation. Both his daughters were trying to suppress a smile, the crowd was loving every moment, and even his personal guards were enjoying the spectacle, but I was not complacent. I could hear the words of my father, who always told me to be careful around a wounded bull. They were highly unpredictable once wounded, and often managed to summon hidden reserves of energy just when you thought they were nearly done.

I managed to suck in some deep breaths of my own, and this seemed to calm my nerves, and steady my right arm for one more thrust of the knife. This time, if the bull charged slower towards me, I was going to try one specific move that my old slave trainer in Athens taught me. Instead of a cartwheel over the bull, try to hold on and mount it!

I had never tried this in practice, but I had imagined it at least a thousand times in my head. When my left hand lands on its head, grab a hand full of hair, and hold on tight. As you spin around

153

upside down in the air, try to land with both legs on each side of the animal, and try not to land with your balls, but with your arse!

The bull scratched its front right hoof and charged at me with all it had. Fortunately, this was not much, but still a fair pace. My plan worked to perfection. In the blink of an eye, I found myself bareback astride a rampaging, wounded bull. Growing up in a palace has some benefits. One such benefit was that I spent a lot of time as a boy in the abattoirs watching our butchers kill and carve animals of all shapes and sizes. They showed me where to cut, how to cut and how deep to cut to give the animal a quick death. I had planned where to do this with my imaginary bull, and fortunately had seen it done with real animals by skilled butchers many times.

There I was, sitting on the bull, heels dug into its massive body, my left hand with a clump of hair and my right hand raised ready to plunge the knife. A hand width either side of the intended wound would only upset the animal, so I had to be accurate. The next moment seemed to freeze in time for me, and I could see clearly where I was to strike and cut.

Down came my knife, deep into the beast's neck, and I could feel its life ebbing away as I sliced a deep gash. I leapt off, not taking my eyes from the bull. The magnificent beast fell to its foreleg knees, and looked me in the eyes. It knew. I felt as though it was paying me the honour of a battle well fought. It was his time to die, not mine.

What happened next was a blur. The crowd rushed through the wooden barriers separating them from the arena and surrounded me. A small and silent crowd stood over the bull. I do not know what they were expecting to see, but it was a sad sight to see such a might beast lose its life all for the benefit of a baying crowd and mad king.

To give King Minos his due, he slowly descended from his wooden throne high above the arena and came out into the arena to stand before me. He too, looked beaten.

"Theseus, you are a mighty warrior, and have proven your worth here today, in front of the citizens of Knossos and Crete. You and your Athenian friends can now safely return to Athens, and the yearly payment of slaves to our court is hereby at an end. Go in peace."

At this moment, a roar went up on the Argo. Apart from Jason, no one else had heard Theseus tell his version of how he freed his people from the yoke of King Minos. Theseus had held the crew, and even Jason, spellbound with his tale.

"I heard it was a minotaur?"

"Someone told me you were in a labyrinth."

"What did Phaedra tell you before the battle?"

The crew fired many questions in rapid succession at Theseus. He answered them all. There was more to his story, especially about how King Minos and his father King Aegeus came to end their agreement, but all Theseus could say was that he was not part of those negotiations, and that was that! The one thing he added later, while he was rowing, was that Phaedra did not come to Athens immediately with him.

However, nature has a way of ruining a good story. While this last interrogation was taking place, the wind dropped considerably, and Typhus called for oars to be manned. Theseus took his rowing seat, Orpheus took up his lyre, and all of Peleus and Telamon's crew manned the oars. The island of Imbros was looming large, but a safe harbour could not be seen in the fading light. Approaching the island from the south, with Limnos still in view behind them, Jason asked Typhus to make a landing on the first sandy beach visible. This was achieved soon after, and before the night sky took complete hold of our vision, the Argo was beached.

Hippomenes and Kristus' crew were tasked with hauling the boat ashore while the last rowers found a dry place to lay their weary bones. Enough drinking water existed in their oak barrels for the night, but fresh water would need to be found before the next part of their journey could commence. For now, all that could be heard were the loud snoring of the rowers, the gentle lapping of tiny waves on the shore, and the soothing sound of Orpheus' lyre.

Orpheus sang.

"Another day on this mighty boat
Where the wind has failed yet again
Its contours match our aching bones
We truly are tired young men."

CHAPTER 12

Imbros, Hellespont
and Kyzikus

Keeping close to the Limnian western coastline, the Argo caught a favourable breeze and sailed with it to the north western tip of the island. Almost as if my magic, the wind dropped totally once they rounded a small uninhabited rocky outcrop off the coast, and the mighty vessel once again was propelled by rowing. Hippomenes and Peleus offered to take the first shift.

Rowing all night, guided by a strong glow from the moon, the rowers worked in high rotation, rowing under moonlight while the non-rowers attempted some sleep, then swapping over. Jason and the four leaders agreed that this was not ideal, but in the distance, a large island was slowly revealing itself. In the strange glow of the shimmering moon, the island appeared to be a large black void edging ever closer with each stroke. Typhus wanted to stay all night at the helm, not trusting anyone else in his role. Well before the sun was due to rise, Typhus saw the unmistakable sight of a sandy beach, near a rocky outcrop at the base of a small hill. He woke Jason and pointed in the direction of where he wanted to beach the mighty vessel.

Hoping for assistance from the gods in the form of a gradual sloping sandy beach, Typhus did not expect any hidden obstacles. His prayer was answered and the Argo soon struck land. Totally exhausted from an all-night effort, one final push and pull was needed to secure the boat before the Argonauts fell onto the sand, completely spent. Soon, all that could be heard above the soft sound of water gently lapping the beach, was a snoring chorus of dead tired rowers yet again.

It was Hercules who woke with a start. Standing a short distance away from the sleeping giant was an old fisherman, clearly no threat to the sleeping crew, but it nonetheless startled Hercules.

Reaching for his weapon, the old man said "you don't need that. I am an old man. Look at these hands. I've got more bumps on my knuckles than pebbles on this beach." The old man had a well-weathered face and stood hunched over, holding a stick for balance.

"Who are you?" asked Hercules. By now Jason and the four crew leaders had woken to gaze upon this lone figure standing on the beach.

The old man gestured towards Hercules with his stick "The question should be – who are you?"

Meetings like this were bound to happen, so Jason spoke to the visitor with his usual bland and short response.

"So, you want to row all the way to Colchis! Why?"

Not wishing to give too much away, Jason said that it was a journey of discovery in a new boat, which by now, the old fisherman was most enamoured with.

"I could catch a lot of fish in this."

"We'll take you fishing, but can you please help us find fresh water first."

The old man gave directions to a bubbling spring not far from where the Argonauts beached the night before. Jason sat with the old man and they talked about his life, his family, his lonely existence and many other things. Grateful for some company, the old man spoke until the water hunting party returned with full barrels.

The old man had never been to Limnos, never travelled to the Hellespont, and in fact, had never left Imbros. "Why would I? I have all I need right here."

He did give one piece of information to Jason that made him concerned.

"I've heard that King Laomedon of Troy guards the straits every day. He won't allow any foreign boats entry unless you pay a tax. If he thinks you won't pay, you can expect a quiver of arrows, so be careful. The entrance is well guarded by Laomedon's fleet."

"Is the entrance guarded at night?" asked Jason.

"No. But you would be crazy to attempt it at night, if you ask me. You won't be able to see a thing."

"Why is it not guarded at night?"

"From what I have been told, the Hellespont is narrow, contains hidden rocks below the surface in many places, and the currents can be too strong to row against. While you may attempt to negotiate this at night, you will need to take all these concerns into account. That is why Laomedon does not guard it at night. No one has made a night time crossing and lived to tell the tale!"

Lynceus had been listening intently to the old man's dire warnings and decided to speak up.

"The Argo has the benefit of an excellent helmsman, fantastic steerage, a flat bottom, the most experienced crew ever known and spare rowers if need be. It is simple Jason. We'll steer clear of the rocks!"

Of all the Argonauts, Lynceus seemed to be able to see in the dark. Until now, Jason and Typhus had not needed such ability. Jason knew of Lynceus' night-time hunting ability and asked him if he would be able to guide the Argo through the Hellespont. Lynceus said enthusiastically that he would be honoured.

One more task needed to be completed, now that the Argo was well stocked with water. The old man was promised a fishing trip, and that is just what they did. Using a crew of only twelve rowers, the Argo launched once again into the sea, but this time, the destination was one or two stadia away from the shoreline, to a place where the old man used to go fishing many years before when he had a boat. True to his word, there were fish aplenty at the appointed spot. The old man was happy, and Jason was equally pleased that he had some fresh fish for the journey over to and through the Hellespont. The old man told Jason that he now had enough fish to dry and keep for nearly a hundred days.

With barrels of water and fresh fish supplies full, Jason and Typhus had to leave the safety of Imbros' shores with enough time to reach the Hellespont unseen, and in the total darkness. Then they had to navigate blindly through the straights and row all night to safely avoid detection.

The heroes set off. Lynceus took over a special position on the bow as his eagle eyes were to remain firmly fixed on the entrance, which was quickly fading from view. No sail was raised, as it would surely be sighted by Laomedon's fleet. Working in short shifts, so as not to tire the rowers, the Argo set course directly for the entrance. By nightfall it was as black as a pig's guts. No one could see a thing, but Lynceus' well-adjusted eyes for night vision could make out the entrance.

"Keep on this course. There are no obstacles ahead" he called out to Typhus. Normally, Orpheus would be playing music, but he was banned from making a sound. Although he could not sing, his mind was being filled with song ideas, and could not wait to sing the praises of Lynceus with his night vision abilities.

After skilfully navigating the entrance, Lynceus called out to Jason.

"We have entered and passed through the entrance. Laomedon cannot see us, because I cannot see any of his fleet. Keep those oars strong."

The Argo sliced through the water as naturally as any boat had ever done. To keep the hectic pace necessary, rowing was completed in ever shorter shifts, designed to keep each rower in peak condition and to give them respite before their next turn. Conversations were conducted in whispers. Jason was beginning to breathe a little easier.

Lynceus called out "I can see the end. Not far to go."

Muffled cheers were voiced until the break of dawn showed

no enemy vessel in site, and only a broad sea in front of them. Now the cheers went up. They had made it. Celebrations soon became muted as all rowers of the mighty Argo were by now dead tired. Even Hercules was sucking in the deep breaths and calling for water.

Fortunately, a light breeze greeted a rising morning sun, and the sail was finally hoisted into place to catch whatever wind was on offer. Spotting what looked like a safe harbour in the distance, Typhus set a course towards a mountainous headland overlooking the harbour. Under sail, the Argo gently glided into the harbour with Lynceus carefully watching out for any submerged and dangerous rocks lurking below the waterline. With a clear run at the shoreline, the Argo gradually came to a halt in deep enough water to drop the anchor-stone.

Typhus was so intent on setting his course for the sand, he completely missed seeing a village set well back and above the harbour. From the water, it was difficult to see any dwellings, but as soon as the Argo came to rest, these houses were clearly visible.

A track led down from the village to the harbour, and Jason spotted several men walking towards them. In front of these men was what appeared to be someone of importance, due to the bright clothing he was wearing.

Jason didn't sense any potential danger, and with ten argonauts, including Atalanta and Philoktetes, decided to meet the delegation. Both Atalanta and Philoktetes were concealing their weapons, just in case the meeting turned hostile.

"You have arrived on a happy occasion. Today is my wedding day, and you are all invited."

Jason was confused. He didn't know who they were, and they

didn't know who he was, but he had just been invited to a wedding. "Philoxenia must be alive and well here in this part of the world."

The colourful man leading the delegation turned out to be King Kyzikus of the Dolionians, the people who inhabited the land. The wedding was planned for later that day, and Jason informed the king that he and the Argonauts needed to rest first, before attending any festivities.

"There is one more thing I ask of you Jason," said the king.

"We have neighbours who are hostile towards us, and your presence at my wedding would no doubt deter them from attacking on this special occasion."

Pointing to a mountain nearby to the south of where they were standing, King Kyzikus said "They live on that mountain, and have been raining down large rocks on us for a long time now. They constantly mount raids and we are living in perpetual fear. Will you help us?"

At that moment, rocks came thundering down from high on the mountain, landing near to where Hercules was standing.

Not wanting to wait for Jason to give the word, Atalanta and Philoktetes cocked their bows and fired several arrows in the direction of the rock throwers. To their immediate surprise, five bodies fell from behind bushes with arrows lodged in their chests. Incensed with losing some of their comrades, the remaining attackers ran down the hill throwing more rocks and even some javelins.

One sideways look from Atalanta to Philoktetes was all that was needed before more arrows brought down the remaining attackers. Or so they thought. At least one of them avoided being fired upon, and fled back into the safety of large boulders high on the mountain.

"That settles it. King Kyzikus, we will be your guards to make sure tonight's wedding is safe."

The king was to marry a girl by the name of Kleite from the Phrygian city of Percote. Hoping to garner a relationship to strengthen the military ties between the Dolionians and the people of Percote, the marriage was arranged, but Kyzikus and Kleite defied tradition and were truly in love. They both had a common enemy in the mountain tribe continually raiding them, and the wedding was seen as a necessary union to ward off this foe.

The wedding later that night was a huge success. The Argonauts were all invited to join in the festivities, but due to the threat of more attacks, Jason and the leaders thought it would be wise for Hercules and ten others to guard the Argo. Throughout the evening, the guests were showered with wine and food, and the Dolionians were happy.

When the time came for the Argo to depart, more gifts were brought by the Dolionians to the beach. Jason could not find any more space aboard the Argo to store this additional cargo. In return, Jason made a gift to the king of their anchor-stone. Argus spotted a perfectly formed larger stone by the water's edge to replace this smaller one. To this day, the Dolionians show people the anchor-stone as proof that the might Argo sailed by their city. Departure time was pushed back to late in the afternoon in view of the weather. Wanting to get underway without much delay, Jason and the leaders chose to risk the potential nasty weather to make head way around the coast and find a safe harbour as soon as possible before nightfall.

Wind and rain greeted them as the rowers leaned into their oars. Rowing in the night-time was necessary due to the conditions, but Jason thought they could ride out the storm as long as they remained in view of land, but not too close to dangerous submerged rocks lying in wait all along the coastline.

Overnight, the weather changed for the worse and Typhus altered course attempting to steer the Argo out to sea in stormy weather. Once they thought they had beaten the worst of the weather, the strong north wind blew even harder. Under all oars, the Argo made some considerable headway along the coast, but the wind now turned into a violent storm.

It was pointless using the sail. Argus said it would rip to shreds in this wind, so all rowers were battling strong headwinds, water poured in like a fast-flowing river, and several barrels of the gifts received from the Dolionians were washed overboard. Visibility was poor. Even Lynceus could not see in the worsening conditions. Before too long, the Argo was blown completely off course, and beached itself rather violently on sand dangerously close to a rocky outcrop. Under rapidly fading daylight, Typhus had no idea where they were, so all Argonauts secured the mighty boat with as many ropes as they could tie down to keep the vessel from any potential damage. They were unable to recognise any features of the land around them, so Jason insisted they try to hold fast until the storm passed.

Lynceus did try to say to Jason that the land looked familiar, but even he was not sure as it was by now, so dark. What they didn't know, until much later, was that the storm had blown the mighty Argo back to the opposite side of the harbour from where they departed that morning. Attempting to seek shelter in and around the rocks and trees close to shore, the Argonauts started to venture out on foot to locate sufficient coverage from the wind and rain.

High above, the Dolionians noticed many men coming ashore and thought it must be their arch enemies, the Pelasgians returning to attack under the cover of a storm. On his chariot, King Kyzikus led the charge convinced they were being attacked by their long-time adversaries.

Kyzikus had his warriors don their armour, and under the command of their king, the Dolionians attacked with rocks, javelins and spears. Immediately, the Argonauts retaliated quickly and decisively. Before too long, there were twenty-five dead. Suddenly one of the Dolionians called out "Stop. We are fighting our friends. Stop now."

Hercules, who by this stage had dispatched a dozen men to their destiny with the ferryman Charon, recognised the voice of the Dolionian.

"Brothers. Stop. He is right. These are our friends."

All combat ceased immediately. The remorse felt on both sides was overwhelming as the opponents were now face to face and saw who they were fighting.

"The king is dead" called one of the Dolionians.

Lying on the ground with a severe gash in his stomach was a man who had only the day before, been married. No one knew exactly who killed the king, but it was most likely Jason or Hercules. Given the ferocity of the fighting only a short time before, Jason and Hercules admitted it must have been one of them, but they were not entirely sure.

Driven with grief at this most unfortunate circumstance, the argonauts and surviving Dolionians carried the dead back inside the walled city for burial rites. On seeing the sight of her husband,

Kleite let out a heart-rendering cry, and rushed forward to embrace her husband. Laughter and great joy only days before had now given way to overwhelming tragedy and unimaginable grief.

For the next three days, the argonauts assisted the Dolionians raise a funeral mound in honour of the fallen king. None of the local people blamed the Argonauts for the death of their king, but Jason and Hercules particularly felt responsible. Funeral rites were performed in voiceless sorrow and funeral games were organised and held in honour of King Kyzikus. The only words of any significance after the funeral games had concluded came from Jason, who decried "From this day forth, let this city be known as Kyzikus, so all will honour and remember a brave and generous king."

To this day, the people of the city of Kyzikus still make libations at the mound.

CHAPTER 13

The race

With heavy hearts, Jason bid farewell to the people of Kyzikus, and the Argo pulled gently out of the harbour into the unknown. Oars were secured and the vessel glided effortlessly under sail courtesy of a good breeze. Orpheus' doleful voice was the only sound heard aboard the mighty vessel. His ability to instantly assess the mood of each warrior aboard and tailor his songs according to the moment.

Once far enough away from land, Jason proposed something strange. With exactly forty-eight available rowers, not including Jason himself, he proposed a race.

"How can we possibly have a race when we are all on the same boat?" asked a puzzled Polyphemus.

Jason was inventing the race format as he spoke.

"We have four groups under the leadership of Hippomenes, Peleus, Kristus and Telamon. The first two groups will row as hard as possible, and the team which tires first will be deemed the loser."

"Then the other two teams will compete to determine a winner."

Oileus, who was also a student of Chiron and an old friend of Jason's was usually quiet, and not prone to speaking up in front of everyone.

"OK. We get to two teams, and then what? You can't have one whole team as a winner, or can you?"

"Good point my old friend. When we arrive at one team, we split that group into two further teams of six."

Pleased with his invention, Jason had not finished.

"Then two teams of three."

"Finally, we'll have the best team, but it will have to be three rowers who will be crowned."

"I have an ultimate challenge for the remaining three members of the successful team" called out Iphicles.

"The final three rowers will then have to stand still on one leg, holding an oar above their head. When the first rower touches his other foot on the boat, or lets his oar fall, we will have two rowers remaining."

"Great idea Iphicles," said Jason. But Iphicles was not done yet.

"Thank you. Then the final two rowers can place their oar back in its rowlock, and we row until one drops with exhaustion".

"And then we'll have a winner," said Jason proudly, who by now was attempting to preserve his own energy.

I won't bore you with the details and results of each preliminary race, but the final three rowers were Hercules, of course, Oileus and Butes.

By this stage, the other forty-five losers, including Jason, were thoroughly exhausted, but nothing could stop Orpheus from singing songs dedicated to each winner.

With a booming voice, Orpheus asked each of the three finalists to unlock an oar and hold it up with straight arms above their heads, standing in the centre platform of the mighty Argo. As if the gods had decreed it so, the wind blew slightly harder and made balancing on one leg impossible, let alone the challenge of holding an oar aloft.

Butes was first to fail, and now only two remained. Hercules and Oileus!

The banter between Hercules and Oileus became a battle of wits and humour. Exactly what was said has been lost in time, because each of the remaining forty-six were laughing so much, they could not really hear anything of the raucous battle of words.

Both took their seats, locked in their oars, and waited for Orpheus to strike the first note on his lyre. At about the time Orpheus started his final musical offering, a stronger wind picked up in its intensity making rowing much more difficult. Normally when this occurred, oars would be put away and the sail raised, but Jason decreed that the race should continue regardless of the weather conditions.

The mighty Argo rocked from side to side barely making any headway. One of the worst scenarios for a rower on this vessel was when you reach back with your oar to bite in the water, only to find there is nothing but air. A direct result of this action is that the oar does not grip anything, causing the rower to bring the handle of the oar rather heavily into his stomach. This is what happened. Hercules was rowing on the starboard side and Oileus on port. The Argo tilted to port, meaning Hercules could not gain any traction with his oar in the water and several times found no purchase. Oileus strained when he felt Hercules wilting.

The Argo righted itself giving Hercules a chance to row again. Pleased he was now back in the race, Hercules dipped his oar into the water and pulled with all the power he could muster. His oar bent like a bow. Sadly for him, and due to his enormous strength, the oar broke into two pieces, unable to cope with such a strenuous demand. Hercules threw the stump of an oar into the water, and gave a wry smile to the victor. Both warriors were exhausted. Hercules did not mind Oileus winning. Oileus loved winning, but was too fatigued to care.

Orpheus sang for Oileus, and the sail rose to receive a belly full of wind. Argos and his apprentice Markos inspected the oars and were worried to discover around eight in need of urgent repair, or if possible, complete replacement. In addition to the broken Hercules oar, Argos suggested to Typhus that they search for a suitable place to beach the Argo. As usual, it was Lynceus who indicated an ideal stretch of coast with sufficient vegetation on the horizon. The sadness of the previous few days was replaced with the more immediate task at hand which was to find land soon to mend the damaged oars and refill barrels of fresh drinking water.

CHAPTER 14

Hylas

Typhus steered the Argo safely inside a small and tranquil harbour, on the coast of Mysia. Lush vegetation appeared to reach all the way down to the waterline from a mountain range, but no running water could be seen or found in the vicinity of where they had beached. A small salt water inlet inside the harbour was a fruitful source of fish, and with food supplies on the boat, the argonauts had a restful and satisfying feast of dried figs, nuts and honey which almost emptied their food stores, topped off with some fresh salt water fish.

Hylas, Hercules' friend and young squire was sent by Hercules to locate fresh water. He was instructed to fill a small krater, bring it back, so that a larger group could then leave with him to fill more containers. Hercules began to walk with Hylas, and after a short time, veered away to search for a tree branch large enough to be fashioned into a new oar. At the same time, Argos instructed six others to also search for suitable branches. Markos took all damaged oars from the Argo and set about fixing them on the beach with the assistance of several volunteers. Atalanta, Philoktetes and Euphemus began a search to find smaller branches to replace their used and spent arrows from their disastrous battle with the Dolionians.

Another small group were on a mission to find berries and any fruit they could source. Jason and the four group leaders, Hippomenes, Kristus, Peleus and Telamon discussed issues arising from the previous day's activities. Jason was still clearly upset at the events with the Dolionians, and vowed for that to never happen again.

After the remaining warriors slept on the sand, groups of gatherers returned with their findings. It was approaching sunset, and all but Hylas had returned. Hercules found two suitable tree branches and asked if Hylas had come back.

"No. We have not seen him."

"I know the direction he went, so can we go there to see if he is injured?"

A search party departed and were heard to yell "Hylas, Hylas, Hylas." No answer. The search continued until dark, and it was decided for all to return to the beach in case Hylas had made his way back.

Hercules insisted Hylas was most likely lost, and has decided to lie low until sunrise the next morning.

Hercules and Polyphemus awoke before sunrise and once more went in search of their friend, but not before informing Jason.

Inland from where the vessel was grounded on the beach, a steep hill was found with what appeared to be a waterfall coming over the ridge high above. Polyphemus suggested they climb the hill to obtain a vantage point in an effort to identify the source of this waterfall where it was obvious water was flowing from some river nearby.

"Hercules. Over here."

The water krater Hylas had with him was found next to the waterfall where the flow of water cascaded down a steep, rocky slope into a pool surrounded by large rocks far below. Hercules was immediately concerned.

"Hylas may have bent down to sip the water, but slipped on the well-worn rocks lurking below the surface. Why else would he have placed the krater here?"

After a fruitless search for Hylas at the bottom of the waterfall, Hercules and Polyphemus returned without their friend. Jason could see how distraught the two men were, and said they still had several days to search for Hylas before the boat would be ready to sail again to resume their quest.

The next day, all food containers were filled, arrows made, with only the damaged and broken oars still to be completed. This was proving more difficult than first thought, so larger teams of gatherers seeking suitable tree branches were dispatched. Argos was not happy with the strength of the original branches located on the first day.

Meanwhile, Hercules and Polyphemus continued their search for Hylas. All day they wandered aimlessly until they realised they too were lost. When darkness descended, Hercules agreed to build a shelter and thus they spent the night away from their comrades on the beach. When the two searchers did not return that night, Jason was also concerned, but readied himself for the worst possible news in the morning.

"We can't wait for them" Jason was heard to say as he prepared to sail due to favourable winds. Telamon, who was the leader of the group containing Hercules, Polyphemus and Hylas did not agree with Jason's assessment of the situation.

"We have just lost three of our comrades, and all you care about is finding the fleece. Shame on you."

"Telamon. I am deeply concerned about the loss of these three, but we cannot stay here and continue searching. We may lose more."

Jason and Telamon argued and it was obvious to all that Telamon was deeply upset, but Jason stood his ground.

The Argo was being readied for departure, when to the joy of the warriors, Hercules emerged from the vegetation. He and Jason spoke for a moment, and Jason nodded while Hercules climbed aboard to gather his, Polyphemus and Hylas' personal belongings, on the chance he was found alive.

"I am staying here until we find Hylas, or at least until we discover what happened to our lost companion. Polyphemus and I will continue searching. May you all survive the quest, and with the luck of the gods, we shall all meet again."

Jason agreed that they would revisit this beach on the return leg of the journey. However, he also acknowledged the possibility of Hercules, Polyphemus and hopefully Hylas independently finding a way to travel to Iolchus to be reunited with the Argo crew.

CHAPTER 15

What happened to Hercules, Polyphemus and Hylas?

I don't normally do this, but I must let you know what happened to Hercules, Polyphemus and Hylas. It is highly possible you have all heard of Hercules and his labours, so you already know that he survives and thrives for a long time to come. His labours have reached legendary and mythical status, much like Jason, but alas, stories can become lost in translation.

After the Argo departed the shores of Mysia to recommence its journey to Colchis, Hercules and Polyphemus searched for many days for their friend. Alas, his body was never found, notwithstanding the efforts of a great number of people. Hercules came across some Mysinians from the nearby city of Kios and asked them to assist in the search for Hylas. It has never been established how Hercules convinced them to help with the search, but help they did. Impressed with his size and obvious strength, the Mysinians were initially concerned Hercules would cause them some harm, but all he wanted was for them to help find his friend. A group of young men were assigned to Hercules and Polyphemus, and the search area expanded. In the end, it was Hercules who called an end to the fruitless efforts, as it was becoming abundantly clear that Hylas may never be found.

During the search for Hylas, Polyphemus grew to love the people of Mysia and convinced Hercules that he wanted to stay with them for the rest of his days. Hercules was sad to leave behind two of his best friends and reluctantly approved of Polyphemus' decision. Together with the Mysinians who assisted in the search, Polyphemus, and these young men, who by now had found enough women to be with them, founded a new city which they named Trachis.

There were stories that Polyphemus became the first ruler of Trachis. There are stories that he continued the search for Hylas until his dying days. There are stories that after his death, his loyal subjects continued to search for Hylas. There are stories that Polyphemus left his kingdom to search for his comrades from the Argo, and met his death at the hands of a tribe known as the Chalybes.

What happened to Hercules? He bade farewell to his friend and the two never saw each other again. Hercules thus began his life of helping people who needed his special set of skills, and eventually found his way back to Colchis. Jason did come back to see his old friends on the return leg of their journey home, but Hercules had long departed.

CHAPTER 16

Pollux and his boxing skills

S ince leaving Hercules and Polyphemus behind at Mysia, the Argo once again found favourable winds and made excellent progress. All oars were now either repaired or new, but due to the sympathetic stiff breeze, were thankfully not required. Although the Argo was equipped for rowing, each of the Argonauts preferred to lie back in any position they could find and let the wind drive them forward. Argos was more than pleased that his boat had surpassed all his initial expectations. Sailing under the power of nature allowed for all on board to be passengers, all apart from Typhus who rather enjoyed his time at the helm. Approaching sunset, the wind was still blowing, but not as much as when the sun was shining.

Well before daybreak on the second day, the advantageous wind had ceased blowing. "Oars out, sail down" was the cry from Typhus, as Orpheus reached for his instrument. His playing and immediate invention of little humorous odes to each rower seemed to make them forget that it was still quite onerous to row a vessel of this size. With the sheer exertion of rowing, drinking water was in constant supply to keep up the necessary physicality and hydration of the effort.

On the coming sunrise, fresh drinking water supplies began to dwindle so Jason and Typhus agreed to seek anchorage at sight of the first city or village. Lynceus climbed to the highest point of the Argo to set his eagle-like eyes to scan the coast for such a landing place.

"Village ahead" cried Lynceus, as the Argo rounded a promontory which fortunately opened into a large sandy bay.

"We'll run her ashore over there" said Jason pointing to a flat, sandy beach surrounded by tall, shady trees.

The whole operation of beaching a mighty vessel such as the Argo was by now a well-drilled, military-like event. Once a location on a beach had been selected roughly one stadion away from landing, and if there was sufficient wind, the sail was up, and all rowers pulled their oars at maximum effort, as if they were approaching or evading an enemy boat on the open sea. They were guessing, and usually quite rightly so, that the beach gradually became shallower, and there were no hidden rocks lurking beneath. Argos, more than anybody, was always nervous at this moment, fearing the unmistakeable sound of wood splintering on a submerged rock.

But this time, Typhus suggested a different manoeuvre.

"We cannot risk striking hidden surprises, so why not row in towards the beach at a gentle speed to see if we have a clear run at the sand. If so, we row back out to sea, and then attack the beach with full oar power."

"Good idea Typhus," said Jason as contemplated the question of 'why didn't I think of that?'

At this speed, the boat could be driven as far up onto the beach as possible, sometimes well away from the water's edge, and sometimes with the bow displacing sand on the beach. On this occasion, the Argo rammed the sandy beach so hard, the bow was nearly one man's body length into the white, soft sand.

Next task was to secure the vessel by jumping overboard and attaching ropes to the rails so that the boat could be dragged further up onto the beach. The purpose of dragging the boat onto a beach in this fashion was to prevent it from floating away in a sudden wind, or a change of tide. Another purpose was to make it difficult for a surprise attack from pirates to take over the vessel themselves, but Jason was not concerned with this possibility, given the quality of warriors he had at his disposal.

Another task for the four group leaders was to assign rotating sentries for the entire time they were on land. Just like a military operation, sentries were necessary in all unknown and potentially hostile environments. The task none of the argonauts enjoyed performing on dry land, but was necessary, was to dig latrine pits. If you were designated this duty, you could safely expect Orpheus to wax lyrical about you later. The only difference was the first word of this little ditty changed every day.

"Butes dug our pit, now we can all take a shit."

Or one like this.

"When the Argo sails back home, Laertes will be a king. But here he digs a hole, so we can do our thing."

Either way, if it was your turn to dig, you could be guaranteed of becoming immortalised in song.

One of the first argonauts posted as a sentry observed a man striding confidently out from the trees and approaching in a slightly menacing manner. He was very tall, and looked like a savage beast with the fur of recent hunts covering his massive body.

"We have company," said Menoetius. No sooner had he yelled this, the observed man was followed closely by at least ten others, all carrying weapons.

Atalanta, Philoktetes, Peleus and Theseus reached instinctively for their own bows, while Jason thought it would be prudent for him to approach the first man and meet him away from the Argo.

The tall, beastly looking man, who was not carrying any weapons, stopped with his feet slightly apart and his hands firmly planted on his hips. With an air of arrogance, he surveyed the boat and all who sat on the beach.

"Listen to me, you whoresons of sailors from where I know not. I am Amycus, king of the Bebryces. Who are you and why are you armed on my land?"

With a slight movement of Amycus' right arm, more warriors emerged from the shelter and cover of trees to his left and right. Sensing trouble, Jason spoke.

"My name is Jason and we are travelling to Colchis. We mean you no harm, but we would like to take our fill of water and top up our dwindling food supply. We will stay only as long as it is necessary."

Before Jason could utter another word, Amycus commenced

an annoying, throaty, sarcastic chuckle.

"What is so funny, King Amycus?"

"Haven't you heard? We have a custom here. No strangers may take anything from our land until one of you challenges me in a boxing match. Nothing to it really. You give me your best boxer. I kill him. Then, you can take what you need and be on your way."

Wishing Hercules was still one of them, Jason searched his warriors for a willing volunteer. He didn't have to search for long, as Pollux, brother to Castor and known horse expert, was also an expert in the boxing ring, stepped forward.

"I accept the challenge."

"But you could die Pollux," said Jason.

"He looks big, but he is just full of hot air and wind. Must have been something he ate!"

Pollux took another step closer to the giant king, and looked directly up into the dark eyes of the big man. He was wearing a lightly woven cloak, a gift from one of the Limnian women, and carefully removed it to place on the mantle of a walking stick he always carried, made from an ancient olive branch. Now it was the king's turn to study his opponent more closely.

With flaring nostrils, King Amycus surveyed all who were standing around the makeshift boxing ring now hastily drawn in the sand by one of his subjects and bellowed to no one in particular "you are going to look mighty stupid without a head you insolent little man. Bring me the gloves."

One of the menacing guards standing close to King Amycus reached into a leather satchel and produced two pairs of recently skinned cow hide gloves. Both men had their gloves tied on and

Amycus said "say good bye to your little friends, sailor boy. You are about to take a trip to the underworld. I'll even pay the ferryman!"

"Get on with it, or are you just going to talk me to death?"

It was obvious to all that Amycus used his sheer size to intimidate opponents, but unbeknown to him, Pollux had been sparring with Hercules nearly every day, and knew how to approach a fight with a giant. He had a simple plan. Stay out of reach as much as possible, and when the time comes, let one rip into the stomach of your opponent.

Allow me to give you some background to the normally quiet Pollux. Prior to joining Jason and the crew of the Argo, Pollux was also known as Polydeuces, which was a nickname given to him by his brother. The origin of the nick name meant 'many fists,' because his opponents could not see his fists until it was too late. His boxing prowess was only secondary to his ability with horses, but on the Argo, his boxing skill grew each day. Probably also because there were no horses aboard the Argo.

Starting on the beach at Myrina in Limnos one day, Hercules needed a boxing partner to train with each morning as part of his fitness regime. Initially, many of the argonauts tried to match it with the mighty Hercules, but none made it past the lightning speed of Hercules' fists. One morning, Pollux had been observing all who fell at the hands of Hercules, and said to his brother Castor, "I think I can handle myself with this big man."

Pollux walked casually over to where Hercules was standing and offered to be his sparring partner. Hercules laughed and asked if he was an idiot or something. Pollux stood and smiled. "I guess you will just have to find out."

I won't bother you with the details, but let me say this about

Pollux on that memorable morning. He not only matched Hercules, he even managed to fell the giant of a man with one sneaky left fist to the jaw that set the big man down on his backside. Since that moment, Hercules had the utmost respect for Pollux, and so too did each of the other Argonauts.

But back to the beach with Pollux and the king of the Bebryces.

The fight began with the big man taking a wild right-handed swing at the smaller opponent. Pollux easily feinted and stepped sideways to avoid the savage right hand. Amycus followed with another wild swing with his left, which was again competently avoided by ducking under the rather agricultural attempt.

Pollux knew that if the king could land one of his wild punches, he would most certainly be felled like a sapling in the forest. In his mind, he could hear the words of Hercules loud and clear 'watch his shoulders, just make him tired, watch his shoulders, make him tired, focus."

This strategy worked on two levels. Amycus was tiring, but he was becoming more incensed with each swing and miss. The footwork of the big man was not that of a skilled pugilist, and Pollux could sense a faltering in his limited boxing ability. One more wild swing was all that Pollux needed to strike. Amycus threw a wild punch again, but Pollux knew it was coming, feinted and as he leaned back, threw two punches in quick succession into the stomach of Amycus.

The king buckled over in pain and fell with his right hand on the ground. Feeling a small rock under the surface of the sand, Amycus scooped it into his right hand and rose to his feet. Pollux noticed the rock and stepped out of reach, pretending not to see anything untoward. Amycus came again in a rush feinting a blow

185

with his left, then followed with his right hand firmly wrapped around the rock. Attempting to crush the rock into the face of Pollux, he skilfully avoided it by swaying away, then rushing towards with a half turn to his left. By doing so, he used his right elbow to swing backwards and made perfect contact with Amycus' nose. The sound of bones breaking was music to Pollux' ears.

Blood streamed out of Amycus' bulbous nose, and bloodied his chest. Some of the blood must have clouded Amycus' vision because his next attempt at a strike was at thin air. Pollux came in for the kill. As the punch from Amycus landed on nothing, he followed through and stumbled slightly, enough for Pollux to step sideways and deliver a quick right hand to the side of the giant's head, followed by an uppercut to his chin. The wounded and severely disoriented king fell face first into the sand. Another rock was innocently hidden under the sand, but sadly for the former king, he struck it with his forehead, and died instantly.

Seeing their king lying prostrate on the sand, the Bebryces guards took up their arms to seek revenge. Before they could launch an attack, Philoktetes and Atalanta had deposited four arrows into the chests of four guards, killing them instantly. The remaining Bebryces were terrified, and Jason quickly yelled for them to drop their weapons, lest they also be killed.

One of the Bebryces said "Spare our lives. Show pity on us. Take our gold, but spare our lives."

"We didn't come for gold. We came for water and provisions for our journey. Your king was an evil man. Swear that you will offer friendship and goodwill to all strangers from this moment onwards. Swear that you will not insist strangers to have to fight when all they want is food and water."

One of the defeated warriors claimed to be the dead king's brother, but was not the menacing brute that Amycus seemed to be.

"I am Clytius, brother to the dead king, and now king of the Bebryces. I swear to all that you requested Jason."

He then ordered his own men to bring provisions and to show the visitors where they could fill containers of beautiful spring water. The Argonauts stayed the night, and as an act of good faith, invited Clytius and his people to join them in a feast. Orpheus shone with a new crowd to perform to, and even performed a song dedicated to the new king Clytius.

Later that night after the Bebryces retired to their farms and homes, Jason thanked Pollux for his martial prowess.

"Don't thank me, Jason. Thank our friend Hercules. If it wasn't for his lessons and kindness in helping teach me, I most assuredly would have died on this beach today."

"What did he teach you? I am interested to know."

"Watch their shoulders, and try to tire them."

"That was one of Chiron's lessons to me as a boy, but I have never had to do it in the heat of battle yet. You must spar with me one day soon Pollux. You have much to teach me too."

For his achievement in defeating the tyrant king, Pollux was given a lamb by the Bebryces which would provide fresh meat to consume on their journey to Colchis. Seeing some irony in this gift, Pollux asked Jason later that night if they could sprinkle some gold dust on it, claim it to be the golden fleece and go home. Jason laughed so much he thought he'd die.

"Sprinkle some gold dust on a sheep's fleece. That is the best joke I have heard in a long time. Now get some sleep before I put you on latrine duty!"

CHAPTER 17

Symplegades

There was one more city to visit before leaving the Sea of Marmara. Salmydessus lay on the southern point of the narrow waterway leading through to the Black Sea. The city was situated at the eastern end of a little harbour, and two of the Argonauts had a familial connection to this place. Zetes and Calais had never been to the city, but their sister Cleopatra lived there with her husband, King Phineas. Having not seen their sister for ten summers, the brothers were keen to see how she was coping with being such a long way from home, meeting her husband for the first time, and maybe to meet their children.

Jason allowed the excited brothers to be lookout with Lynceus as the Argo rowed gently into the harbour. High above the waterline and indeed the foliage of wondrous trees stood the mighty palace of King Phineas, buttressed by large rocks and a formidable fortress rising high out of the water. All the way into the harbour, the brothers had one eye on the palace as it came into view, but also one eye on the prevailing winds.

Jason asked Calais if he was excited at the prospect of meeting up with his older sister, and the response was *'yes.'* "I am excited as you put it Jason, to see our sister after so long, but we are both more interested in how we are going to sail or row through that narrow strait."

The narrow strait to which Calais alluded was the obvious visible entrance through to the Black Sea, so feared by mariners and known to be practically impassable. Jason was most interested in their opinions regarding wind direction. But they had never been to this part of the world before, so how would they know how to read the winds accurately.

"That is easy," said Calais.

"After we speak to our sister, who is just as competent as we are in this matter, we will observe birds flying, watching how they rise and fall along the air currents coming off those cliffs and mountains. We'll see how they swoop down to catch fish, how they fly into winds and how they glide with wind. I told you. It is easy for us. We have been observing these things for a long time."

King Phineas stood at the top of his palace wall facing the harbour. Noticing the size of the Argo gently gliding into view, he summoned his guards to meet them on the beach once the ship had run up onto the sand. Cleopatra also noticed the Argo, and thought it was strange to see two men high up on the mast holding on with one hand and one foot while scanning the horizon and water for depth. She had a feeling that this was a friendly visit, and rushed down to the beach with her husband to welcome the strangers.

Calais was first to see his sister with the king, and let out a very loud bird call. Zetes did the same, and Cleopatra recognised her two younger brothers, neither of whom she had seen since before they had beards!

The crew completed its usual landing routine where all those who were not rowing leapt into the water, waded ashore with ropes and secured one end of each rope to any useful tree. Jason was usually the first to set foot on dry land, and this was no exception. King Phineas' guards were always wary of strangers, but once Cleopatra told them that her brothers were aboard, and that it was possible that all aboard were Greeks, the guards stood at ease and helped secure the vessel.

As the Argo was heaved up onto the sandy beach, Jason was formally welcomed by the king. Cleopatra ran to embrace her brothers, and a small crowd of local people gathered to gaze upon the fine specimens of men now resting and drinking heavily of cool water. Women raced to offer any assistance possibly needed, and Eurydamas was not alone when he mentioned how similar it appeared to the beach at Myrina in Limnos. There was one major difference: There were men in Salmydessus.

In a scene reminiscent of Myrina, young women from seemingly nowhere appeared on the beach offering drinks, food, and laundering services. Luckily, they spoke Greek, or a version of Greek whereby most on the Argo could understand the local dialect. However, hand gestures abounded between Argonauts and local women so that nothing was misunderstood.

Sitting in the palace later that morning with Jason and the king were Hippomenes, Kristus, Peleus and Telamon along with four advisors to the king. It was normal for Jason to include his four group leaders in any discussions with local kings. Although Jason was the leader of the expedition, he relied on the experience and wisdom of these four trusted friends when negotiations were needed with these official representatives of cities visited. On this occasion, King Phineas was impressed with his visitors and promised to help them in any way he could. He most likely did this as his wife was happy to see her brothers, and Phineas wanted to make his wife happy.

King Phineas asked Jason for the purpose of their journey.

"One purpose of our journey is to locate and bring back to my king, the fabled golden fleece from Colchis."

"What makes you sure the king of Colchis will give it to you, Jason?"

Jason explained that he was not entirely confident that the king would relinquish such a precious object, but that he would try to obtain it by fair means.

"I have heard of the fleece Jason, but not seen it as we have never visited Colchis."

"Have you heard any stories from visitors who have seen it?" asked Jason

King Phineas and his advisors had heard from several who had visited Colchis, but their stories of the fleece were conflicting. Some thought it a wonderful object, but others didn't agree with those sentiments.

King Phineas, Jason, and each of the advisors discussed other important purposes for the journey, mainly to see how a vessel such as the Argo would withstand such a long voyage, and whether any modifications would need to be made to new boats like this in the future. Jason explained that Argos, the boat builder was with them, as were many others who possessed extraordinary talents.

In the meantime, Cleopatra had introduced the brothers to her children, and for the rest of the day they spent the entire time together getting to know each other. The remainder of the Argonauts were busy refuelling the Argo for the next stage of their journey at sunrise the following day. It was also essential to carry out any necessary repairs to the boat, due to the conditions faced over such a long period in the water. Argos conducted a thorough inspection and declared that only minor repairs were needed to the vessel, but the sails needed some urgent adjustments.

Each of them was brought ashore, and a group of local women who were experts appointed by the king, repaired small tears and rips in the fabric. Eribotes the Argo's surgeon was most fascinated in the implements used by the women to repair the rips. He fashioned some of these tools into smaller versions, so that he could potentially use them to sew up patients who had injuries caused by arrow penetration and knife cuts.

Atalanta and Philoktetes took ten men with them and joined a hunting party made up of the king's best archers. And yet again, it was Atalanta and Philoktetes who killed more wild pigs and boars than anyone else. The king's guards were impressed with her skills and on their return with enough game to last three days of feasting, Atalanta taught some of the guards how she makes her own weapons and how she practiced as a young girl. The guards were amazed, as they had never seen a woman like her. They had only ever heard of a race of women far away who rode horses and fired arrows with the deadly accuracy of any battle-hardened man.

While the official discussions were underway, and the hunting party was searching for meat to be roasted at the king's feast later that night, Zetes took the opportunity to ask his sister how they would go about choosing the correct moment to enter the strait and advance through to the Black Sea. Like her brothers, Cleopatra was an expert when it came to reading the prevailing winds. But her news regarding the winds came as a surprise.

"It is not the winds you need to watch out for. Two currents are flowing at any one time. The surface current is the weaker one and can flow both ways. It is easy to see as you will notice small waves moving on the surface in either direction. The second and hidden current is by far the stronger flow of water. It lies just under the surface, and can flow in the opposite direction to that flowing on the surface."

Zetes looked confused. He asked his sister to explain it again, and she did.

"What you are telling me is that if we see waves moving slowly out of your bay towards the Black Sea, the main current may be travelling in the other direction, and is therefore impossible to row against."

"Yes. Possibly. It also depends not only on the main current, but if you travel with the undercurrent, and the winds are favourable, you will find the journey less strenuous. For favourable winds, you will see the birds flying towards you, against the wind."

Zetes listened to his big sister as he had never listened before. He thought reading currents and winds was purely the domain of men, but his sister dispelled all those prejudices.

"If you approach the currents at the wrong time, you can row all you like, and even if the winds are favourable, you may not make any progress."

It was slowly becoming clearer to Zetes, that he needed to wait for the currents and wind direction to be in their favour. The entire journey through the straits to the Black Sea depends on impeccable timing. The optimal time to make the trip could be either during the daylight or at night.

Armed with this important maritime information, Zetes sought the company of his brother, who at the time was playing with his sister's children.

That night, King Phineas had his kitchen workers prepare the animals caught that day, and the entire city of Salmydessus was invited to attend the feast in honour of Jason and his Argonauts. By all accounts, the night was a raging success, not because of the food, or wine, but because Orpheus had yet a new crowd to entertain and the opportunity to showcase his musical talent. Even Orpheus was stunned when one of the city's beautiful young girls asked him if she could sing a traditional song. Orpheus did not know the song, but after a few moments of the girl singing quietly in his ear, he had learned enough of the tune to be able to play. Orpheus was heard many years later to say that he had never heard such a lyrical, melodic and deeply moving voice as that which came from this young girl on that night.

One thing Cleopatra firmly stated to her brothers was that the favourable conditions required to attempt a crossing into the Black Sea could occur at any time during the day or night. Fisherman from Salmydessus often ventured into the mouth of the strait well before sunrise as this was the optimal time to catch some of the abundant fish swimming into their bay. It was a perfect time to watch and carefully observe tidal and current flows. Before retiring to the beach to sleep soon after the feast ended, Jason was told that the Argo may have to set sail at any time during the night, depending on conditions. Luckily for most of his men, who were sleeping off a stomach full of wine, the Argo ultimately prepared for departure mid-morning.

Overnight, a dozen of the city's women were busily making repairs to each of the two sails, along with Eribotes, who did not partake in the previous night's entertainment. Declaring the sails fully repaired, Jason gave the word to heave the mighty Argo out into enough water. Supplies were replenished, water amphorae filled with fresh spring water, and food stocks were supplied for the next four days.

Together with King Phineas, Cleopatra farewelled her brothers, who promised to call again soon. Making its way out of the harbour, the Argo turned to face the tall, narrow entrance to the straits, and almost at once, the main current lurking beneath the small waves on the surface propelled the giant wooden vessel onwards. Initially Typhus had difficulty in maintaining a steady course, but once all oars were rested, and a sail raised, the journey through the straights was perhaps the simplest part of their epic voyage.

CHAPTER 18

Typhus, Idmon and Sinop

The heroes now entered a vast and unknown expanse of water. Although they knew it to be the Black Sea, they had only ever heard rumours of it, the people who lived there, and the geographical wonders of hidden rivers and large, wooded mountains. Not knowing how long the favourable conditions would last, Jason and his advisors believed they should stay as long as they could on the water being carried along by the current and wind. Typhus steered a course close to the southern edge of the huge sea in case they needed to seek dry land, but as long as the Argo was travelling without the assistance of twenty-four oars, they kept moving.

A half-moon that night allowed for night time travelling. Sensing a smooth evening ahead, Jason allocated the night watch to Telamon's group while the others tried to find a small area on deck to attempt sleep. By now, the Argonauts were adept at sleeping in awkward positions when required. Food and water were still plentiful, and wind was blowing gently enough to fill the sail.

Two days after departing Salmydessus, a minor incident upset the otherwise event free day. Typhus suddenly became ill, and was replaced at the helm by Ancaeus.

"Must have been something I ate" said Typhus to Jason. "I will be good after a short rest."

Worried for his friend, Jason thought it prudent to make land at the first sighting of a village. By nightfall, a village had been sighted and Ancaeus helped glide the Argo up on the soft sand for the first time. There was enough moon-light for the usual beaching routine, and while ropes were tied to secure the vessel, a man approached from behind a stone building nearby on the shore.

"I am King Lycus, ruler of the land of Mariandyne."

A brief discussion took place between Jason and King Lycus. Within a matter of moments, the two men embraced heartily, slapping each other on the back. During their brief chat, Jason happened to mention the encounter between Amycus and Pollux where the unfortunate king was no longer a threat to passing travellers. Little did Jason know, but King Lycus was the sworn enemy of Amycus. Lycus showered the new arrivals with honours and declared a feast would be held in their honour the next day.

Typhus did not improve. He seemed to be worse after a fitful night. Jason was deeply concerned for his friend and Eribotes felt helpless. King Lycus offered his own surgeon, and Typhus was taken into the palace where he received the best care available to any man.

To prepare for the feast, Philoktetes and Atalanta together with several of Telamon's group set off with the king's archers to hunt for wild boar. Joining in the hunt was Idas, who up until now had not snared himself a boar. Jason had met Idas during the Calydonian boar hunt many years prior to this voyage, and was one of the first young princes of Messenia to join in this amazing adventure. Being a friend of Atalanta, Idas knew how to hunt and often shot multiple arrows with Philoktetes and Atalanta when they had some quiet time. Atalanta had no problem hunting for boar in the land of the Mariandyne with Idas.

One of Telamon's group on this boar hunt was Idmon, a quiet but strapping young man who had been a soothsayer for most of his short life. Proudly predicting his own downfall on the voyage of the Argo, he could not foretell exactly when this event was to take place. Jason did not believe in the ability of soothsayers, and often jokingly mocked Idmon for his apparent gift.

King Lycus sent a dozen of his best hunters to join the hunt for wild boar along with the Argonauts. Wild boar seemed to be in abundance in the fields and forests of the land of the Mariandyne. With nearly eight boars killed by arrows, the hunting party was making its way home to prepare for a fine feast when disaster struck. Idmon was carrying a dead small boar over his shoulders when a much larger and ferocious animal appeared from nowhere and charged him, piercing his stomach with its large horns protruding from its mouth. In an instant, Idas saw the accident and drew his bow to shoot an arrow, striking the boar between its eyes, killing it instantly. Sadly, Idmon could not be saved and died. The hunting party were in shock, but remained on high alert for more attacks as they gathered their fallen comrade. On return to the beach, Jason was informed of this most unfortunate event and vowed to always believe in a soothsayer's ability to foresee their own future. He never forgave himself for disbelieving Idmon.

To make the day much worse, Typhus did not regain his health, and he too died. To mourn their deaths, the bodies of Typhus and Idmon were burned on a funeral pyre and their ashes were placed in urns buried in earthen tomb-mounds. An oar was placed in an upright position for each man. For the next three days, their deaths were celebrated with funeral games. After the third day, it was once again time for the mighty Argo to continue.

After a few more days at sea and in need of fresh water, the Argo landed at a city on the coast named Sinop. Not knowing anything about this place, they soon found that it had a strong connection to Thessaly.

Arriving as it happened on the day when a great feast was being prepared in honour of the river-God Asopus, the people of Sinop invited the newcomers to join with them in their annual worshipping of the nymph Sinope after whom their city had been named. The ruler of this village was amused and bewildered that Jason did not know of the history of their village, and its connection to mainland Greece.

"There is only one way we can teach you. Bring out the minstrel."

With that, a beautiful young man appeared with his lyre, and sat on a log, cradling his instrument as if it were a new born baby. He began to play and sing a song about the river nymph who came to Sinop from the area known to many as Thessaly. The song was sung, and the music filtered through the air like the sweet-smelling aromas of freshly cut flowers. All were entranced, but none more so than Orpheus. "What a beautiful song" he said.

With a nod from Jason to Orpheus, the musician quietly departed the feast and made for the Argo, where his lyre was carefully stored in a cupboard near the bow. Jason made a short speech saying how much he enjoyed the performance, and that he learned something about how the city of Sinop was founded, but more importantly its connection to mainland Greece.

"We have our own minstrel. He will now perform for you some songs from our land."

With that, Orpheus played several songs from Thessaly from where the river nymph was said to have come. Many of the Argonauts had never heard these songs before, but four of them were singing along quietly because they were Thessalians.

Three of the young Sinop men were seen to be extremely emotional while Orpheus was performing, and soon told Jason that each of them was from Thessaly.

"What brought you to this city, so far from home?"

"My name is Deilon, and these are my brothers, Autolycus and Phlogius. We are the sons of King Deimachus from Thessaly, and we were searching for Hippolyta's belt."

"Hippolyta's belt. Tell me more. What is it? Why are you searching for it?"

Orpheus had ceased playing and was listening intently to the conversation between Deilon and Jason. So too were four other argonauts. Coronus, Eurytus, Eurydamus and Admetus all hailed from areas in Thessaly, and knew of King Deimachus and his sons. Deilon continued.

"The story is like this. Apparently, the Queen of the Amazons wears a belt which makes her invincible, and we wanted to find her to see for ourselves, but we became lost and now we are here."

"You became lost? What do you mean lost?"

"We were led to believe that the Amazons are a race of women warriors, and that they live near here, but we have never found them. So, we must have been misled or we are lost."

"Atalanta, what have you got to say about this belt?"

Atalanta put down her wine, and stood up. She was wearing a leather belt which she never at any time took off. It was made in such a way as to store her two hunting knives, and when in battle, to carry additional arrows. These weapons were cleverly hidden behind her, so an unsuspecting enemy could not see how dangerous his opponent could be.

Deilon took one look at Atalanta, and thought she must be a slave for Jason, due to her diminutive size and long flowing hair. Atalanta spoke.

"I am wearing Hippolyta's belt. Come and get it from me if you think you are able."

All Deilon could see was a small leather strip on her waist, and thought this would be easy. He stood, took a few steps towards Atalanta, and then rushed in attempting to take her belt. Atalanta stepped sideways, parried her left hand down on his right arm, then punched him in the side of his head. Now Deilon was angry.

"Go on, you can get her. She's just our cook" cried Philoktetes. Atalanta always loved this comment. It made her laugh, because she hated cooking!

Inspired by the crude suggestions of many argonauts, and his two brothers, Deilon made one more attempt. This time he was more careful, and he slowly approached, keeping a watchful eye on her arms. When he thought the time was right, he lunged forward and wrapped his massive hands around Atalanta's neck.

"Look at your balls" cried many of the onlookers, but Deilon did not hear. "Look at your balls you fool" yelled his brother Phlogius. This time he recognised the voice and glanced down, noticing Atalanta had a very small and inconspicuous knife about one finger's width away from his balls. In a heartbeat, appreciating at any moment he could lose his manhood in one simple slice, he relinquished his grip and backed away. Atalanta did not take her eyes from his, and smiled.

"Now can you see Hippolyta's belt?"

She turned around to show Deilon the back of her chiton where the belt had pockets and places for two concealed knives. Jason explained a little to the three brothers that Hippolyta's belt is nothing more than a belt worn by female warriors, like Atalanta, so that it fits the curvature of their body tightly.

Philoktetes explained to Deilon and his brothers that the story of Hippolyta's belt was one of the many he had heard himself, but it had a far more practical usage, especially for his partner in the hunt, Atalanta.

Sheepishly walking towards Jason, Deilon asked if it would be possible for him and the two brothers to join their fellow countrymen for the remainder of their journey. Jason did not ask for permission of the leaders of Sinop, and immediately accepted their offer. Afterall, they had lost four men since Hercules stayed behind to search for his friend Hylas. Three more would be a welcome addition. Immediately, the existing four Thessalians welcomed their new brothers and conversations soon evolved along the lines of who do you know, where did you live, and how did you come to being so far from home.

CHAPTER 19

Getting close

Immediately on leaving Sinop, heavy rain fell on all those aboard the Argo, but the one piece of good news was that they had a strong and favourable wind. Zetes and Calais were convinced that if they could find relative safety each night on a sandy beach, the winds would continue for many days to come. Jason and the four leaders declared that if the winds were sympathetic to their journey, they would make the most of it. For the next seven nights, Lynceus carefully guided the mighty Argo to safety on a sandy beach. The rain gradually eased, but everyone was thoroughly water logged by the end of each day.

Even though the wind was advantageous, rowing was still necessary to depart and to arrive at these beaches. Orpheus strategically covered his lyre and instead, made up little sea shanties about every rower that complained of sore muscles and an aching bum. On arrival at a beach for the night, it was Peleus' group that was responsible for erecting a waterproof covering with the second sail, so that a fire could be lit to dry out any waterlogged items, which was pretty much everything!

Another group led by Hippomenes took his men to search for dry wood, or at least, wood that could burn. Kristus' group organised a hunting party for any wild animals and edible vegetation, which from time to time, could be found in abundance inland from the beaches. Telamon was responsible for preparing shelter, and Peleus took pride in maintaining lookout for any potential trouble.

On the seventh night, the well-practiced nightly routine was in full swing, but just as complacency was setting in, Laertes noticed four figures struggling to hold onto what appeared to be a large log of wood drifting towards the beach near the campfire and shelter. A group ran quickly to the water to help the four men to shore. There was no need to guess what language they spoke, as one of the four began speaking a strange dialect of Greek.

"We are four brothers, shipwrecked last night. I fear that we are the only survivors. Our ship was swamped by a huge wave two nights ago, and we have been drifting ever since."

The four waterlogged sailors had not been holding on to a log, but rather the broken mast.

"Where are you from?" asked Telamon as he helped one of them to safety underneath their shelter.

The answer stunned Jason.

"From the city of Aea in Colchis."

"Colchis. You said *from* Colchis. Where were you going?"

"To Boeotia, to claim our grandfather's legacy. To reclaim our titles."

Not fully understanding any of this, Jason asked one more question.

"Who is your grandfather?"

"He was King Athamas."

Jason was never one for showing much emotion, especially not in front of the warriors under his charge, but he embraced each of the four brothers.

"My grandfather was King Cretheus, the brother of King Athamas. We are family!"

With that final statement, Jason now fully understood the connection between his own grandfather and King Athamas, and the meaning behind Chiron's night-time story all those years ago on Mount Pelion.

When Jason realised that these four men were the sons of his uncle, his emotions were on display for all to see. "Orpheus, play. Anyone? Wine. This is a wonderful day."

Even the drizzling rain did not dampen Jason's spirits that night. He thought of his upbringing with Chiron, all his brothers from that time, the lessons learned, his family, and the man he had become. It all was leading to this very moment when his destiny was nearing reality.

A meeting took place the following morning. Argus, the older of the four brothers, explained to Jason, Ancaeus and Erginus who was now sharing the piloting duties, how the remainder of the voyage to Colchis would proceed.

"We still have a few days sailing ahead if winds are favourable, and there are plenty of safe harbours to spend nights if we feel it is necessary. There are many rivers flowing into the sea between here and Colchis, so we need to be careful of changing currents, sand bars and submerged rocks. Luckily, we brothers know this part of the world like the backs of our hands."

"I've never heard that expression before – like the backs of our hands. I like it," said Jason.

Without too much more discussion, the overnight camp was hastily cleared away, and the mighty Argo was once again manoeuvred into position with the brute strength of men heaving on many ropes. Erginus was an experienced navigator, and Ancaeus gladly gave up his temporary role for the final few days. Jason talked at length to the four brothers, Argus, Cytisorus, Phrontis and Melas. He promised them a safe return journey with the Argo should they be successful in their quest for the fleece. The brothers gladly agreed to do all they could to help.

Jason was hesitant to tell the brothers of the fanciful story of Phrixus and Helle as told to him by Chiron, as he did not believe much of what he had been told.

"No please do," said Melas. "We'd love to know how much the story you know has been altered over time."

With that, Jason gave a very thorough rendition of the story as told to him by Chiron. Other students of the seer Chiron, namely the argonauts Oileus and Kristus agreed that the tale now told by Jason was faithful to that of their mentor all those years ago.

Waiting for the tall tale to conclude, the brother's side-glanced each other and laughed uncontrollably. Jason, Oileus and Kristus also joined in the merriment, because they knew that any moment now, a more faithful rendition would emerge.

"Flying golden sheep" said Phrontis. "Now that is a variation on a theme."

But Argus did say that some of the Chiron fable was almost true. "Which bits?" asked a polite Jason.

"Our father and his sister did leave Boeotia, and it was because our grandfather had fallen under the spell of our step-mother Ino. That part was accurate. Ino did not like them. She wanted our father and his sister gone, so they left on a ship bound for the Black Sea, and a life of adventure."

"What happened to your aunty Helle, Argus? Did she survive the journey?"

"Sadly, she did not survive the arduous trip. Our father would only say that she succumbed to some illness and had to be buried at sea."

"So, what is all this about a flying, magical, golden sheep?"

"Aah. The golden fleece. Is that what you want to know?"

"Yes. That is why we are here!"

Cytisorus continued from his brother.

"Our father arrived by boat and was immediately taken to live with a family near Colchis. This family lived and worked below the Caucasus mountains, from which great rivers have flowed since time began. Having known about the precious metal called gold back in Boeotia, our father soon learned how the bright golden stones were found in these rivers, and how precious they were to passing travellers from many a distant land."

"In the palace with his father Athamas, the king had a slave who worked with gold to make jewellery and artefacts for the palace. Our father was so impressed with this, he followed the slave everywhere for many years, silently learning his craft. On his arrival in the Caucasus mountains, our father was stunned to see just how much of this gold was silently flowing down in rivers and could be easily gathered. The family he was living with had many sheep, and he was amazed at how much grease there was on these sheep. Everything stuck to the fleece. Insects, dust, small rocks and detritus of every kind were just some of the items he noticed attached to the fleece of the sheep."

"One day, after a sheep had been slaughtered for food, its fleece was placed in a shallow section of a river to clean and to help remove some of the grease. He said it was a complete failure as a cleaning process because the cold water did not dislodge the grease, but rather made it worse."

"Our father thought he might try to submerge the fleece underneath some fast-flowing water near a rock pool to see if any of the grease might be removed. Again, this proved to be a useless cleaning procedure, but many items found their way onto the fleece, due to the amount of grease."

Jason could see where this was going.

"Our father noticed small flecks of gold dust and even some very small nuggets had attached themselves to the fleece. He told the family and they were amazed at how much gold they now had. The process was refined and soon, there were many people using the same mining methods all over the land. Our father, together with his new found wealth, decided to travel to the big city of the Colchis area in search of his destiny. It was here that he found our mother Chalciope, and her father, King Aeetes."

"At first Aeetes did not believe this fantastical tale of gold mining, but after a brief demonstration, the king was amazed, and invited our father to live with him in the palace."

Phrontis resumed the story of his family and the sheep's fleece.

"King Aeetes was given a fleece to hang in a garden at the palace, where its display undoubtedly impressed palace guests. It was not long before our father and mother were married and within the space of a few years, we four were born."

"The king decided to buy all the gold collected from these miners using the fleece to trap specks of the precious metal. He paid them just enough for it to be a worthwhile venture, but then sold the gold as jewellery and nuggets to merchants visiting Aea. This has proved to be a most profitable situation for the king."

"Life in the palace was easy for us all. Our father did not claim or want any royal title, but King Aeetes became most jealous of father because if it wasn't for him, the king would not have gained the wealth that this form of gold mining provided. Our father did not care much for wealth and was planning to take our mother and we boys far away, back to the place where he was born, and to claim his rightful inheritance."

"One day, we noticed our father was missing, and no matter where we searched, we could not find him. This was most uncharacteristic of him, as he was devoted to us and to our mother. King Aeetes told us that he had heard our father simply left on a boat bound for Boeotia and told us to forget him. But we could never do that."

Argus had been quiet for some time, and decided to round out the story with one piece of fascinating information.

"Our mother has a younger sister, Medea. She is most strange, but we seem to get along well with her. She also lives in the palace with her half-brother Absyrtus. Medea has taken on the role of the 'keeper of the fleece', the one shown to visitors. What many of the visitors don't know, is that the fleece on display does not have real gold attached to it. Our father also knows that some stones in the nearby rivers, have a colour on it that looks like gold, but is most certainly not the precious stone. There are many slaves whose sole purpose is to mine for gold in the rivers and then King Aeetes takes all of it for himself. My brothers and I have become sidelined completely, and that is why, with our mother's blessing, we were bound for Boeotia."

Jason sat on the Argo, and on dry land each night, listening intently to these stories from the four brothers, and was more than ever determined to return to Iolchus with a genuine golden fleece, and not the one used to impress visitors in Colchis. But it was one thing Argus said to him that sparked his thinking in a different direction.

"We can help you take a real fleece home with you, but we'll have to fool the king into thinking he is giving you the fake one. This will take some planning, but we do this for you."

A plan was hatched between Jason and his closest confidantes, Hippomenes, Kristus, Peleus and Telamon, and of course the four brothers, to steal a real golden fleece. Jason's friends. Jason's cousins. His family!

CHAPTER 20

Colchis

Cytisorus assisted Lynceus guide the Argo gently out of the Black Sea into the river Phasis. The river mouth was a difficult navigational proposition due to water currents, submerged objects and changing wind direction, but with some local knowledge, and some gentle rowing, the mighty vessel glided effortlessly along the waterway. "We will make camp by those reeds" said Cytisorus, pointing to an area adjacent to a good high cover of trees. "We can safely stay there out of sight, until we know it is safe to enter Aea.

Jason and the argonauts soon realised that Colchis was not a city, but the area south of the great Caucasus mountains, covering the mighty grassy plains and many rivers flowing effortlessly from the snow-covered peaks high above. At that time, King Aeetes lived inland, well away from the sea, on the shores of the river Phasis, in the city of Aea. Partly to obscure the city from potential pirates, the city was well fortified and agriculturally abundant beyond the city walls. The Argo was totally hidden from view, and according to the brothers, it was unlikely any fishermen would be travelling along the river at this time of day. The brothers were confident they would have plenty of time to slip into the city on the following morning to pass a message to their mother.

Given their location so close to the towering mountains in the near distance, a thick mist descended, covering them in a shroud of secrecy. As Jason and the leaders prepared to make camp for a night, Argus made for the city, to get word to his mother of their plans involving the fleece, and more crucially, for their important and deeply personal journey to Boeotia.

Rubbing mud over his face and arms to camouflage his true self, Argus walked the short distance to the city walls where he found his friend, a former slave who lived on a farm which provided vegetables and milk for the palace. He asked his friend to get a message to his mother, and the friend agreed to do so immediately. Not wanting to arouse any further suspicion, Argus returned to the Argo and told Jason he was confident his plan was now under way. He hoped his mother would be a willing participant and not back down in the face of the powerful king Aeetes should the monarch mount some sort of objection.

The excitement in the air that night was high. Normally on a night such as this, the hunters would disappear to track down anything edible and warm blooded, but this night, it was agreed that only fish would be caught, and the remaining wine storage would be depleted in celebration of an anticipated successful mission.

On his return to the vessel, Argus joined Jason and the leaders in a deep discussion of his plan to gain access to the fleece. Well aware of the false fleece decorated with fool's gold, Argus actually knew where he could obtain one of the many genuine fleeces kept by King Aeetes. These naturally were well hidden from the prying eyes of visitors and indeed the local and loyal subjects of Colchis.

Morning came, and the eerie, thick cloud of mist persisted. It would only be a short journey to row into Aea. Rowing had to be the method of propulsion, as there was no wind. Activity in the city was slowly returning to the normal daily routine. Slaves scurried around the dock area primed for the day's work. Washing, food preparation, latrine emptying, fish cleaning, bartering, fishing net repairing, and water collecting were the typical duties performed in the early morning. Given the thickly mist and lack of wind, no boats were preparing for departure any time soon, preferring to wait until the weather was more favourable.

Suddenly, a dock-side slave noticed a large boat emerging from the fog, slowly making its way towards the main dock. It was abundantly clear from the sheer size of the vessel, that this was no ordinary boat. The slave sent a boy to run and warn the king. The buzz of activity on the docks was like someone had disturbed an ant's nest. People did not know what to do, but standing on the prow of the mighty Argo, stood a proud Cytisorus.

"It is Cytisorus. Cytisorus has returned."

"Look. There are his brothers."

By this stage, the king's slovenly band of a dozen sleepy and dishevelled guards had ambled towards the water's edge with weapons at the ready. "Put away your weapons. You are in no danger" cried Argus as he leaped onto the dock and landed with a thud.

Arriving at the wharf, some slaves were thrown ropes to secure the Argo to bollards. A rope ladder appeared on the starboard side and Jason was first, apart from Argus, to set foot on the wooden wharf. Spotting the King, Jason approached with a gift for the king, being a wonderful bow made by Philoktetes himself.

"My name is Jason and we have travelled from Iolchus."

Before the king could give a formal welcome to his land, the boy's mother Chalciope rushed forward to embrace her sons. King Aeetes was totally confused, and the first thing he said was "I thought you had departed for Greece. Why have you returned here so soon?"

Argus told the king of the terrible storm and shipwreck, only to be saved by Jason and his fearless men. "They are not foreigners, but Greeks. Our fellow countrymen."

King Aeetes noticed the well-built young men on the Argo, and for a moment, did not believe what Argus was telling him. However, he did ask Jason to choose six of his comrades to join him at the palace. With two claps of the king's hands, slaves rushed to offer food and wine to the newcomers. Standing well back in amongst the crowd of interested onlookers stood Medea, who did not take her eyes off Jason for one moment.

Together with Jason, his chosen group accompanied the king to the palace and in a scene reminiscent of their visit to Limnos, women effortlessly emerged from the gloomy mist bearing gifts for the beautiful young men they saw coming over the ladder onto the wharf. Four of Hippomenes men were instructed to remain onboard to ensure the safety of their vessel.

Medea melted into the crowd, and followed her father at a distance. Who was this strange man? Why were there so many of them? What was their purpose? She must have had many questions, but her focus was fixed firmly on the enigmatic Jason.

Walking a few paces behind her was Orpheus, carrying his trusted lyre. He could sense some stalking of his friend Jason and wondered what this strange woman wanted. Orpheus asked Phrontis, who had joined him on the steady walk to the palace, who was this woman so obviously fixated on Jason.

"That is our aunty. Her name is Medea."

"But she looks not much older than you."

"She is our mother's much younger sister."

"Is she married?"

Phrontis laughed heartily. "Oh no. No man in his right mind would have her as a wife."

"If you don't mind me saying but she is very beautiful."

"Don't let her good looks fool you."

With that rather informative exchange, Orpheus found a tavern, ordered a wine with bread and olives, and started to play his lyre. Soon, a crowd of locals and some of the argonauts joined him at the tavern. Startled at the early start to the day's activities, and sensing something other than the normal morning's fare of a few customers, the tavern owner sent word to his wife to see if they could find additional larger kraters of wine, as he was sure to run dry without a supply of fresh wine and bread.

In no time, Orpheus was singing and entertaining the crowd with many of the songs he had written on the journey thus far. Many of the Argonauts were singing along, and laughing when the tunes mentioned their names and exploits. They even started to call out requests. Orpheus was thankful to have a different audience, and an appreciative audience at that. Consequently, he did not have to purchase any more wine for himself. Soon, street vendors were setting up their trestles outside the tavern, and it wasn't long before the sweet smells of roasting meat and onion wafted gently into the stillness of the morning air.

By the middle of the day, the people of Aea had welcomed the Argonauts into their community. The four brothers rescued from their ship-wreck were back home with their mother, and Jason and his advisors had concluded their talks with King Aeetes. Jason informed the king that he was given the task of bringing back the famed golden fleece to Iolchus, and that the success of this task would enable him to reclaim the rightful throne, usurped by his uncle.

"So, you want to take home the fleece Jason?"

"Simply put King Aeetes, yes. If there is anything we can help you with, such as defeat any pirates, brigands, marauding tribesman from far away, we can help as we have the finest fighters in the whole of Greece here right now."

"But we don't need any help, Jason. I am supremely confident that our guards are well equipped to handle any situation that arises, and they have already shown they are more than capable."

"Then what about a contest to see if our warriors are better skilled in martial warfare, fitness and skill than your warriors. May I suggest we stage athletic games, in the finest tradition of martial ability that Greece has displayed for many years? There is one more thing I would like to add your highness. If by chance we should lose any singular event, then we will return empty-handed.

What do you say?"

"Only one event?"

"That is right. All you have to do is to win one of the events and we lose. You will never see us again, and we will return to Greece empty-handed and in disgrace."

King Aeetes had confidence in his soldiers, but when Jason said that if his warriors were to lose only one event, how could Aeetes possibly resist the challenge? Choosing to consult with his advisors first, the king didn't reply immediately and retired to his chambers to consider his response.

Jason, Kristus and Peleus departed to the palace's garden, next to where the fool's gold fleece was supported by and secured to four wooden stakes to await the king's decision. Aeetes had little appreciation or understanding of the Argonauts' considerable and varied abilities, but was convinced his own soldiers would ultimately prove victorious. Walking briskly into the garden with supreme self-assurance and an air of arrogance, Aeetes stood facing Jason.

"Our soldiers will win all events. Why stop at only one? I accept the challenge.

Within time taken to consume one or two kraters of fine wine, courtesy of King Aeetes, it was decided on the following five events: a one stadion footrace, long jump, discus, javelin and wrestling. But the wily Jason decided to trick Aeetes by suggesting an event that on the face of it, was a legitimate battle skill, but that he insisted his one and only female Argonaut would enter. That of course was archery.

"You want to put a woman in an archery event" joked Aeetes.

"Yes, I do. It is only fair that we include as many of my warriors as possible."

"You are saying that your woman is a warrior?"

"Yes, I am" said Jason, further drawing Aeetes deeper into his trap. "Actually, she is our cook, but she desperately wants to compete in something. I've never seen her shoot an arrow, but she assures me she has done so several times when she was very young."

After King Aeetes stopped laughing, he agreed to the sixth event.

So, it came to be that in three days hence, a total of six events would be held, consisting of one competitor for each team. Although Aeetes was still supremely confident in winning, he knew that the fleece he would offer would naturally be the fool's gold version. He chuckled quietly thinking he could not lose regardless of the outcome. Jason was fully confident his team would win all events, and he suspected Aeetes would try to offload the false golden fleece in place of the real thing were his warrior athlete to be beaten in any event. With the assistance of the four brothers, Jason would leave Colchis the supreme victor.

CHAPTER 21

Medea

In recognition of their arrival, and in anticipation of a win at the forthcoming games, King Aeetes invited Jason and the Argonauts to a special celebration at the palace. No talk of the games would be permitted, only the traditional celebration and formal libations to the god of good times, Dionysus.

Before the night's activities commenced, Jason and the four brothers devised a plan. It was to break into the king's strong room during the evening, safely secure a genuine golden fleece to replace the fool's gold version in the palace garden. Security around the strong room was lax to say the least at the best of times because the king never really thought anyone in their right mind would attempt to break in. He always had his most idiotic and stupid guards on this duty. On the night in question, Argus and Cytisorus offered the buffoon guards a chance to enjoy the feast while they agreed to take their position and stand watch over the strong room.

All four brothers, being the grandsons of King Aeetes, aroused no suspicion on the night, as the other two, Phrontis and Melas took wine to all guards situated at their posts around the palace. Once all guards were well and truly lubricated, Argus entered the strong room, took a real golden fleece and hid it in a large leather bag. Walking briskly towards the garden, he simply swapped the false fleece for a real one. Surprisingly, each fleece looked almost identical, which would help the deception should anyone question it.

On leaving the garden, Argus walked past two very inebriated guards, and asked them if they wanted more wine. The very forthright "yessh' response resulted in a promise to bring two extremely large kraters of the king's finest vintage.

"Before I do, hold this bag and make sure not to lose it. Is that clear?"

"Yessh, shir" said one of the guards.

Argus quickly ran to where the royal wine was stored, poured two large kraters, and walked back being careful not to lose a drop.

"Sssshhh. We won't shayyy a thing" said one guard to his mate as the bag containing the false fleece was swapped for two large kraters of the king's special wine.

With the deception done, Argus and Cytisorus stood guard once more outside the door of the strong room. Within only a matter of a few moments, two new, sober guards replaced them, and at once, Argus and his brother made their way to the celebration. The two new guards did not question why the brothers were standing guard, but being royalty, the brothers were not under any suspicion. It seemed like a perfectly normal thing for the brothers to do.

Sitting on the royal lounge chairs were King Aeetes. Queen Idyia, and their daughter Medea. Medea could not take her eyes off Jason, as he sat only a few paces away with Hippomenes and Peleus, carefully observing the entertainment. With a simple nod of Jason's head, Orpheus strategically brought out his lyre.

"King Aeetes. In honour of your wonderful hospitality towards all of us, may I present to you the finest musician in the whole of the Greek world, Orpheus."

King Aeetes was suitably delighted with this introduction, and invited Orpheus to play and sing. Seeing the musician with his instrument in hand, many of the crowd already knew of his abilities, and started to cheer, 'Or-phe-us, Or-phe-us.' King Aeetes looked surprised, wondering how his loyal subjects knew this man. Medea leaned over to her father and said quietly in his ear "This man is a gifted and talented minstrel. Trust me, you will truly love what you are about to hear."

With that confirmation, Orpheus did what he did best. Played, sang, invented songs, and performed them immediately. One of his performance techniques was to strum his instrument and walk around asking people in the audience their name and what they did. He would do this three times, and always had a method of weaving their names and occupations into a song. He did this because the music he played was always the same, just the words were different. A common tactic for him, but absolutely fascinating for anyone seeing and hearing this for the first time.

Another musical technique he employed was to repeat lines of the song and encourage the audience to join in the singing.

When he performed it with King Aeetes and Queen Idyia as the substantive content of the song, the king was so impressed he called for more wine!

While Orpheus was performing to the crowd, Medea silently moved to sit next to Jason. Jason had not taken much interest in this beautiful woman until that moment, but as soon as the two were sitting next to each other, he had no other choice. They were locked in quiet conversation for the remainder of Orpheus' performance. When an exhausted Orpheus finally laid his lyre down and slumped into his seat, clutching a krater of the king's finest, Aeetes and Idyia departed for their private quarters. Clearly under the influence of one too many drinks, Aeetes was heard singing one of Orpheus' songs all the way to his bedchamber. The celebration ended abruptly with almost every Argonaut being led away by a local woman for a night of rest and recouperation.

Medea and Jason remained, and after a short chat, were seen walking down to the wharf. On board the mighty vessel were Argos, Markos, Philoktetes and Atalanta, who took it upon themselves to help guard the boat and its contents. Jason and Medea stood on the docks looking up at the mast, and Medea was heard to say "that is indeed a wonderful sight." Whether she was looking at the Argo, or looking directly into the eyes of Jason, no-one can be sure.

Jason told Medea about his destiny, to take the golden fleece back to Iolchus and to fulfill his promise to King Pelias, leaving out the rather important part of him reclaiming the throne that was taken from his father Aeson. Medea was fascinated, and by now, infatuated with Jason. Being a gentle man, Jason walked the return journey with Medea to the palace, and still the conversation flowed effortlessly.

Jason did not stay with Medea that night, but chose to return to the Argo where he felt comfortable amongst friends. On awaking the next morning, Jason requested Atalanta and Philoktetes to gather all the Argonauts for a very important discussion regarding the games planned. It took some time, but by midday, all of the warriors were assembled on the wharf next to the Argo. Jason did not want to inform them all of the plan in case one of them inadvertently spoke to a woman or member of Aeetes inner circle of advisors. He was still not sure who he could trust, yet he did trust the four brothers. To ensure they departed with the very cargo they came to claim, it was best that as few as possible knew of the finer details. He did not trust the King, and did not trust Medea yet.

"In three days, we will be undertaking games so that we may win the fleece fairly. The games will follow the usual format, with running, long jump, discuss, javelin, wrestling and archery. I am going to leave the decision as to who will compete to you men. You must choose one competitor for each event. Any of the chosen must not consort with any of the local women of Aea until after the events have been completed."

"Do I need to explain to you how important this is to us, for the purpose of our quest, and to your legacy for the rest of your lives? If we are successful, not only will Orpheus sing your praises, but every musician and bard for the next thousand years will do the same."

There was mumbling amongst the warriors, but they understood the urgency of this situation, and now it was up to their group leaders to confer with each other in order to choose the competitors.

After a morning of careful consideration, the following competitors for the games were named by Jason.

"My advisors and I have met and we decided on our best competitors to enter this competition. I don't need to say how much our quest for the golden fleece rests on your shoulders, but may I wish the chosen few all the luck of the gods."

"For the one stadion running event, it will be Calais. For long jump, Acastus."

Choosing the son of King Pelias was a master stroke of Jason's. Over the length of their voyage to Colchis, Acastus had become a friend to Jason, and was not viewed as a problem. It was the ultimate test for Acastus to show his faith in Jason as the true leader and potential king. Jason continued.

"For discus, Telamon. For javelin, Nestor. For wrestling, an obvious choice since his destruction of Amycus, King of the Bebryces, Pollux. And finally, Atalanta will represent us in Archery."

"For the rest of you all, it is your task now over the next three days to help train these competitors. I know you will not let me down."

Each of the selected competitors chose their preferred training partners to prepare for their individual event. Calais chose his brother Zetes. Acastus by now was well regarded by the Argonauts, and had no problems finding training partners. Telamon chose his own brother Peleus, but Pollux had difficulty in finding a sparring partner given how he was the only one to match Hercules in hand-to-hand combat. Finally, Nestor chose Ekhion, Meleager and Ephemus, who were all excellent hunters of wild boar. Atalanta chose Philoktetes to be her training partner, the only man on the Argo who she considered her equal in the fine art of archery.

Time not dedicated to preparation for the contest was devoted to a range of important tasks. Preparing the Argo for the next stage of their journey involved addressing urgent repairs, filling all water and wine containers, replenishing stores of oregano and salt, dried figs, salted meats and sundry other tasks for the first leg of their return to Iolchus. Jason needed to know the mighty Argo was ready as soon as the events were concluded. Of course, the non-competitors were permitted to assist the city people with any jobs they needed completing. In a scene reminiscent of Limnos, many of the argonauts offered their unique and deeply personal services to the people, especially single women, of Aea.

Jason strode confidently to the palace to see if he could speak with Medea, but before he arrived, he noted she was coming down to the docks to see him. Meeting about half-way, Medea asked Jason if he would like to go for a walk. Jason agreed and the two set off to walk around the city. As Jason had all his plans for the games and securing a real fleece, he allowed himself to relax in the company of a beautiful, and enchanting woman.

He told her of his life with Chiron and his life now with the greatest heroes in the whole of Greece. She asked him of the trials and tribulations of the journey so far, and Jason glossed over them, only providing some minor detail. But with all their sharing, he neglected to inform Medea that he had married Hypsipyle in Limnos. It is not clear why he did this, but it has been suggested by many that he did not see himself ever returning to that island. He had no idea that when he departed Limnos, the queen was pregnant.

Medea told him of her unhappy life in the confines of a royal palace. She appeared to be honest in her explanations of her life and Jason had no reason to distrust her. She asked him about rescuing her nephews and wanted to thank him for it, so she invited him to the palace later that night for a meal. He agreed, and they parted company.

Later that night, Jason arrived at the palace and was immediately taken to a private garden where Medea was waiting. Slaves were in abundance, and offered to satisfy every whim requested. Jason requested a krater of wine and in two claps of Medea's personal slaves' hands, wine appeared.

"How about some cheese, bread, olives and dried fish?"

Jason said that he could get used to this.

Medea waited until she was sure Jason had had enough wine before she informed him of something troubling her.

"I want you to take me back to Greece with you."

Just like that, without any warning, she asked to be taken onboard the Argo back to Greece. Jason said that it could possibly be arranged, but wanted to know why.

"Because I have not seen the world. You have. You have many wonderful stories. You have visited many places, and seen many things. I have seen this palace. As marvellous as it is, I find it stifling."

More food, wine, hand claps and much conversation followed, and Jason was beginning to like Medea. Not just 'like', he was fascinated with her. She was beautiful, and wondered why she had not been married.

"The only men I have ever met from outside Colchis, only come here for one reason."

"What is that?"

"The fleece," said Medea.

"But that is the very reason why I am here."

"You are different Jason. No one has ever come here from as far away as you. No one has ever known the mythology of the fleece in quite the same way that Chiron taught you when you were a boy. You know that the fleece is nothing more than a gold mining implement, common to all of Colchis, yet you risk losing your dignity and future should you be unsuccessful in winning at the games. Why do you still seek this prize?"

Jason had never been challenged like this before. What a woman!

CHAPTER 22

The Games

The day of the games had arrived. To say that the ultimate success of Jason's voyage hinged on this upcoming event was an understatement. His confidence in each individual competitor was rock solid, and he was supremely confident that despite the limited time for training and preparation for the 'games', his competitors would triumph. The strength of each competitor was never in question given that they had been rowing with heavy oars for nearly a year.

A short distance from the palace was a grassy area, surrounded on three sides by soldier's barracks. This was the training ground for King Aeetes' military school. In the middle of the fourth side stood the sanctuary dedicated to the god of war, Ares. Each of his chosen athletes knew every blade of grass, each rock and each patch of bare ground like the back of their weathered and battered hands. Jason's chosen had not been given permission to train on this most sacred area, but they were not perturbed at this perceived slight.

The games were set for midday, when the sun was at its highest peak. A crowd dribbled in from first light, hoping to gain a favourable position from which to observe the spectacle. Many among the crowd secretly hoped for Jason's team to triumph, but did not dare to openly show them any support. King Aeetes was known to use spies to report any citizen who showed disloyalty to the king. In the past, a good number of these people suddenly found themselves working for years at a time in the gold mines south of the Caucasus mountains. To say the least, this would not have been their preferred choice of occupation. Living conditions were unbearable and the remuneration was negligible. Many of these poor sods never returned.

Jason and his crew arrived early, and the sight of muscular, fit, strikingly good-looking athletes made a few hearts flutter. Some of the women who had received personal attention from an argonaut in the previous few days had taken up positions in the front so they could pass on their best wishes, and gratitude. Jason sensed the enormity of this occasion, and allowed himself to scan the faces of each eager crowd member. He sensed they were on his side.

To the sound of horns blaring, King Aeetes made his grandiose entrance, surrounded by slave girls dancing and playing flutes. Before taking up his position on a permanent throne directly in front of the sanctuary, Aeetes poured libations to Ares, and declared the games had begun.

First event was the foot race, one stadion in length. One thing to mention here was that Aeetes was also confident that he could win at least one event, and thus keep the fleece in his possession. He organised one of his slaves to act as the starter, and appointed more slaves to be games officials. Jason was not permitted to have any of his heroes act in any official capacity, but that did not bother him.

Calais sat on the ground, gently stretching his leg muscles, and once called to begin his event, he jumped up in one almighty leap. Removing his chiton, Calais made his way slowly to the start of his race. Aeetes had chosen one of his guards to compete in the foot race, and this particular competitor ambled his way to the start. A murmur rippled its way around the crowd as it was perfectly obvious Calais looked more like an athlete than the rather casual looking soldier running for Aeetes.

The race was to start in front of the king where the two competitors would run to the opposite end of the arena, turn around a wooden post dug into the ground, and run back to the starting position. The starting mechanism were two slaves holding a rope tight so that no one runner could gain an advantage at the start.

Everything was in readiness for the first event. Calais was focussing all his attention on the post at the end of the arena and the opposing runner appeared nervous, as if he knew he would lose.

The rope dropped and the two runners took off towards the opposite end of the arena kicking up dust as they ran. Calais was the early leader and was gaining ground with every stride. He rounded the post in first place, but his nervous companion was catching up and not far behind. Once the king's man rounded the post, Calais was in the lead by three full strides. He kept this lead and cruised to the finish line, that being the rope held by the starting officials, in first place. One event complete, one win for Jason. Zetes jumped out of his seat and punched an imaginary branch of a tree above his head and let out a throaty "yes." Jason knew that no-one onboard the Argo could have ever beaten Calais, other than his brother Zetes. Immediately after the race concluded, Jason permitted a wry smile as he turned his head to face Aeetes. The king did not acknowledge Jason's gaze.

Calais' friends ran towards him and they embraced feverishly. The runner was lathered in sweat, and the dust from the arena was coated thickly on his muscly body. King Aeetes wasn't too perturbed, as he only had to win one of the remaining events to retain the fleece.

Event number two was the long jump, and Acastus stood early to perform last moment stretches. Removing his chiton, Acastus joined Jason and they walked together to the long jump pit. Athletes had to jump from behind a wooden plank lying on the dusty ground and leap into the air, landing in a pit of soft river sand. Three slaves were standing at the pit with short wooden planks attached to a stick, where they would flatten down the sand following each jump.

Rules for this event were simple. In a best of three jumps, the winner would be the first to win two. Again, the king's chosen athlete was a nervous looking soldier who appeared to want to be anywhere but competing in front of this very large crowd.

Jump number one, and the king's chosen competitor attacked the jump first. He sailed into the air landing in the middle of the sandy pit. Next, Acastus. He waved to the crowd, sucked his right index finger and raised it in the air. Then, he bent down, and waited for a short time before he ran off towards the wooden plank, jumped a good distance behind the starting spot and sailed effortlessly into the air, clearly jumping further than the king's man.

Dejected, the king's jumper attempted to copy the starting style of Acastus, and he too stuck his finger in the air, but without the suck! He ran purposefully, landed a hand's width before the starting plank and leapt into the air. This time, he managed to successfully jump further than his first effort, and when he emerged from the sand, he broke into a smile.

Not to be outdone, Acastus stood to commence his run-up, turned towards the crowd and began to clap his hands over his head, slowly at first, and when the crowd joined in, the clapping gained speed. As soon as he was satisfied with the audience's clapping speed, Acastus took off down the runway, jumped from two hand's length before the plank into the air, further than his competitor. A roar went up from the crowd, led by every Argonaut. Acastus had given Jason his second win. Ten of his friends ran towards him, patted him on the back and poured watered down wine into his mouth from a leather wineskin. Two events completed, two wins for Jason. Still, Aeetes did not show any signs of distress. On the contrary, he appeared quite relaxed.

Next was the discus, followed by the javelin which Jason's athletes won easily. Like the long jump, competitors were to be first to win two attempts. Both Telamon in the discus and Nestor in the javelin won their two throws after only two attempts. King Aeetes was now sweating as much as his athletes in the midday sun. Four events, and four losses.

The king's chosen boxing competitor was a man the size of

Hercules, and he looked like he had been in many fights. Both his ears were severely deformed and his large nose was bent to one side. His forehead was a mass of scar tissue, and his muscles bulged out of his leathery tanned skin. He was the king's hope. A big man. An unbeaten man. But Jason had Pollux.

The two fighters had already been preparing their fists with leather bound tightly around their wrists, knuckles and palms to give more power to punches. The event was to be decided when one fighter would be deemed unable to continue, or one competitor was forced to submit.

Holding out their left hands to touch, the fight began. Both started warily of each other. Moving around in circles, feinting with left and right jabs, no punches were landed on anything other than gloves. Pollux was quickly analysing his opponents' strengths and weaknesses. 'Keep away from his big right hand. Don't get hit in the head' was all that Pollux was saying to himself. The larger man had a longer reach, so Pollux was determined not to stay within the reach of his arms for too long. In close to the body was where he should be, taking away the longer reach advantage of the giant.

Although the Hercules lookalike fighter had the physique and size of the mighty Greek warrior, he lacked the cunning ability. Pollux sized him up for a few moments more by throwing some simple left-hand jabs to his opponent's face. Patting them away easily, the Colchian giant did the same, and Pollux patted the first two punches away with his right hand, but on the third jab by the giant, Pollux parried with his left hand moving to the right-hand side of the giant's body, temporarily putting him off balance. Sensing his moment, Pollux released a severe right-hand jab to the left side of his opponent's face, breaking his jaw. This was immediately followed up by a left-hand punch to the giant's stomach. The fight was over with barely enough time for Pollux to raise a sweat. The giant fell to his knees, holding his jaw with both leather-bound hands, and looking back up at Pollux as if to ask 'what did you just hit me with?'

Aeetes was mortified. Five events, and five humiliating defeats. In his mind, it wasn't the loss of a fake fleece that was his concern. It was the fact that if he was to lose the final event, the loss of face amongst his people would be far more serious. He called his son to his side and asked if the archer was any good. Aeetes had no idea if his final competitor had any ability. Absyrtus confirmed that the final competitor for the Colchians was the best archer in the whole land, and has never been beaten in any event. A wry smile came over the jaw of King Aeetes. "He'd better be good. If he loses, it will be a life time in the gold mines for him."

The Colchian archer approached the king confidently and bowed his head in respect. Aeetes whispered something to him that no one could hear. The only thing Jason remembered hearing was a vague reference to a mine.

Jason called for his archer, and as planned, Atalanta walked nervously towards the King. Aeetes laughed.

"A woman? Are you serious?"

"Yes. She is a woman, and yes, I am serious," exclaimed Jason.

The whole ruse was working perfectly. Jason had complete confidence in her ability, as he had witnessed her incredible skills over many years now. Aeetes suddenly felt confident that his man would be victorious and the fleece, albeit a phony one, was safe, but more importantly, he would not lose face.

"Alright then. Let the final competition begin."

Rules for the archery would follow a set format. Two arrows at a distance, followed by a longer distance and two more, until the fifth set of two arrows at the longest distance. The target was a circle drawn on a large piece of wood, attached to a post, fifty paces away. Inside the circle was a very small circle, the size of a fist. The outer circle was the size of a boar's head. The winner was to be the archer who had more arrows lodged inside the small circle. Following the first set of two arrows, the two competitors would then take ten paces further back, to fire the next set of two, and so on.

If there were to be no arrows lodged inside the smaller inner circle, of the target, then the competitor with the greatest number of arrows inside the larger circle would be declared the winner.

First up was the Colchian archer. His first arrow landed on the board, but not inside any circle. Next Atalanta. Fumbling for her arrow, and appearing to have an attack of shaking hands, she cocked her first arrow by facing the arrow head towards the ground in front of her, gradually lifting it to aim at the target. Aiming slightly higher than the wooden target, she smiled, looked directly at Jason and fired. The arrow fizzed as it flew through the air and landed with a thud just below the board, and was wedged firmly in the wooden post.

Aeetes shifted excitedly on his seat.

Second arrow for the Colchian. Much like the first. Just outside the larger circle, but it was an improvement.

Atalanta wiped imaginary sweat from her eyes as she squinted at the sun. Second arrow routine was like her first, only this time, it landed under the first, at the base of the post.

Aeetes was growing in confidence. Two arrows down, and his man was winning.

A further ten paces back, the Colchian took his arrow confidently, and nervously felt the weight of his bow. Adjusting to the small breeze now blowing across his left shoulder, he fired. Thud. Just inside the larger circle. "Yes," he cried out as he too punched the air with his right fist.

Atalanta looked suitably impressed.

Atalanta and Jason had devised a plan that she would get progressively worse with each shot, giving the Colchian and his king false hope. This tactic worked a charm, as her third arrow to her eighth failed to hit anything at all.

The Colchian archer was now far too full of his own confidence. Walking around in front of the crowd, he was imagining the accolades and gold he would be afforded by the king when he was awarded the competition.

His ninth arrow barely made the target, but it was nonetheless lodged in the wooden board. At this stage, he had six arrows inside the larger circle, but none penetrated the small inner circle.

Time for Atalanta to shine. This time, she adjusted her routine, placing her bow and arrow on the ground, walking all the way to the target to stand about a body length in front of it for a while. She nodded to herself, turned, and walked purposefully back to her bow. Caressing it like a mother does a newborn baby, she cocked her arrow, aimed, and fired.

Up until now, Atalanta had aimed higher than she normally would, due to her purposeful lack of strength. Not this time. Pulling back on the bow, the arrow went almost dead straight at the target, with barely a noticeable curve in the air.

Thwack!

The sound of her arrow landing just outside the small circle reverberated around the arena. It had missed the inner circle by the width of her left-hand little finger. The Colchian archer stood with his jaw agape. Never had he seen such fine archery. With one arrow remaining, he was still the leader with more arrows inside the large circle, leading six arrows to one.

Now sweating profusely, he wiped away the stinging liquid from his eyes with his chiton, cocked his arrow and fired. Again, narrowly missing the small circle, but he now was well in the lead. Only a miracle could defeat him.

Again, Atalanta walked to examine the target. Standing in front of it, she dipped her sweaty finger in the dust, and drew two eyes inside the little circle. The crowd were so quiet, only the sound of some rather nervous coughing from the crowd could be heard.

Aeetes was supremely confident, convinced that Atalanta's last arrow had a one in a thousand chance of success, whilst he was secretly rehearsing his victory speech.

Reaching her hunting equipment, she bent down, picked her weapons up from the dirt, carefully wiped away any dust and turned to face the king.

"Which eye?"

Looking from side to side, Aeetes did not understand the question.

"Which eye?" asked Atalanta again.

"What do you mean, which eye?" asked a bemused king.

"Which eye would you like me to hit? The left, or right?"

The ultimate fate of the contest came down to this, and Atalanta was challenging the king to choose an eye. What madness was this? Jason played his part well. He looked decidedly perplexed, nervous and slightly defeated. If that is possible, he was maybe overacting just a bit!

Aeetes could not see that he was being set up to fail in a very public humiliation. The crowd sensed it. The Colchian archer sensed it.

"I don't care which one" yelled Aeetes.

"The right one.' "Go for the right one," said a calm Jason.

Noticing the change in attitude of Jason, Aeetes lost all colour in his face. He sat down to witness the inevitable, fully realising he had been duped.

The final hush descended upon the expectant crowd.

Atalanta did not wait long. She cocked her arrow, aimed, and let loose.

Thud! Arrow now embedded firmly in the right eye drawn on the target only moments before.

Aeetes' shoulders drooped. None of the Argonauts cheered. They all played their parts by going about their business as if nothing out of the ordinary had happened. Some of them quietly collected winnings from small wagers laid at the outset. Some of them returned to eating cold meat washed down with copious quaffs of wine, and some were even seen walking off into the distance with a woman under their arms. Philoktetes and Jason congratulated Atalanta, and a defeated King Aeetes offered his subdued compliments to Jason and his crew.

"Tomorrow morning, I will hand over the fleece Jason. You are a formidable foe." With that, he walked shamefully back through the crowd towards his palace, but as soon as he left the arena, he laughed. His son Absyrtus asked why he was laughing.

"I may have lost, but I have won. The real fleece, or should I say one of the many fleeces will not be making its way to Greece. Instead, they will be taking a false one. No-one will ever take our gold from us. No-one."

CHAPTER 23

The Golden Fleece. What didn't happen

Before I talk about the last day Jason spent in Aea, I must first address some misconceptions some storytellers have invented relating to the fleece. Over the past number of years, truth has been sacrificed whilst some severe misrepresentations prevail. These stories are preposterous, yet they still remain to this day.

Let me explain in the simplest language I can.

Medea did not have any special powers. She was not a witch. She did not cast spells forcing Jason to love her. There were no bulls released from a stable that he yoked in order to plough a field.

He did not then have to plant dragon's teeth in the field. After he didn't plant the teeth, skeleton warriors did not emerge from the earth holding swords and shields. Medea did not whisper into his ear to throw a boulder amongst the skeletons, so that they could fight each other. Jason did not then fight all remaining skeleton warriors until only he was standing.

Medea did not rub a special salve on Jason's skin to make him flame resistant to the fire breathing dragon guarding a cave where the fleece was temporarily kept.

King Aeetes did not order a war council where he did not decide to burn the Argo and kill all Argonauts.

Jason did not steal the fleece from Aeetes' Garden, and with Medea, did not run to the Argo for a quick getaway. Jason did not kill Absyrtus, cut him into pieces and throw the remains into the sea. Aeetes did not pursue the Argo with his fleet.

To escape Aeetes fleet, the Argo did not return to Greece via the Danube, or indeed any river in Europe!

Aeetes had many foreigners attempt to win the fleece over many years. In all of the attempts, the standard five athletic events would be held, and Aeetes warriors and guards had never lost any event, therefore, the fleece was never forfeited. Aeetes had always gladly welcomed any foreigners attempt to win the fleece. What he had not counted on was such a wonderful band of superbly athletic and gifted warriors, made stronger by many moons of rowing the mighty vessel, as well as daily physical training to hone their skills in preparation for any event. He had not planned to meet Jason and the Argonauts!

CHAPTER 24

Handing over the fleece, and leaving Aea

Jason, Hippomenes, Kristus, Peleus and Telamon, flanked by a dozen Argonauts entered the palace one last time. Aeetes did not waste any time. He wanted these foreigners out of his city, and on their way home as soon as possible. Absyrtus met the delegation and asked them to follow him into the throne room, where a surprisingly happy King Aeetes was sitting. Next to him, was what he thought was a false fleece resting on a massive wooden trestle. Two guards, the same two who were drunk on that first night guarding the strong room, attempted to look menacing, but only managed to appear foolish, standing watch over a real fleece.

"Come gentlemen. Let me offer you some wine for the last time," said Aeetes. Two claps of the king's hands later, slaves effortlessly brought kraters of wine for each guest.

Aeetes rose and spoke briefly.

"This fleece is the envy of all who have seen it. It has stood here in our palace garden for many years. None have ever won it fairly as you have done, so we reluctantly offer it to you to take back to your king Jason."

With that rather innocuous speech, King Aeetes and his son Absyrtus formally handed over to Jason the very thing Jason had come all this way to find and to collect for his king. The special moment was not lost on Jason, who merely offered his thanks to King Aeetes, drank his wine, and carried the fleece out with him, followed by his trusted warriors.

The ruse was almost complete. All that had to happen was to return to the Argo and set sail. In the meantime, the remainder of the Argonauts had prepared the mighty vessel for departure. Argos had declared it ready to sail, and all containers of food, water and wine stowed safely. Tearful farewells from some of the rowers to their new female friends were made as Jason and his band of trusted warriors made their way to the docks.

Medea had informed her father that she was travelling with the Greeks only the day before. King Aeetes was happy to see the back of his wayward, unmarried daughter, and his four nephews as well. Missing from the launching place was anyone from the palace. Aeetes did not send anyone to officially farewell the foreigners. Faced with a perceived humiliation at losing the fleece, Aeetes planned to inform his disloyal subjects once the Argo was long departed that the Greeks did not have in their possession a real fleece, but a fake one.

The wharf was now packed with well-wishers. One mother stood alone. Chalciope had already farewelled her four boys once before, only to have them return. Not displaying any public emotion, she waved her boys goodbye again, but this time, she was supremely confident they would succeed in their quest.

Medea embraced her sister then joined her new man on board the enormous boat. Jason helped her aboard and once she was over the rail, ropes were loosened and thrown into the river by a number of maritime slaves. With no wind to speak of, it would be rowing power until the Argo made progress away from the docks. All rowers heaved on their oars, and in a sudden jolt, the Argo sprang to life.

Jason stood at the helm looking back at the docks while the helmsman Erginus pulled on his steering oar, carefully pulling the Argo around. Jason could not help himself, and laughed out aloud.

"What is it, Jason?" asked Orpheus.

"Can you imagine the look on King Aeetes' face when he realises he actually gave us a real golden fleece?"

With that as poetic fodder, Orpheus immediately sprang into action inventing a new song, dedicated to Jason and the golden fleece, incorporating references to the stupidity of King Aeetes. Once the rowers learned their communal words to sing along with, it must have sounded magical to anyone left standing on the wharf at Aea that morning.

Assisting Erginus were the four brothers, two standing on the bow watching for hidden dangers, and two at the stern assessing the wind. It was not long before a gentle enough breeze arose such that the sail could be raised. The return journey had begun, and

Jason wanted to see if they could land on the beach near where the brothers were shipwrecked. For the remainder of the morning, the Argo, under sail, rowing power, and a favourable river current, made its way along the river Phasis and out into the Black Sea.

No sooner had the Argo tacked along the coast bound for the shipwreck beach, the weather turned nasty. Wind blew into their faces, and rowing proved to be impossible. Two of the brothers remained lashed to the bow sprit with their eyes firmly searching the water for hidden obstacles. Rowing duties were regularly rotated to share the load. Orpheus ceased his playing due to the incessant rain storm that battered the entire crew. "We'll have to make land at the first sighting of a safe harbour, or even a sandy beach" said a waterlogged Argos as he pleaded with Jason to agree.

Phrontis was the first to see a familiar headland where he knew the Argo would be sheltered once it rounded the dangerous rocks at the end of a slight promontory. Sure enough, once the cape was behind them, the Argo found itself in the lee of the wind, and was safely beached for the night. Once again, the crew slipped effortlessly into its nightly routine of beaching, securing, hunting, sheltering, fire making, eating, and drinking. Medea had not witnessed this and was suitably impressed. Not having a role to play, she asked Jason what she could do, and not wanting to give her an easy job, gave her a sharp stick and said she should try to catch some shellfish!

Given the inclement weather expected, the sensible strategy was to land at any city or small village found along the coast during the next few days. The crew was getting physically tired with the sheer exhaustion from a day's solid rowing in constant rain. The weather was much the same from one day to the next.

Cold, wet and windy, and blowing in the wrong direction. At irregular intervals, the Argo found small coastal villages where after beaching, they could hunt and fill up with fresh drinking water. Jason was most concerned that a crew of fifty or so tired warriors would overwhelm the food supply of any small village, so they only requested basic supplies. In return, the nightly hunting parties always brought back an abundance of game, enough to eat themselves, and more than enough for the villagers.

On the tenth day, the Argo landed at the familiar city of Sinop where they were once again welcomed with open arms by King Lycus. "Stay for as long as you need before your journey home Jason," said the happy king. Before any regular tasks could be commenced, every Argonaut visited the burial mound of Typhus the original helmsman, and Idmon the boar hunter and seer. Jason spoke at the site and described to Medea the brave warriors who were now resting in this earth.

Staying several days for urgent boat repairs arranged by Argos and Markos, Jason spent most of his time with Medea aboard the Argo. Not wanting to leave the fleece unguarded, and despite trusting King Lycus' people, he was not about to make any mistakes and lose the valuable treasure to thieves or robbers. Philoktetes and Atalanta were also onboard to assist with any perceived trouble. Thankfully, none came, and soon after the repairs were concluded, Jason and the Argonauts were underway again.

CHAPTER 25

The journey home

For five days, the mighty Argo sailed along the southern coast of the Black Sea, making good progress during daylight, and finding suitable landing spots for overnight rests. Jason and the four leaders decided not to risk sailing or rowing throughout the night in case they chanced upon pirates. Although Jason was totally confident in his warriors fighting off any unwanted attacks, he always tried hard to avoid any potential confrontation.

Each day was much the same. Using wind power when possible was the preferred option, and if becalmed, use the rowers. The major problem facing Jason was one of boredom for the Argonauts.

After the second day of travelling had concluded, and a landing place was being set up, Jason asked Orpheus to sing more songs about the rowers.

"Orpheus. We need you to help the rowers become happier. Find out what they like, what they don't like, what their fears might be, and anything else you can imagine that will lighten their moods."

Orpheus loved the challenge, and started to sing using his tried-and-true formula of starting with snippets of information and then turning the words into witty banter through song. Wisely, he never at any time used Atalanta as fodder for these sordid songs. On this leg of the journey, Orpheus enjoyed the rhythm of these four-three-four-three beat, little songs, and it has been said by those who remember, he composed at least two or three of these for every Argonaut, excepting Atalanta and Jason. His Atalanta songs were never as crude as this one for Amphiarus.

"Amphiarus loves to hunt,

"And kill the wounded pig."

"His charm is great and his hair is long."

"But his dick is not that big."

One thing Orpheus and the helmsman Erginus, who controlled the speed and rhythm of rowing did was quite ingenious. If the helmsman wanted a slow speed, Orpheus simply sang and played a slower rhythm. The chanting came on the last word of each phrase, so in the above song, the words 'hunt,' 'pig,' 'long,' and 'big' were screamed out by all on board. If Erginus wanted a faster rowing effort, he simply asked Orpheus to play the song again and again slightly faster until the required speed was reached.

After the sixth day, the narrow entrance to the straits connecting the Black Sea to the Propontis, where the brothers

Calais and Zetes would once again see their sister, was reached. This time, it was to be negotiated without the help of Typhus. Jason called on Calais and Zetes to assess all visible surface and invisible currents below to determine when the optimum moment to attack the straits would arise. Observing not only the water current, Calais and his brother also watched the flights of birds above, and the speed of waves.

Remembering the words of their sister, Calais and Zetes decided to wait for a day and observe the currents and wind direction to determine the optimum moment of entering the straits, and to also observe local fisherman in their boats. One more night was spent on a beach in the Black Sea, giving all rowers a chance to rest in readiness for navigation along the straits.

Early next morning, and after careful consideration of all tidal and wind directions, Zetes announced to Erginus and Jason that the time for departure had arrived. A quick clean-up of their camp site, and once again the mighty Argo lurched into action with three forceful pulls on all oars.

With little or no wind to assist the crew, the Argo approached the entrance of the straits under oar power. Erginus positioned the vessel in the centre of the body of water flowing through the straits with a strong surface current. Rowing allowed for quick and error free navigation, and in as little as four rotations of rowers, the Argo emerged through to the Propontis and in the fading light, the rowers had enough energy to make for the city of Salmydessus.

The Argonauts only stayed for two days. Enough time for Jason to show King Phineas the fleece where it was guarded all day by at least ten heroes.

"Thank you for showing me the fleece Jason. It is truly a

remarkable object, but not as spectacular as I had imagined. Some of the travellers from Colchis have rightly expressed their thoughts to me, and now I have seen it, I must say, I wanted it to be a more magnificent thing."

Jason agreed with the King, and said the object was not as he expected, but that it was still special.

"King Pelias will think it extremely special. He will have to honour his word to me, and that is all I care about."

Phineas and Cleopatra again called for an impromptu feast on the first night, and most of the Argonauts attended. The four leaders of Jason's crew operated rotating shifts to guard the fleece, but no threats were made, and by all accounts, the evening was a roaring success. Orpheus once again stole the show with his little four-three-four-three rhythm songs, and when he sang, the Argonauts joined in the chorus of voices. Riotous laughter at the ribald humour in his songs made Orpheus happy. If only he could remember all the songs.

Two days after arriving in Salmydessus, the Argo set off for the land of the Bebryces, where Pollux had killed their old king, Amycus. Erginus remembered where to land the Argo when it neared the ill-fated beach. From a position high above on a hill overlooking the water, a scout notified King Clytius of Jason's return.

This time, the formal reception was much more welcoming, and in no time, the Argonaut hunters and king's personal guard once again made for the forest to hunt for game. Citizens from near and far who did not witness the Argonauts last visit were now thrilled that the tyrant king was no more. Once Pollux was identified, let it be said that he didn't have any trouble in finding a young woman to soothe his aching muscles, peel him some grapes, rub oil over his body, or practically anything else that came to mind. Come to think of it, Pollux did not suffer from a lack of invitations to spend the night away from his friends.

King Clitius was very happy that Jason had informed many others that the king's former brother was dead, and now the Bebryces would welcome any strangers with 'xenia.'

When it came time to depart in the early morning, Pollux was nowhere to be found. Kristus sent the twin brother Castor to find Pollux, and soon came back with a quite inebriated individual, smiling as wide as a moon crescent, dressed in a new chiton and smelling sweetly of aromatic rose oil. Trailing behind him were two obviously dishevelled sisters, giggling and showing more bare skin than they would normally display at this time of the day in public.

Smiling at the spectacle unfolding in front of them, Jason, Castor and Kristus helped Pollux up the gang plank and shoved him over the rail in a heap. Still grinning, Pollux waved farewell to his new friends, and they returned the gesture by baring their breasts. Orpheus could not believe his luck at the amount of new material he now had at his disposal!

Given his tiredness, Pollux was permitted to rest until needed. With three powerful oar strokes, the mighty Argo lurched into action and headed out to sea. It didn't take long for Orpheus to start.

"Pollux loves to kick and fight."

"He'll strike you in the head."

"But if you are two plump young girls."

"He'll strike you in his bed."

Pollux loved this song more than anyone else. To him, it was the first time he had been immortalised by the great Orpheus in song, and when it came for the chorus to be sung, he yelled his part loudest of all.

Soon after the rowers established on a constant rhythm, driving rain descended from the heavy clouds above. Visibility was poor, and Erginus kept the Argo close to the shoreline, but not too close to flounder on hidden rocks. For the next five days, the rain did not abate. Orpheus did not want to have his lyre damaged, so it was carefully wrapped in cloth and placed in dry storage. Even though he did not play music, to keep spirits up, he invented yet more ridiculous songs.

"There's so much rain from clouds above."

"We'll never dehydrate."

"Could sink, could drown, could end it now."

"And that will be our fate."

On one of the wet days, the wind had stopped entirely, and rowing was the only way to progress. During a mid-afternoon rest, Jason stood up and said something quite out of character and unexpected.

"I can't swim. If I was to be washed overboard now, I would not know how to swim to safety. I have been thinking of Hylas, who may have drowned in the river in Mysia after slipping on rocks at the top of the waterfall. We will be returning to that place soon, and I want to know that if it happened to me, what would I do?"

He asked everyone if they could swim, and only a handful of Argonauts said they could. Erginus was one of them, and offered to teach anyone who wanted to learn.

"Erginus. When we beach next, you will be tasked with teaching many of us how to swim."

Erginus had an idea. Instead of running the Argo up onto sand as they had done hundreds of times, he decided to weigh anchor far enough offshore so that everyone who wished to go onto dry land would have to jump in the water. There was a lot of argument about this strategy, but Jason with his four leaders, none of who could swim, held firm. All in!

The fear displayed by those who could not swim was manifested in their vehement objections to jumping into the water. Once the Argo was safely anchored, the distance to sand and firm land was no more than the distance of a javelin throw. Erginus and the only Argonauts who could swim were the first to jump overboard. These swimmers were Orpheus, Ekhion, Mopsus, Ancaeus, Admetus, Calais, Argos and Markos.

With the eight swimmers treading water, Jason was the first to make the jump. Feeling immense dread at what he was about to do, Jason could not show any fear in front of the Argonauts. Swimming was one of the few life skills not taught by Chiron on Mt Pelion!

Leaping off the bow, Jason's feet touched the sand beneath the water level, and he bounced back up with his mouth spluttering sea water. Erginus and Ekhion immediately held Jason's head above the water. He was still petrified, and held onto his friends as if his life depended on it. Once they calmed his breathing, Jason was taken towards the beach until his feet touched sand.

Standing alone on the beach, Jason felt immense joy at having survived his first attempt. Beckoning for the others to follow, one by one the Argonauts leaped into the water and were helped to dry land. After all non-swimmers were safely on the beach, the eight swimmers climbed back onto the Argo, raised the anchor and rowed until the bow struck sand.

The happiness felt by all was overwhelming and Orpheus

was once again considering the additional material he had at his disposal. Erginus and Jason devised a new strategy that for every day until landing at Iolchus, swimming would be taught until all Argonauts could feel safe in water out of their depth, and at least capable of treading water for a short time.

They beached the Argo in the same harbour as they had first landed. Before setting out to find food and drinking water, Jason sent a party of five to visit the city of Kios to inform them of the Argo's arrival.

Returning to the beach a short time later with the five Argonauts were several men from Kios, and former Argonaut Polyphemus. Jason welcomed him, along with all his new friends. Since leaving the Argo, Polyphemus explained that they never did find Hylas, and that Hercules had since left to return home. The search for Hylas' body had continued at length, and Hercules reluctantly agreed that he was probably dead and as such he should return home to inform Hylas' family. Jason was happy to see his old friend again, and promised to return one day.

With food and drink supplies replenished, it was once again time for the Argo to leave the shores of Mysia. The next scheduled arrival was one that Jason and his leaders were not looking forward to, but necessary nonetheless. To return to the place where you had been responsible for the death of a beloved king was deeply troubling for the leaders.

News of the Argo's return was quick to spread in the newly named city of Kyzikus. Children ran to the beach where the Argo was due to arrive. Instead of seeing the mighty vessel ramming the beach at speed, the Argo dropped anchor so that swimming lessons could continue.

Standing on the beach now was Queen Kleite, surrounded by children and a few adults scratching their heads at the unusual method of arrival. Jason was first to leap into the water, and this time was confident enough to battle his demons and swim to shore. Clearly struggling, Jason managed to set his feet on sand, and crawled up to the beach on hands and knees on his own.

"That is quite an entrance Jason," said the bemused queen.

"Hello Queen Kleite. Allow me to explain."

While Jason was being greeted by the queen, the remaining Argonauts, some with assistance, and some independent, also made their way to the beach after jumping into the water.

Since the Argo had last been to the harbour, a small wharf that could fit only one vessel had been constructed to allow for boats such as the Argo to berth and unload cargo.

"Why did you not use our new wharf, Jason?"

The eight competent swimming Argonauts climbed back up a rope ladder on the Argo, and gently rowed towards the wharf where it was firmly secured. Jason attempted to explain the rather unusual landing procedure to Queen Kleite, and the more he explained, the more she laughed. Laughing at the ridiculousness of the situation himself, Jason quickly realised that any concerns he may have had at meeting Queen Kleite were unfounded.

"If there is anything we can do for you, please do not hesitate to ask."

Queen Kleite thought about this for a moment and replied.

"There is something you can do for me Jason. Show me the fleece."

For two nights, the Argonauts enjoyed the hospitality of Queen Kleite and the Dolionians. Jason and the leaders paid their respects at the funeral mound to King Kyzikus, and in a further tribute, poured libations to the brave warriors who also died on that fateful night of the unfortunate conflict.

The farewell this time to the crew of the mighty Argo was a far happier occasion. Nothing could undo the terrible loss of life and loss of a well-liked king, but Jason was content in the knowledge that Queen Kleite did not blame them. With a disappearing Argo rowing out of the harbour, the queen waved farewell surrounded by children once again. Kleite must have known something. Inside of her, a new life was forming.

One thing that Atalanta and Philoktetes did in Kyzikus was to stock up on arrows, because they had to once more cross through the Hellespont, and were concerned for their safety should Laomedon attack. Lynceus offered to stand lookout again as the Argo sailed under a soft wind through the narrow straights. Fortune was with the Argonauts this night. The only vessel encountered was a lone fisherman sailing back to Troy with his catch after two days at sea. Jason thought of the great story the weather-beaten old fisherman would tell when he arrived in port, boasting that he encountered the mighty Argo.

Once they were clear of the dangerous Hellespont, Jason and Erginus set a course south to reach Tenedos. For the first time in quite a while, the weather was clear, and with sufficient moonlight to navigate successfully. Erginus kept the west coast of the Troad peninsula on the port side until the dark mass of Tenedos slowly emerged from the sea.

Seeking rest on Tenedos in a sheltered bay on its east coast, the crew made camp for several days. Nestor and Peleus volunteered at first light to lead a search party for fresh water and to see if there were any people living nearby. Water was found, and a few fishermen were spotted heading out in small boats.

Little did they know at the time, but these two Argonauts and the son of Peleus would return to this relatively uncharted island under vastly different circumstances. Within the short time period of twenty-five years, a mass of armed Greeks would use Tenedos as a base to launch naval attacks on the Troad peninsula in an effort to stop Priam charging exorbitant taxes on shipping through the Hellespont. On this first morning, the scene in the sheltered bay was one of a highly organised routine, practiced countless number of times. Worn out from a night of rowing, most Argonauts were busy studying the insides of their eyelids, snoring and farting until the sun was high overhead. A small group remained on the Argo guarding the fleece and other valuable items. Thankfully, the weather could not have been more perfect.

On the morning of their third day on Tenedos, it was time to depart to make their way to Imbros. Fatigue was beginning to show, and the lethargic start to this morning was a clear indication to Jason that all Argonauts were counting the days until they were home.

CHAPTER 26

Imbros and Limnos

The Argo reached the same beach on Imbros at which they had landed on the outward-bound leg of their journey. Near the same rocky outcrop at the base of a small hill overlooking the protected bay, Erginus took a calculated risk that there were no hidden obstacles, and soon found the bow wedged firmly on sand.

This time, the rowers were not as fatigued and leapt out into the waist deep water, ready to secure their prized vessel. The usual duties of beaching the Argo were performed without a word being spoken, just nods, hand gestures and well-practiced rituals. The same old man observed the landing whilst reclining in the shade of a plane tree a short distance from where the Argo came to rest. He rose slowly, and ambled towards the boat.

"You seem to have improved your landings boys."

"Good to see you again old man," said Jason as he walked through the soft wet sand towards him.

Standing now in front of his shady tree, the old man made a hand gesture and a younger man emerged through the trees to join him.

"Who is that?"

"My son. He has just returned to live with me after spending many summers on Samothraki. But we will come to see you tomorrow. We have some important work to do tonight."

Jason did not know what possible work they might have to do, but instead of trying to solve that conundrum, swung into the normal nightly activities. Fortunately, they were well stocked with some dried fish, olives, fresh water, wine, and honey, and did not need to supplement these provisions with fresh game. Not yet, anyway.

Next morning, the old man and his son returned to the beach with some fresh fish for the morning feast. The old man knew they must have come for many days without fresh food, so offered his latest catch to Jason.

"Thank you old man. If we can help you in any way, do not hesitate to ask."

"Oh, I won't forget. I do have some duties you may help me with soon enough."

The old man's son approached Jason after the fish was devoured by the ever-grateful crew.

"My father told me that you visited Limnos on your journey many moons ago. Tell me. Did they have any men on the island at that time?"

Jason was concerned and somewhat curious by this question,

and decided to press the son for more information before offering too much information.

"Have you ever been to Limnos?"

"No, and I never will."

"Why not? We had a very nice time there. The Queen looked after us, and the crew seemed to enjoy themselves, if you know what I mean."

"Jason. What did the queen say about the lack of males on the island?"

"They went to Samothraki to fight pirates who were attacking the island and killing young women."

"Jason, Jason, Jason. Have you ever been to Samothraki?"

"No, I haven't ever been to that island."

"I spent many summers there, and it is a largely uninhabited, mountainous island apart from one small village. There were no pirates. It was the men from Limnos who went there to take young women against their will. It was the Limnian men who killed people from Samothraki. When those men returned to Limnos, they brought with them many young girls and women to be kept against their will as sex slaves on farms."

Jason was shocked to hear this story, but did not interrupt the son.

"I have heard since that the women from Limnos, with their queen as leader, devised a plan to kill all the males on the island, and they so did. You and your crew arrived later."

The son allowed the shocking story to take hold in Jason's mind.

"Since you left, many children have been born, and these children were fathered by your crew. Even possibly yourself Jason."

"How do you know this?"

"Since you left, the women have become far stronger. They now allow foreigners to trade with them again, and some men have been known to live with the women you left behind. They used you, Jason. They used you and your men and they got what they wanted."

"Why did the men from Limnos go to Samothraki in the first place?"

The son thought long and hard about his response to this obvious question.

"Because the women of Limnos chose to ignore their men for ten days while they worshipped Aphrodite."

"Wouldn't the men take what was rightfully theirs? Why go to all the trouble and bring young women from another island to be their slaves?"

"Jason. How can women ignore the advances from their menfolk for ten days? The answer is very simple. They ate garlic and onions, and even smeared their body with raw onions. They washed their hair and body in the sea, if at all, and did not wash their clothes."

"They were not like that when we were there. If anything, they were overly clean and smelled of sweet oils and rosewater."

"I don't know the full story of why the men did what they did, or why the women did what they did. But one thing is for certain. They lied to you and lied to your crew. They only wanted you for one thing!"

By now, Jason was completely confused in his thoughts. Do I tell the men, or not? If I tell them, and they still want to go past Myrina, how can I face Hypsipyle? If I don't tell them, how can I explain why we aren't going to land on Limnos? Jason did not want to make this significant decision on his own.

Away from the crew, Jason asked his leaders to meet with him, to discuss this troubling situation. The five met high on the hill overlooking the sandy beach where the crew busied themselves with everyday tasks. The sight of Jason and the leaders discussing strategies was not new and as such, were largely ignored.

Jason explained to the leaders all that the son had told him. For once on this entire journey, the four leaders agreed with Jason completely.

"That explains a lot. No wonder they were overly eager to see us. And here I was thinking that we were such good-looking young men, irresistible to women. That puts a dampener on things," said Hippomenes.

"I must admit Jason, I was looking forward to going back, but I am in agreement with my brothers on this," said Peleus.

Kristus mentioned that Hercules had told him of another port on the northern side of the island, where they could re-stock water supplies and food if necessary. After all, it was not far from Limnos to Iolchus. "How did Hercules know of this port," asked Kristus.

"Remember the lady he met? The one who he helped? She told him about it, but I can't remember if the big man ever saw it himself."

Next morning, Jason informed the crew that they would not be landing in Myrina. There was much discussion, and even outright hostility towards the leaders, but when Jason told them that the previous men on Limnos had all been killed, boys and old men included, the mood changed. The main point that swayed each of the Argonauts who wanted to visit Limnos was made by Jason.

"We will not be landing in Myrina on our journey home. However, if any of you wish to visit the women with whom you probably fathered children, you will be able to do so after we deliver the fleece to King Pelias, in your own time.

Philoktetes desperately wanted to visit Limnos. He had grown fond of the island and of the people, even after he discovered the truth. Of all the Argonauts, he was one of only two Argonauts to take up Jason's suggestion and did eventually visit the island again, living there for many years. The other was Orpheus!

The Argo departed Imbros and made its way towards the north-eastern tip of Limnos with a solid wind filling its sail. Oars were laid aside, which enabled each rower to seek a place to attempt rest. The mood was sombre, and Orpheus noted the change. Contributing to this change in mood was his choice of songs focusing on death and sorrow by way of his darker than usual lyrics. Reaching the island of Limnos represented a place where each rower knew they were closer to home. Orpheus laid his lyre down, and instead asked each Argonaut what they were looking forward to doing once they were home.

While these conversations were taking place, the north eastern tip of Limnos came into view. Zetes was on lookout duty and noticed a possible lone horse rider disappear behind a hill. He must have thought his vision was playing games with him, because when he pointed it out to Jason, the rider had long gone.

Rounding the promontory, the wind ceased to have any impact on propelling the vessel forward, so oars were needed. Theseus remembered Hercules mentioning fertile land at the end of a bay where they could also find fresh water. Erginus was not convinced a bay existed, because all land to the east of their direct path was rocky cliff faces with no potential landing places in sight.

Keeping well out from huge cliff faces rolling down onto dangerous rocks, the Argo continued on its way and soon enough,

Calais spotted what appeared to be a bay emerging in the distance. A quick changeover of rowers, and the hill Hercules said was at the end of the bay was evident.

"We'll land just over there," said Jason, pointing to a flat beach of sand and sea weed.

Erginus called for the anchor stone to be dropped several boat lengths out from the beach.

"Why here" asked Kristus.

"See how flat that beach and land is? It suggests that this is silt and therefore, the closer we get to land, we will gradually run out of deep enough water."

Erginus was correct. The land around this bay and beach was extremely fertile, and had been building up for many years because of silt. Beautifully coloured flowers bloomed in the nearby fields, and for the first time in a long journey, aromas of things other than salt water and sweat filled their nostrils.

"Look. There. I told you there was a horse rider."

A young boy, no more than ten years old, dismounted from his horse, and approached on foot carefully while his ride munched on tall grass.

"I know who you are," said the boy.

"How could you possibly know who we are?" asked a puzzled Jason.

"You must be Jason. Komi has told me all about you."

"Komi. How do you know Komi? Now that I think of it, who are you exactly?"

"That is a long story, but may I go and fetch Komi? She desperately wants to know where Hercules is. Is he here?"

"No, he is not with us. But he is alive. I think."

The boy re-mounted his horse, and galloped off into the distance over the fields of flowers, trampling them in his haste to make good time. Castor and Pollux looked at each other and said in unison 'nice horse.'

The existence of this obviously hale and hearty young male child was something of a conundrum. The old man from Imbros told him all Limnian males were killed. Jason didn't have to wait long to find out. The young boy returned soon with Komi sitting on another horse carrying a baby.

When females decided to kill all males on Limnos in direct retaliation to their husbands and fathers taking sex slaves from Samothraki, one father and his son escaped to live in a remote part of the island. The father, Damianus and his son Timotheus did not take part in the slave trade, and abhorred the notion. Sensing something horrible was going to happen, the father and son chose to live on the north eastern tip of Limnos, far away from Myrina, far enough away to avoid discovery.

Komi asked Jason the whereabouts of Hercules, and was told that he had departed the Argo many seasons before, and was most likely on the mainland. As upset as Komi was at this news, it did not surprise her. Komi noticed Medea spending time with Jason, and decided not to inform him that Hypsipyle had given birth to twins, but later, did tell Orpheus about the boys. She also told the musician that over ninety babies had been fathered by Argonauts!

The land around the beach teemed with wildlife. Atalanta and her group of hunters had no trouble finding animals to kill and eat. Komi showed Jason where to find water, and showed him where many kinds of fruit trees had been planted. For the next few nights, Komi with her baby daughter stayed talking with Jason, but mostly with Orpheus. Needing some work done at her farm, Komi asked Jason if he could lend him some men to help, and he gladly approved.

Once again, it was time to leave, and with full water storages, fresh food aplenty, and enough dried food to last until Iolchus, the Argo set sail for the voyage home. The day prior to leaving, Komi insisted that Jason should take with them some of the red earth found near a natural water spring bubbling out of a nearby ancient volcanic crater.

"What is so special about this red mud?"

"Just use a small handful of it in your cooking pot."

Eribotes told Jason that he had rubbed some of the wet red earth on a cut to his right hand on the day of their arrival.

"I rubbed some of the mud on my wound, and now the cut has fully healed," said the rather surprised surgeon. Jason was not convinced, but agreed to take some of the earth with him. He had indeed been aware of the strange, yet beautiful flavour to the stew made on their last night by Komi.

"I agree that the flavour was different" said Jason as he remembered the meal, "but as a medicine, I remain unconvinced. The next thing you know is that someone will try to sell this red earth in clay tablet form, and claim it cures all ills!"

On the morning of the departure, Timotheus and his father watched from afar, and Komi and her daughter were nowhere to be seen. Orpheus did not inform Jason that he was the father of twin boys, but did joke in his songs that the Argonauts sons and daughters would live on in the stories of this island for a thousand years. Maybe that will come true!

CHAPTER 27

Iolchus

Early one overcast morning, a young boy runs down from a hill overlooking the bay in the city of Iolchus. On any given day, this boy could be found playing with his friends high above the bay, in a flat grassy clearing where the boys are hidden from the view of their anxious mothers. But this particular day, he is alone as his friends have chosen to sleep longer. Looking out to sea, all he can see are heavy clouds resting gently on the calm waters. He loves to stare into the distance, and this morning, he sits on top of his favourite rock and contemplates brave warriors, gods and savage monsters.

But this morning is different. He sees something rather odd. He is yelling something, but his excitement at what he has seen, coupled with his breathlessness, renders his words meaningless. Almost tripping over his oversized feet on unsteady rocks the size of his fists, he dashes downhill narrowly missing trees and huge boulders. Reaching the port he leans on his knees, gathers his breath, and his words become less gibberish.

"A big boat. I think. A boat. A boat. Look," as he points directly out into the bay.

Dock workers and slaves stop coiling ropes, loading and unloading small boats and mending fishing baskets to notice a sail full of wind on a massive boat slowly making its way along the gulf into the port of Iolchus. The boat seems to be peeping through a window of clouds and gradually makes its presence visible.

"He is right. It is a boat. I think I can see a man standing on the bow," said one of the dockside slaves. Soon, hundreds of people lined the jetties and wharves staring out over the ripples, watching the boat calmly drift towards them. One of Argos' boat builders who was working on a fishing vessel that morning, immediately noticed the very boat he helped build. With a deep sense of satisfaction and happiness, he stood up from his daily grind, put a hand over his eyes and looked directly at Jason. "It is the Argo." Almost two years since it departed from this very spot, the Argo had returned.

Under the assistance of a gentle breeze, the mighty vessel sailed comfortably into harbour with oars strategically pulled back. It was a wonderful sight to behold. With the midday sun showing its face, the Argo and all its occupants waited in anticipation for the reaction from a now growing band of well-wishers standing and cheering on the docks.

All on board were happy, but the happiest of all was the boat builder, Argos. He didn't give much away, keeping his emotions to himself, but he felt fully justified in asking the king to assist in the funding of this boat all that time ago. It survived. Not only did it survive, but it thrived. Argos was smiling to himself, planning how he could build a bigger, better boat, with room for more storage, and one that could journey to lands much further away than Colchis. The possibilities for Argos and his maritime musings were endless.

Jason stood tall over the bow sprit with his left foot on the hand rail, and his right hand on a rope attached to the mast. His mass of blonde hair gently rested on his neck as he scanned the many hundreds of eyes peering intently in his direction. Seated next to him rather awkwardly was Medea, smiling at finally reaching a destination she had only ever imagined. Orpheus played one of his many songs written only recently and the entire crew sang along. The Argonauts expressions were of relief that their marvellous journey had reached its end, relief that the many months of rowing had finally finished, and anticipation of the roads and stories ahead for each of the heroes.

Sensing a possible bonus payment, one of the many slaves working on the wharf thought it would be a good idea to inform King Pelias of the arrival, so he ran at full speed towards the palace. He didn't need to go all the way, as word had already reached the clearly bemused king. Pelias had given up on ever seeing Jason again, and more importantly, had given up on ever seeing his son Acastus as well. Could this rumour be true? Had they both survived and now only a matter of a few moments away from setting foot in our city? Pelias did not know what to think, so he had his slaves arrange for a quick chariot ride to the port.

He was too late. The Argo had docked, and Jason was first to set foot once again in Iolchus. By the time the king arrived, over a hundred people were surrounding Jason and his crew. Out of nowhere, wine and bread were produced and libations were being made to Dionysus. Still no king. Waiting for King Pelias to arrive, Jason did not make any speeches.

"Get out of my way you peasant," yelled an obviously angry king, whipping anyone who came too close to his chariot. Fortunately for the citizens of Iolchus, they knew to move out of his path. There was no love for their king, but they were not prepared to feel his relentless wrath. Jogging in quick step behind the chariot were a dozen soldiers carrying swords ready to protect their leader.

The crowd parted to allow the king to greet Jason. "So, Jason. I see that you have safely returned. No doubt we'll talk at greater length soon enough, but did you bring me the fleece?"

Jason was expecting this kind of impersonal reception. Before he could respond, Acastus jumped off the Argo and ran to greet his father, interrupting the king's train of thought. Not wanting to cause any hostility with his son, the king greeted Acastus, and Jason waited for his turn to speak.

"Please allow me to bring the gift to you at the palace soon, but first, I must seek my parents."

"Oh, I am sorry to inform you Jason, but soon after you departed, your parents vanished."

"Vanished. What do you mean?"

"It means that they are missing. No one has seen them for a very long time."

At this time, while Jason was attempting to take in the troubling news, his sister Daira rushed to him from amongst the growing crowd and embraced her brother.

King Pelias melted away quietly, looking rather sheepish in his withdrawal. Daira did not let her brother go, and whispered into his ear that she had her suspicions who was responsible for their parents' disappearance. Thrilled at seeing his sister, and equally saddened by the possible deaths of his parents, Jason agreed to visit Daira and Sophia later that night.

The Argonauts disembarked slowly while securing the Argo with ropes attached to pylons on the wharf. None of the mighty warriors came from Iolchus, so had no family to greet them on arrival. But it was finally good to be back on the Greek mainland once again, and as if by magic, Acastus had secured sufficient wine and food for his friends at a nearby tavern. He told his father that he would personally pay for the feast, and shortly after he spoke to his family at the palace, he returned to the docks to be with his comrades.

Medea sat with Jason at the tavern and asked him why he wasn't happy.

"I have just found out that my parents are missing, most likely dead."

Medea knew of his upbringing on Mt Pelion, and how he had never really spent much time with his parents, so couldn't quite understand how he was feeling. But as soon as a krater of wine was thrust into his hand, and after a few libations were poured to honour Dionysus, Jason rose to speak to his men.

"We have returned safely. Our mission has been successfully completed. People will remember you all for years to come. With the help of Orpheus' songs, you will be sung about for a thousand years. To me you are all heroes. But we miss our dear departed friends."

Five of the original Argonauts did not come home. Two of them,

Hercules and Polyphemus voluntarily stayed behind, and most certainly are still alive, but three died; Hylas, Idmon and Typhus. Each of the three deceased Argonauts were remembered and had their names shouted aloud ten times.

"We welcome the four brothers and Medea from Colchis to our homeland. You are now amongst more friends than you can possibly imagine. I am not going to mention all of you by name, because I have done that in private in the past week."

In the past seven days, Jason had spoken to every Argonaut at length, about their brave deeds, the difficulties they overcame, and their lives going ahead. He wanted to know what they each had planned. Many of the answers were the same. Either, 'I am going into the family business,' which was a humorous way for them saying they were expected to take over from a father or uncle as a King somewhere, or the most common answer was simply 'I don't know.'

"But I will mention some of you, here and now. First of all, Argos. Your boat has weathered storms, rough seas, and terrible weather. It is a testament to your skill and ability as a boat builder. Atalanta. It must not have been easy living in close proximity for so long with so many farting, snoring, and let's not forget the bad-breath, and angry men, but you have shown by your sheer skill with weapons that you are a force with whom to be reckoned. To Hippomenes, Kristus, Peleus and Telamon, my four leaders. Your wise council has been sought each and every day. You did not deviate from our objective, and you have helped turn this rag-tag bunch of sheep shaggers and now may I say, warriors, into the best friends we could ever hope to have. Finally, let me mention one of my dearest friends, without whom on this journey to the ends of the world, we most certainly would have fallen apart. Orpheus!"

With that, all Argonauts stood up, raised their kraters, and shouted his name so that the whole of Iolchus would know it. The gathering crowd was huge, and soon, most of them also had wine to drink. Orpheus did not respond verbally, but took his lyre in hand, placed his left foot on a small wooden stool, and sang. Within only a few strums of his instrument and one or two words, every Argonaut joined in, and sang as loudly as they had ever done.

For the rest of the night, Jason and Medea sat together, gazing into each other's eyes, and declaring their love for each other. Jason had not had many kraters of wine, and stood one last time to address his men. By this time, almost all the Argonauts had a female companion sitting with them. All except Atalanta. She was sitting with Hippomenes.

Jason's sisters had walked to the tavern, and he introduced them to Medea. The four had much to talk about, but decided to retire for the night early, leaving Orpheus doing what he did best. On the way home, Daira informed Jason that she believed King Pelias arranged for their parents to be murdered. The king was never going to give Jason the crown, even if he returned with the fleece. Jason confessed that night that he no longer wanted the crown, even if King Pelias offered it to him.

Next morning, and with a thoroughly clear head, Jason and Medea returned to the Argo, where Meleager, Mopsus and Euphemus had remained guarding the boat. Although it was difficult to say if they spent time performing security duties, because by the time Jason and Medea arrived, the three guards were snoring so loudly it could be heard two stadia away. Also, nestled in with the three Argonauts, were three very comfortable women who had decided to spend the night onboard the mighty

Argo. Jason managed to sneak past the three sound asleep guards and gathered the fleece in the same leather bag used to snatch it from the king's strong room. Cautiously stepping over the six intertwined bodies on the deck, Mopsus opened one eye to see Jason jumping over the portside rail. As soon as Jason landed with two feet on the wharf, Mopsus stood up and said "I know you will be successful Jason."

Jason turned to face him, nodded and smiled, then resumed his slow trek towards the tavern for a well-earned feed of whatever was on offer. Two years aboard a crammed boat with variable food and water quality at times had made him appreciate the importance of eating well on dry land. Jason and Medea ate a hearty breakfast and afterwards, departed for his parents' home once more. It was here that he planned on deciding how to hand over the fleece, discuss the death of his parents with the king, and ultimately ask the king if he intended to keep his end of the original bargain. Knowing that he would reject the offer if it were made, Jason also planned how to respond if the king reneged on the deal to hand over the kingship to him.

A king's courier arrived at Jason's parents' home later in the morning to request a formal meeting with the king prior to sundown that day. Jason asked what the meeting was about. The courier informed Jason that the discussion would follow the lines of his original agreement with the king. Confused by the meaning of this, Jason decided not to press the courier, as he was a simple slave who knew nothing of importance of the golden fleece quest. He was simply delivering a message. Sent on his way, Jason agreed to the meeting, but added a stipulation that he would bring his trusted advisors with him.

The four leaders arrived shortly after the midday sun reached its zenith. Also arriving at the house were Philoktetes, Atalanta, Meleager, Laertes and Nestor. Jason addressed them all.

"Friends. Our mission has almost been accomplished. We put together a crew to find the impossible and we have done so. We found the mythical golden fleece, won it in a contest fairly, and brought it back here. The King of Iolchus thought we would fail, and fail spectacularly, but we proved him wrong. He offered me the chance to take back the crown of Iolchus stolen from my family, never expecting the need to fulfil his promise to me. He was wrong. It appears to me that my parents were murdered by this king, to rid him of my family forever, but he was wrong. I have returned."

The friends of Jason were primed to march into the palace and seize the crown by force if necessary, and they believed that is what Jason wanted. But what came out of his mouth next shocked them.

"I originally thought I wanted the crown to reside with its true and rightful heir, but I am not sure now that is what I desire. The crown is tainted with the blood of too many people. My family's blood. I do not want it. Here is what I propose."

Jason made a proposal to his most trusted friends and asked them to back him fully. Reluctantly, they all agreed.

"Is that what you truly want?" asked a bemused Hippomenes.

"My friend. It is. I have all that I want right here," pointing to Medea and all his friends.

"Travelling to Colchis has taught me to value what is important. You are more important to me than being a king. I know that some of you will return soon to your homes and you will reign over your lands. I honour you. Laertes and Nestor, your destiny is written. You will become good kings for your people. You grew up with them. You know them, and they you. I grew up on Mt Pelion away from my family. This home where we are today, was not my home when I was a boy. Yes, my sisters and parents lived here, but not me. While I will always love them, I know what I must do with my life, and living here, as king, is not for me."

"Who knows what adventures lie ahead for each of you, and indeed for us."

By this stage, Medea had joined Jason and asked if she could accompany him to the palace. Jason agreed. They were now ready.

Jason and the group strapped weapons to their belts, not with the intention of using them, but with the intention of averting any possible disasters befalling them on entering the palace. "I know the gate where we may enter easily," said Jason.

It was the gate near Aegeus' cousin's tavern, the very gate Jason entered a few years ago. As luck would have it, the same two hungry and thirsty guards were still propping up a wall. "Fetch some food and two large wines" suggested Jason as Hippomenes entered the tavern. Returning with two large portions of something uneaten from the previous night's meal, and two huge kraters of fine wine, the guards saw their opportunity and gratefully accepted the gifts. "Thank you again" said one of the guards, as he and his hungry companion tucked into their meal as if they had not eaten for a week.

Jason knew the way to King Pelias' quarters. Carrying the fleece and confidently walking with his friends, Jason walked past a number of other guard posts, but considering they were already in the palace, they were not challenged. Many of the slaves shuffling from room to room carrying cleaning utensils and trays of food also did not challenge the newcomers. They were fully aware of who these people were. Some of the slaves even bowed towards Jason as he walked past them. Jason stopped to talk briefly to one old slave, and they embraced.

"What did you say to him" asked Kristus.

"I told him there was to be a new king very soon."

King Pelias expected his guests to arrive at the appointed time, but Jason liked to surprise people by arriving early. This meeting was no exception. Arriving slightly early, the Argonauts and their leader entered the throne room and waited to be introduced formally. A female slave rushed to inform the king that his guests were waiting in the throne room. Pelias was furious, and castigated the poor slave girl. "What do you mean they are already here. They can wait. I am not ready."

Jason entered the king's private quarters. His friends followed.

"What happened to my parents King Pelias? And don't tell me that they simply disappeared."

"I told you Jason, I don't know."

"Why do my sisters not believe you? Why do most of the local people who knew my parents not believe you?"

"Who is suggesting that I killed them?"

"Just about everyone I have spoken with, King Pelias."

"Let me know who they are and I will deal with them."

"Not anymore king. Remember you promised to hand over your kingship to me if I brought back the fleece. Well then, here it is."

With that, Jason gestured to Kristus to open the leather bag.

"Here is your precious golden fleece Pelias."

King Pelias stood with his mouth open, staring at the wonder before him.

"It is true. It does exist. And it is mine."

Jason had suddenly lost the will to fight any longer. Regardless of whether King Pelias would eventually tell him the truth, he honestly did not want any part of being king of Iolchus, even though it was his by birthright of his father's inheritance, an inheritance which Pelias had stolen many years prior.

Turning around and walking out of the room, Jason promised to return in five days. His ultimatum was simple.

"You can keep the fleece and the kingdom. All I want from you is the truth about my parents. Lie to me and there will be dire consequences for you. Tell me the truth, and you will never see me again. This I promise."

Pelias was delighted, and all Jason's friends departed, but not Medea. She was nowhere to be found. Unknown to Jason, Medea had gone to speak with some of the kitchen slaves about the local herbs found in the local area used in food preparation. One of the slaves mentioned a particular herb used, and Medea said that she also knew that ingredient, but she used it mixed with other condiments for a facial cream, common in her city for women to use in an attempt at smoothing out facial wrinkles.

"The paste works very well and does make woman look younger again, but must be used sparingly and mixed in correct proportions," said Medea.

The slave woman said that she only ever used the herb in food preparation, but would now try it as a facial treatment. One of Pelias' daughter's totally misheard Medea talking to the slave about a remedy for making people younger again. A remedy she claimed to work miracles, but was dangerous if mixed in the wrong way. The daughter also tried to commit it to memory but must have misheard the exact ingredients of the concoction.

Pelias actively sought out remedies to make him young again, but nothing worked. When one of his daughters told him she had overheard Medea speaking with a slave, the king agreed that she should mix it for him. "Nothing else has worked. What possible harm could come if this one doesn't work?"

Either Medea was purposefully playing a deadly trick on the king, or it was an honest mistake. The daughter thought she had remembered the correct proportions in terms of the dosage and made up the brew. But something was wrong, and the daughter made a grave error.

The daughters of King Pelias were worried about their father. Not that he might confess to a terrible crime, but that he was getting old, and may not have the strength to reign much longer. The daughters were afraid their brother might eventually become king, marry someone, and dismiss his sisters. When the sister informed the others of the special concoction, they all agreed to make up the brew and give it to the king.

When the daughters prepared the special brew and gave it to the king, he was dead within two days. That night, he just didn't wake up. The girls blamed the sister who they believed heard it incorrectly. Jason was delighted that the king had died, but equally saddened that he would now never know what did happen to his parents.

News of the king's death was greeted with much joy by the people of Iolchus. Taverns were full of happy, drunken patrons toasting the death of the tyrant king. Jason and his friends gathered at the tavern close to the palace gate where they had given the guards food and wine. Orpheus arrived with his lyre, and Acastus together with his sisters made a brief appearance. Acastus gave the tavern owner a small bag of gold, and with that magnanimous gesture, a night of music, song, wine, laughter and celebration was guaranteed.

CHAPTER 28

The brothers

Remember the four brothers from Colchis, rescued from a shipwreck, brought back to Colchis who then travelled with the Argo to Iolchus? I am sure you do! What happened to them I hear you ask. For this part of my story, I need to revisit something I told you earlier, but this time, it is not the myth I am retelling, as was told to Jason by Chiron, but the true story.

Argus, Cytisorus, Phrontis and Melas wanted to travel to mainland Greece to reclaim their birthright. Travelling aboard the Argo with Jason was the agreement made between them and their aunty Medea, their mother's sister and of course, with Jason.

The brothers lost their father many years prior, and were not old enough or mature enough to understand the nature and circumstance of how their father came to live in Colchis, and specifically in Aea. Their mother told them that it was a topic never spoken about, and the boys grew up not knowing much about their father's heritage or cultural background.

Once the Argo berthed in Iolchus, the brothers departed as soon as possible to find any trace of their grandfather, King Athamas. Was he alive or not? They did not know. From their father Phrixus, the boys learned their grandfather was a king in Boeotia at one time, and that was about it. Nothing else.

Grandfather Athamas was married three times. His first wife was Nephele, but she was not a nymph. Soon after their marriage, Nephele became pregnant and gave birth to twins. The boy Phrixus was first to be born, and sister Helle soon after. Mother and father adored their children, but Athamas had one major personality flaw. He could not keep his eyes and hands off other women, and it wasn't long before Nephele noticed him taking a particularly keen interest in the daughter of a neighbouring king. Nephele could not bear to be with her husband a moment longer, and left him. The children were very unhappy with their mother for leaving them, but Nephele knew she could not easily explain her reasons for leaving to such young children.

The new wife, Ino, took an immediate dislike to his children, while Athamas was oblivious to this hatred, given his infatuation with the new woman. Nephele was banned from visiting her children, and had to resort to dressing up as a peasant woman, just to enter the palace under heavy disguise in an attempt to catch a glimpse of them.

Within one season, famine struck Boeotia, and farmers were blaming anyone and anything they could. Ino sought the advice of an oracle, and the advice given was for the first-born child of the king to be sacrificed.

In possession of this knowledge, Ino convinced her husband to sacrifice Phrixus so that the famine could end. Athamas was shocked. He still loved his children, and could not bear to perform this horrendous task. Although the oracle only mentioned the first born needed to be sacrificed, Athamas could not bear to think of his children being apart from each other. In a blind panic, Athamas arranged for an importer of wine and olives from the Black Sea area to take the children with him far away to a safe place. The king had known this man for many years, and trusted him to carry out this deeply personal task. For a sizeable fee, the importer agreed, and under the cover of darkness one night, Athamas had his children placed on the boat bound for the Black Sea.

On the trip, Helle became violently ill, and tragically died. Somehow, Phrixus ended up in Colchis where he was taken in by a slave to the royal family. It was here that Phrixus became enamoured with princess Chalciope, and after considerable time, king Aeetes agreed they could marry.

In the year before the marriage, Phrixus worked a very long way from Aea, in the foothills of the Caucasus mountains, where he observed the use of a sheep's fleece to catch specs of gold floating down in the rivers from the ice capped mountains. When he informed King Aeetes of this phenomenon, the king managed to convince his gold miners to give him one of the fleeces to take to the palace.

Now you know how it came to be that the brothers were born in Aea. Sadly for them, their father also died while they were young, and now none of Athamas' children were alive. Once the boys were old enough, they decided to search for their grandfather, to see if there was any possibility of an inheritance due to them.

Setting off for Boeotia with little more than hope, the brothers did not have far to travel. They found the palace in the city of Orchomenus. Not wanting to give too much information away as to their identity, the brothers discovered their grandfather had long since departed and was now living in the Phthiotis area, in a city known as Halos.

Within two days walk, the brothers arrived tired and footsore in Halos. After a night of wine and some freshly cooked lamb consumed in the first tavern they spotted, the boys were taken behind the establishment to a barn where they were told they could easily find some straw to make a bed for the night. Sleeping amongst some donkeys, sheep and goats, the boys were awoken by an old man early the next morning.

"What are you all doing in here? Get out."

The old man was hunched over, and carrying a pitch fork. He had led some more sheep inside to escape the rain now falling steadily.

"Don't worry old man. We aren't staying."

"That's all right then. Before you leave, can you help me milk these animals? My hands are not as strong as they used to be, and you lads look like you've done this sort of thing before. Well, you certainly smell like you have."

Laughing at his attempt at early morning humour, the old man grabbed his milking buckets and small stool and set them down next to where the boys had been sleeping.

"If you don't mind me asking, who are you and why are you sleeping in my barn?"

Cytisorus explained that they were in Halos looking for someone, and that they had come a long way to find him, adding that they were offered the barn for the night to sleep off the effects of rather strong wine.

"Who are you looking for? Maybe I can help you," said the old man.

The brother continued.

"This is going to sound strange, but we are looking for our grandfather."

"Your grandfather you say. How long since you saw him?"

"We have never met," said Melas.

"What is his name, as you probably do not know what he looks like if you have never met him."

"He was a king. King Athamas from Boeotia. Do you know him?"

When he heard his own name, the old man stumbled and fell off his stool. Melas and Argus were the closest to him, so they rushed to pick him up.

"Leave me, I am all right. Just lost my balance. I am old."

"Can I ask you boys one more question?"

"Are you Helle's boys, or is Phrixus your father?"

"How could you possibly know to ask that, old man?"

"Because you have come to the right place. I am Athamas."

For the remainder of that day, the boys and their grandfather talked at length as they had a lot of catching up to do. Athamas told them about his family, and the boys talked about what they could remember of their father, and life with their mother in the palace of King Aeetes. Athamas was devastated that his daughter Helle did not live for long, but was pleased that Phrixus survived and had a life with his family. They spoke for a long time, and ultimately the boys did not blame their grandfather for his decisions all those years ago.

"I am afraid I cannot offer you much in the way of your inheritance. Over my life, I have lost so much to my second and third wives. Let that be a lesson to you boys - try to marry only one woman if possible!"

"But I do have something that might interest you."

Athamas hoisted his tired old bones onto the back of his trusty old donkey and asked the boys to follow him. On leaving the barn, the old man took the boys for a long walk, finishing on top of a low-lying grassy hill, overlooking lush green pastures rolling down to the sea. The quality of the soil was clearly able to grow any produce, but being an old man, Athamas had no energy nor time to devote to this land, and nothing was growing apart from grass and weeds.

Lifting his crooked, arthritic fingers to the land around him, the old man sitting on his donkey gradually began to smile, pointing out land marks in the near and distant countryside. He pointed to the trees, rocks, gullies, fresh water creeks and hills.

"I have always wanted to develop this land as a farm." The boys stood with arms on their hips, gazing out into the distance through squinted eyes until Melas asked "is all this yours?"

The four boys never sought any fame due to their time aboard the Argo with Jason. They did not want any. While they were not officially part of Jason's crew, they did sail over half of the journey with him. They never sought to take advantage of their connection to Jason. All they wanted was to be reunited with their family in Greece, and this they achieved. For the remainder of their lives, the four brothers married local women, had many children, and most importantly, spent time with their grandfather on the land he managed to hide from his last two wives!

CHAPTER 29

Daily life of the Argo

Not all Argonauts who arrived safely back on the Greek mainland when the boat landed in Iolchus stayed on, soaking up the hospitality of local people and starting their lifetime of storytelling. Two of them couldn't wait to get home to their families, and departed Iolchus immediately.

Stories of daily life on the Argo were sought after topics for tavern conversations with Argonauts who happened to be in town. Eurytus from Evia and Eurydamus from Thessaly were two rather quiet individuals who were more than keen to commence the rest of their lives, and purposefully kept away from the adoring crowds eager to hear the exploits of Jason and his crew. They returned to homelands immediately and never sought the limelight. As a result of this, their stories of the daily life aboard the Argo are stories that were not tainted by wine, women, and song. Before the end of their lives, a descendant of one of the brothers from Colchis found the two old Argonauts on their farms, and invited them to tell him their stories of daily life aboard the Argo. This transpired to be a version of the journey, far less popular than the normal tall tales.

Stefanos was the grandson of Phrontis, and a keen storyteller in his own right. I met Stefanos when he was an old man, and it was from him, through the stories told by his grandfather and great uncles, along with Eurytus and Eurydamus which enabled me to gain much of what I can tell you today.

Eurytus and Eurydamus were two of Kristus' group. When they heard of the possibility of joining Jason on his quest, the two men, who did not know each other at the time, found themselves on the wharf next to the Argo, talking with Jason and Kristus about being a part of their crew. The two men were the same age as Jason, and had spent all their lives up until that stage as farmers, but were adept in all matters relating to hunting, food preparation, and most importantly, hard work. Jason immediately liked them and welcomed the two men into the brotherhood.

Never having rowed a boat before, they were not alone, as only a handful of the crew had been on a vessel like the Argo, meaning, a boat with many oars. Rowing was therefore new to them. It was only after Limnos, when the Argo had passed through the Hellespont that the two men could begin to claim that they were now rowers, and not just farmers.

Gaining much needed strength and conditioning thanks to the daily grind of rowing through every nautical condition from calm seas to driving winds and pounding waves, Eurydamus and

Eurytus settled into life onboard, growing to enjoy each new challenge.

This is the story as told to me by Stefanos, and is told in the words by both Eurytus and Eurydamus.

Let us begin with rowing. At any one time, there were twenty-four of us manning the oars. With our backs facing the bow, we were always facing the wrong way. After a while, this did not matter to us because we had much faith in Typhus, and later Erginus to guide us to our destination. To us, Typhus was a master at his craft. Big shoulders and muscles on top of muscles, he used his steering oar like he was stirring a giant ceramic pot of crushed grapes. Not only was he strong, he was a humble man. He wanted to teach us exactly what it was that he was doing, and oftentimes, one of us who was rowing swapped with him and took turns at the helm.

When we were rowing at night, and the weather didn't hide the stars, he taught us how to read the stars for direction. Up until these lessons, the nightly stars were simply lights in the sky, but his lessons taught us much more than that. We still don't know what the stars actually are, but what we learned with Typhus always remained with us. If we were rowing at night with poor visibility and the moon offered no assistance, Argus adopted a clever trick using shallow clay bowls. Rather ingeniously, he floated a tightly wound linen wick in a pool of olive oil, and lit the end. The only problem with using these lamps was that if it rained, or the wind was blowing hard, the wick would extinguish, but thankfully, we learned how protect them from inclement weather.

Rowing at night was not a common thing for us. But on the rare occasions we were, sleeping during a break was difficult. As farmers, we are used to sleeping on the ground, using anything at hand to make us comfortable, like hay, a sheep's fleece, and a leather bag stuffed with our clothes for a pillow. You could mold the dirt into anything you wanted, but on board a wooden boat, with little spare room, rocking back and forwards like a baby in its mother's arms, sleeping took a while to master. Curling into rather strange sleeping positions was initially a difficult challenge, but it soon became second nature to us.

One skill we have used daily since returning is the tying ropes. Argos, Markos and Typhus were all as you would expect, experts in the art of ropes and using them to secure the boat. We were total novices, but after our time aboard the Argo, rope tying and the use of different knots has become a useful life skill.

Rowing was back breaking work. Our feet were fastened to a sloping wooden stool by leather straps, where we could use the strength in our legs to push as well as pull on the oar. That meant our bare bums had to slide forwards and backwards across a highly polished wooden bench top. You can imagine what this does to your bum, and how sore and blistered it was after just two days of rowing. Thankfully, Jason and his Mt Pelion friends searched for a plant that could be made into a paste to ease the sliding motion on our seats healing our blisters. Without which, we would never have made Limnos!

If there was no wind, and the Argo was travelling over the water by oar power, to conserve energy, we rotated our positions with the next rowers once it became obvious our strength and power was fading. Then, most of us swapped for the next group to take over, but given our numbers, and having to always have a helmsman on duty, someone had to row for two shifts in succession. We all took turns at this, but after a month of rowing, it did not matter much anymore as our strength and endurance was growing daily.

Approaching a beach was always interesting. Firstly, we'd row close to see if there were any hidden objects like submerged logs, rocks or reefs that could potentially cause catastrophic damage to the boat if struck. Once Typhus and Jason were convinced it was clear to row onto the sand, we would turn around, go back out a short distance to sea, and then row as hard as we could towards the beach so that we could get some of the boat up an onto the dry sand. I always loved doing this. We made a game of it. Orpheus and his funny songs made for a wonderful distraction and we sang loudly despite the strain on our muscles. It did not last long, as we would then strike the beach and the boat stopped. Those who were not rowing jumped out with ropes while the rowers slumped back into the arms of the man behind. Then we would joke with each other as to who rowed the hardest and who rowed the softest. In the early part of our trip, we always would say that Hercules was the softest. That would anger him, but the angrier he became, the more we teased him. After he left us, we would pick on Pollux, knowing that at any time, he could kill us with one punch. He saw the humour in our teasing, and would even vote for himself as the weakest link in the rowing chain.

But the best part of rowing was when we had the use of sail power. That way, the oars would be brought in, and we could all rest.

Sometimes at sea, when there was no wind, and we were resting and not rowing, Jason allowed us to go fishing. As many of us were farmers, fishing was an entirely new world of hunting. The normal rules of farm life were completely irrelevant to us out on the sea.

When I say fishing, I meant using nets to try to catch some fish. To move the vessel slowly meant that at least eight of us were touching the oars in the water to propel us forwards with a large net tied to the stern and thrown into the water. As the Argo slowly crept along the surface, some fish became caught in the net. On a good day, we might catch enough to feed all of us that night, but on a bad day, we would not catch anything. Jason did not want to spend too much time fishing, because the crew consisted of expert hunters, and we could always rely on catching wild animals on land at night.

Taking a shit on board was a simple process. At the stern of the boat were two short planks attached which became our seat. The way the planks were constructed by Argos was a genius invention. The person going to take his or her toilet break would crawl out on the planks, and hold on while their bum hung below the planks. But the design of this device failed one particular aspect. Yes, the design was efficient, sending your shit directly into the sea and not touching the boat. Very clean and efficient. But you had to take some sea water with you to wash afterwards. The design fault was that the planks were too high up, and all those on board who were rowing could see the shitter. I don't know why this was so funny, but to take your shit in full view of all on board was a constant source of entertainment for us. Again, Orpheus would often make short songs up about the whole process. Especially someone who had a case of the runs, and was constantly going on to the planks. Highly embarrassing for them, but thoroughly amusing for us.

Taking a piss was easy, but you could not leave your seat if rowing to do this. You had to wait until you were not rowing. At times, the rower just couldn't wait, and took a leak at his seat. If this happened, that rower was first that night to dig the latrine, and then responsible to fill it in when we left. I must say, there were not too many times when a rower would relieve himself at his seat. Atalanta and Medea, who both were rowing at times, never did take a piss at their seats!

Latrine duty was a job no one wanted to do, but was essential every night when we were on land. The job entailed digging a big enough pit well away from our nightly camp site and well away from the food preparation area. Jason and the leaders were not shy on volunteering for this duty, and because of that, when we observed them doing the most menial tasks, it did not bother us to do the same. A shitty job, but someone had to do it!

Argus had designed enough space on board the Argo for fresh water storage in large ceramic pots. This water was only for drinking purposes on the sea, and for most of the time, we had enough for two full days of normal consumption. Something we took for granted on land, was that we could take a drink at any time we needed to, but on the Argo, water was the most precious commodity. The large pots needed to be covered so that no sea water could enter and spoil the liquid. On many occasions, the waves were so large salt water washed over the sides with monotonous regularity in rough weather, so waterproofing of these pots was essential. On dry land, one of the first jobs was to search for fresh water to replenish the pots. Every time we had to search for drinking water, it was foremost in our minds that we lost a good man while on this urgent task. Hylas was a very good friend to Hercules, and one day while searching for water in Mysia, Hylas went missing. We searched for a whole day with no success. Distraught at losing his friend, Hercules decided to remain and continue the search while we continued our journey, promising to return and pick him up. Hercules did not find his mate, and departed long before we returned. Polyphemus also left us at that time. Not because he died, but because he decided he really loved the Mysinians and asked permission to stay. Every time we looked for water, we were constantly reminded that we lost three good men one time in Mysia while searching for the precious liquid.

Once we made landfall at a beach, and we had been hauled up onto the sand, the next task was to tie the Argo to trees with long ropes for safety, which meant being safe from a rising tide, strong wind or even potential pirate attacks. Thankfully there were no incidents when our boat was at risk of floating away, or from a sudden attack.

After the boat was secure, there were set jobs to perform. We have already mentioned the latrine duty, and searching for fresh water, but the first task was sentry duty. Posting sentries fulfilled two purposes. One was to guard the Argo. Second, was to scout the land around our beach and guard against possible attacks from the hinterland. At times, we put ashore on a sandy beach, but were surrounded by distant hills and many trees. In an area such as this, a search party had to scout the area to locate any evidence of potential trouble, identify where the nearest villages were located, and whether or not these villages were considered hostile. For example, we arrived on the way to Colchis at a beach that appeared harmless enough, but in no time, a rather menacing looking giant of a man emerged who announced himself as the king of the Bebryces. With one slight hand gesture, many of his warriors appeared from behind trees. It was this specific event that resulted in Jason and his trusted leaders prioritising security. When arriving at a new beach, the immediate concern was to search the land thoroughly for hostile warriors, and evidence of past battles before making camp for the night.

Once the land had been searched, a hunting party was sent to hunt and source food. Amongst the Argonauts were skilled hunters as well as those of us who could butcher any animal for food. Given the short time available prior to nightfall, the main choice of hunting was with bow and arrow. Atalanta, Meleager and Philoktetes were clearly the best at this form of hunting, and there were many occasions when they too would spend time teaching us their methods. Although never quite mastering the skills of these three, we all became quite proficient.

With so many arrows used, a group of us were constantly searching for wood and reeds to fashion into new arrows. Again, this became easier once we knew exactly what tree branches and the specific reeds were required to make a useful arrow. One of the many items that Jason made sure we had at the commencement of our journey was arrow heads made of stone and bronze. Making arrows for our hunters became one of the new skills learned. Importantly, a new kind of arrow head was tried on our journey. This metal was much stronger, and required a lot of effort to fashion into the items needed. Jason called it iron, and we could immediately see uses for it on our farms later. Atalanta was very happy to use the new, stronger arrow tips and said that they were far superior to the bronze or stone arrow heads. However, we still made arrow heads in the traditional way using whatever we could find, which on our journey was stone in the form of flint, which was in abundance in several locations.

Preparing food for fifty people most evenings was yet another task shared around the groups. Our barrels of wine and olives ran dry and empty on several occasions, and obviously fresh bread was considered a luxury. It was the role of Jason and his four leaders to negotiate with city kings and officials we met to re-stock our supplies when arriving in a port or village. Quite often, our labour was loaned out in exchange as part of these transactions. This was evident on Limnos when we spent months building houses, repairing stone fences and planting trees and vines while the Argo underwent repairs. We probably stayed too long on that island, but again, we farm boys loved it.

Perhaps the most inconspicuous member of the crew, the one who did not say much, the one who repaired our bodies when they were scratched, bruised, damaged, bleeding and aching, was Eribotes. There were countless moments when one of us sustained an injury, only to be mended by the skilled hands of Eribotes. Together with Jason's knowledge of healing practices learned on Mt Pelion under Chiron, we had the best possible medical care available. Eribotes was a humble man and ever the lifelong learner. He was constantly developing and honing his art through careful thinking and doing. If not for him, the journey would have been far more difficult. On our return journey, Medea was a constant source of help for Eribotes, as she taught him how to use many new herbs and flowers gathered along the way to use in his salves and lotions.

The skill most practiced on land was athletics. Obviously rowing for as long as we did built strength in our bodies, but once on land, Jason had us compete with and against each other in running, jumping, boxing, javelin, discuss, archery and wrestling. This athletic ability helped us win every event in Aea. Given so much time could have been wasted on land, Jason made sure that our training guaranteed we were active, alert and ready for any circumstance. When we look back on our days as Argonauts, we didn't appreciate the full extent of our preparedness to handle any situation. Which of course was true whilst aboard the Argo and the quest for the fleece, but also for the rest of our lives.

CHAPTER 30

Time to move on

Within a week of Pelias' death, Acastus was named as his successor. At first, Acastus insisted that Jason had earned the role himself, and had proved to be worthy of the title by completing the task set by Pelias. But Jason was not interested in being king. The people of Iolchus were more than happy to have Acastus as their new king. Since his journey with Jason, Acastus had matured, and grew to be a humbler man. He learned the value of people working together, and would become a good king. He was always apologising for the behaviour of his father and vowed to never be like him.

Soon after the death of Pelias, Acastus opened the palace to both visitors and city people alike. Many out-of-town visitors wanted to see the fleece, and the people of Iolchus wanted to see the palace. Pelias' tyranny had resulted in 'losses' of family members for many Iolchians. The palace was a place to fear and loath, so to be able to freely walk around inside was a complete relief for them and contributed somewhat to their healing.

Acastus thought of the time he first saw the fleece in Aeetes' Garden, so decided to do the same and display it in his own garden. There was mixed and divided opinion at first. Visitors loved seeing the fleece, but citizens of Iolchus were underwhelmed by it.

"It is a sheep's fleece. So, what!"

For some time, Acastus would delight in explaining the story of how the fleece came to be in his possession. Part of his story was how the Colchians used fleeces for gold mining, capturing specks of gold as they were washed downstream in rivers flowing down from the Caucasus mountains. This explanation delighted and amused Acastus, but not his own people.

"Gold mining? So what!"

After a time, crowds to see the fleece gradually dwindled to a trickle. Acastus was bemused to notice how many people were visiting the wharf where Argos and Markos were giving tours of the Argo. The public's fascination was with the boat, not the object on display in the palace. Wealthy people were lining up to talk to Argos to build a boat for them. Within a matter of days since the Argo sailed into port, Argos had enough work to last him a lifetime. Markos was promoted to boat builder, and a dozen more men were employed to work with them.

Orpheus played in every tavern in the city to packed crowds. He didn't have to buy a drink or plate of food. He was never alone at nights either. Many of the Argonauts remained in the city for a short while. They too were sitting at taverns, retelling stories about their trip to Colchis. Perhaps it was here that some of the stories told by clearly inebriated Argonauts during that week began straying from the truth. Perhaps the people who heard first-hand from these heroes then retold those same stories so many times over the next few years, the original story line had morphed into something completely different.

Can you imagine that? Stories passing on from an original Argonaut to a tavern full of eager listeners who miss-hear bits, and later when they re-tell the tale, add in events of their own.

"I swear by the gods that what I am about to tell you is the truth. Hercules was so strong he could row the Argo himself while the others rested!"

"The fleece was made of pure gold, by the god Hephaestus!"

"Poseidon himself protected the Argo by providing favourable winds every day!"

"Phrixus and Helle flew over the Hellespont on a flying, golden sheep, and Helle fell off. Truly!"

"To obtain the fleece, Jason slew the multi-headed monster, which was guarding the cave where the fleece was held, all by himself!"

"On their journey home, the Argo could not return the same way, so they went via the Istros River, carried the Argo over mountains and then sailed down the Rhone River!"

"I heard they ended up in Esperia, carried the Argo over sand dunes because the winds were against them on the sea, and then sailed around Crete before making their way home!"

Within that first week, the story of Jason and the Argonauts was changing daily to suit those who told it and for the benefit of those who were listening to it. I know this must sound strange to you now, as I am a story teller, but please believe me as I am telling you my version, it has been well-researched and not subject to gossip.

One by one, the remaining Argonauts departed Iolchus and made for their homes, families and homelands. Farewells were made and backs were slapped. Promises were made to 'catchup' soon, but sadly for many they never did. Some like Peleus, Nestor, Laertes, Iphitos and Theseus went home to become kings of their own people.

Some like Menoetius became more well known for who they fathered. Menoetius was the father of Patroclus, childhood friend of Achilles, whose own father was Peleus. Unlike their fathers who went on to enjoy long lives, Patroclus and Achilles died far too young.

Laertes fathered the wily Odysseus, hero from the Trojan blockade. Laertes handed over the kingship of Ithaca to Odysseus before the Trojan battles commenced. While his son was king, Laertes lived a simple life as a farmer, busily planting crops and trees and looking after the animals on his own farm.

We have already seen that Theseus had his personal adventures turned into mythology. By killing a bull in Crete which later became a minotaur, that story has grown out of all proportion. After the voyage, Theseus returned to the village of Athens, and with years of hard work and dedication, he built that village into the vibrant city state we now know today.

Some like Asterion and Amphion went home to their village

of Pellene in the Peloponnese and lived out their lives as farmers, raising many children. So too did the brothers Eurytus and Ekhion, who returned to live their lives in relative obscurity on Evvia.

Ancaeus returned home to his island of Samos where he had planted a vineyard prior to the voyage. On his return home, Ancaeus saw that the vines had reached maturity, been harvested and made into wine. Before he departed Samos to become an Argonaut, a seer told Ancaeus that he would never taste his own wine. Once safely home, Ancaeus summoned the seer, raised a cup of the wine, but before taking a drink, was told by the seer that 'there is many a slip between the cup and the lip.' Ancaeus mocked the seer, but was interrupted by a voice yelling that a wild boar had got in amongst the vines and was causing severe damage to the vineyard. Without taking a sip, Ancaeus put his cup down and ran outside to address the problem. Being a participant in the Calydonian boar hunt, it was completely ironic that this Argonaut was then killed by the charging boar running amok through his own vines.

Admetus married one of Pelias' daughters, Alcestis. They returned to Pherae in Thessaly where he became king.

Nestor returned to Pylos where he became king on the death of his father Neleus. Nestor rose to fame through his involvement during the trojan blockade. He was considered a wise, old counsel to many of the younger kings in that conflict. An excellent javelin thrower, Nestor lived a long life.

Whatever happened to Hercules, after his fruitless search for his friend Hylas? After Hercules and Polyphemus stayed behind in Mysia to search for Hylas, Polyphemus remained for the rest of his days in Mysia and Hercules managed to secure a safe passage to mainland Greece. If there are some rather twisted tales arising from the voyage in search of the golden fleece, perhaps the prize for the most outlandish stories can be attributed to those about Hercules. Let me explain.

On his arrival in his home town of Thebes, Hercules had no form of income, and immediately lent himself out as a man for hire, to carry out any tasks needed, and people paid in gold or silver for his services. He travelled the countryside undertaking these tasks and being paid handsomely in valuable metals. His fame continued to grow, and the mythology of his labours grew to ridiculous levels. What is not known is that his twin brother Iphicles joined him for many of these tasks, but we never hear of the twin. Iphicles was the quieter of the brothers and was constantly in awe of his slightly older big brother.

Hercules and Iphicles chose not to join fellow Greeks in the blockade of Troy, which led to their gradual demise in status around the campfires where men boasted of knowing the strong man. How quickly did Hercules' labours suddenly disappear from storytellers of the day, when they could invent new stories of Helen, Paris, Odysseus, and Hector!

And what of Jason? Medea and Jason left Iolchus and travelled to Corinth where they married and had three boys. Life for the new family was initially quiet and content. However, Medea never really fitted in, and being an outsider from Colchis, was never totally accepted into the community where they lived. Fate played a role in their lives when sadly, illness befell the children, and all three boys died. Spiralling into a world of depression, Jason could not accept that it was fate, and thought Medea played a part in their deaths. With Jason seeking solace in the arms of princess Glauce of Corinth, Medea finally had enough and escaped to live in Athens, where she lived for a time with Theseus in his palace as a guest of the king and queen.

Medea is a much-maligned character in all of this. She firmly believed that she and Jason could make a good life together when he became king of Iolchus as it seemed he would. Now you know that ultimately, he didn't wish to take on that role, Jason did not really know what he wanted to do, and it was he who didn't really fit in anywhere.

The deaths of their three boys was an enormous tragedy not only to Jason, but especially Medea. She loved those boys, and to have Jason blame her for their deaths must have been the last straw for her. It was her decision to leave for Athens, a place she could have remained for the rest of her days, but her life was not over. She did intend to attempt a reconciliation with Jason, but a chance meeting with Orpheus in Athens, whilst he was singing and playing music at a tavern in Piraeus changed everything. Orpheus unintentionally informed Medea that Jason had married Hypsipyle on Limnos. Feeling totally betrayed and ashamed of her husband, Medea departed Athens for the last time and returned home, where she discovered her father had died, and her brother Perses was now king. Unable to live with him as king, Medea travelled to the Iranian plateau and remained there for the remainder of her life. I can only imagine what lies storytellers will say about Medea in the future.

Jason never regained the riches or fame of his youth. He intended to marry Glauce, and for a time, their lives were contented. King Creon gave his full and free consent to their marriage after granting Jason a divorce from Medea, but prior to their wedding, princess

Glauce of Corinth was killed unexpectedly in a fire that destroyed her home.

Jason had nowhere to go. His life in Corinth ended, and he drifted back to Iolchus where he found the one thing in his life that gave him joy. The Argo was still in existence, but like Jason, was rotting away. Jason spent the last few months of his life sitting under the bow of the beached Argo. A sad and lonely figure, Jason wanted to die.

One day, Orpheus returned to Iolchus to perform for king Acastus, and asked if he had heard of their friend Jason. Acastus informed Orpheus that their friend was last seen out of town where the Argo was beached. Orpheus decided to go and search for his old friend. Finding him slumped on the sand, under the Argo's bow, Jason appeared completely dishevelled and reeked of wine and piss. This was clearly not the Jason he knew and remembered. Orpheus could not bear to stay a moment longer and decided to leave Iolchus as soon as he completed his tavern appearances.

The Argo had become Jason's safe place. He could feel normal again, after several large gulps of unadulterated wine. Being in proximity to the Argo reminded him of happier times. He knew that Orpheus had visited him the day before, and waited for him to come back again, even if it was for one more time. On the day Orpheus packed his meagre belongings, which consisted of a lyre, clean chiton, spare sandals and eating utensils wrapped in a leather bag tied around a long, thin tree branch, he returned to the beach to say farewell to his friend.

"Orpheus, my old and dear friend. I do not have much time to live. My days are numbered here. My journey across the river with

Charon the ferryman is coming soon."

"Don't say that, Jason. You have so much to live for."

"No. I don't. Not anymore."

Jason was dying. No doubt about that. He had one last duty to perform, and he had waited for this inevitable moment to ask his old friend to help.

"I now realise that I have made a big mistake."

"No, you......."

"Let me finish. I have made a big mistake. I now realise that the one woman I truly loved, when I was happiest, was well before I even saw the fleece. Before any of our crew had died. Long ago Orpheus."

"Before we sailed?" asked Orpheus, clearly not understanding where Jason was going with his rambling thoughts.

"Not quite. On Limnos."

"Limnos? What happened on Limnos? Did I miss something?"

"I know you didn't miss anything. You never miss anything. That is why you can do what you can do. I mean with Hypsipyle."

Reaching around to gather a tattered old woollen blanket, carefully covering something thin, Jason unwrapped the mystery object. "This is for you. I want you to give this to Hypsipyle."

Inside the blanket was the sword given to him as the Argo was slowly departing the beach at Myrina.

"Remember Hypsipyle running down to the water's edge and giving me a gift. This was her father's. This was the king's sword. I want you to give it back to Hypsipyle when you visit Limnos. Can you do that for me?"

What Jason didn't know, and what Orpheus chose not to disclose, was that Hypsipyle had given birth to twin boys. Jason was the father, and his boys were now growing into fine young men. If only Jason knew he had sons.

"If you can promise to do this for me, I will be forever grateful."

Orpheus nodded and wiped away the tears welling in his eyes. Carrying the sword under one arm, he stood, looked at Jason for one last time, turned and walked slowly along the beach without looking back. This was to be their final moment together physically, but musically, Orpheus sang songs about this moment for many years to come, never ever letting people know the deeply personal meaning behind those sad words.

As for Jason, he lasted another few days. Resting as he did each morning on the sand with his back leaning against the bow of the worm ridden, once mighty Argo, Jason was waking after a night of far too much wine. He was oblivious to the raging wind and driving rain rolling in from the sea, and would have not noticed or sensed the heavy wooden figure of Athena's figure head falling and crushing his lifeless body.

POST SCRIPT

Who were the Original Argonauts?

Who were the original Argonauts and what happened to them during the journey or after the fleece was delivered? Jason used four leaders to assist in daily activities on the Argo. Here is a list of the leaders and the Argonauts who were assigned to his group.

Hippomenes – Leader of Group 1

Courted Atalanta, the huntress. Student of Chiron for a short time. Boar Hunt participant, and friend to Jason from the hunt. One of the four trusted leaders on the Argo.

AMPHIARUS

Seer, and boar hunter. Amphiarus returned to be one of the Kings of Argos, and was Hypsipyle's saviour. He was one of the seven against Thebes.

TYPHUS

Original Argo helmsman and navigator. Died onboard the outward journey of the Argo and was buried in the Mariandyne area.

PHILOKTETES

Master archer and maker of bows and arrows. Originally lived a few days walk from Iolchus. One of the many suitors of Helen. Made his name as the maker of poisonous arrow heads on the island of Limnos during the Trojan blockade. Lived out his life on Limnos.

ASTERION AND AMPHION

Brothers from the Peloponnese. Both returned to their homes and remained for the rest of their lives

IDAS

Boar hunter and Messenian prince. Brother to Lynceus.

LYNCEUS

Boar hunter and Argo lookout after leaving Limnos

MOPSUS

Became a seer after the Argo's voyage.

OILEUS

Student of Chiron, and lifelong friend of Jason. Became King of Locris.

PHLIAS

From Argolis, in the Peloponnese. Later returned to the Peloponnese and founded the city of Phlius. It became renowned for its wine growing.

PELEUS – LEADER OF GROUP 2

One of the four leaders. Future king of Phthia. Father to Achilles, hero of the Trojan blockade. Brother of Telamon and boar hunter.

LAERTES

Boar hunter. Met Anticlea immediately prior to the Argo's departure and married her on return. Became King of Ithaca and father to Odysseus.

THESEUS

Future King of Athens. Slayer of the bull in the labyrinth of Crete (some say it was a minotaur)!

EKHION

Boar hunter. Some say he fought in the Trojan blockade

ERIBOTES

Surgeon of the Argo, from Locris.

MELEAGER
Calydonian prince. Boar hunter. Married Idas' daughter and had a daughter.

ACASTUS
King Pelias' son, eventual King of Iolchus.

AUGEUS
Cattle farmer and King of Elis in the Peloponnese area. Employed Hercules many years later to help clean his enormous cattle stables.

CANTHUS
Arcadian prince from the Peloponnese area.

CORONUS
Became king of the Lapiths, near Pelion, Thessaly.

AMPHIDAMAS
Arcadian prince, and brother of Cepheus.

CEPHEUS
From Arcadia, boar hunter, and future king of Tegea in the Peloponnese area.

KRISTUS – LEADER OF GROUP 3
Lived on Mt Pelion with Jason as a boy under the tutelage of Chiron. Nothing is known of his life after the Argo.

ATALANTA

Warrior, masterful with bow and arrow, only woman on the Argo until Medea joined. Calydonian boar hunter. Never married, but had a child with Meleager.

CASTOR

Brother to Pollux, horse expert. Founded many athletic events with his brother Pollux.

POLLUX

Brother to Castor, excellent boxer and horse expert. Their sister Helen lived in Troy.

BUTES

From the Athens area, was a shepherd, ploughman and warrior. Excellent skills with knives and butchering animals for meat.

ARGOS

Boat builder and builder of the Argo. Returned to great fame as a boat builder.

MARKOS

Argos' apprentice, but on return, took over as a master boat builder himself.

ERGINUS

Piloted the Argo after Typhus died. Excellent swimmer. Taught the argonauts how to swim on the journey home.

EURYTUS
Calydonian boar hunter. Brother of Ekhion. Returned to Evia after the Argo adventure.

EURYDAMUS
From Ktimene in mountainous Thessaly.

POLYPHEMUS
Stayed behind with Hercules to look for Hylas, but remained in Mysia. Nestor thought of him as a hero. For a while he wanted to marry Hercules sister, but never did. Later, founded the city of Cius, where he became the king.

MENOETIUS
His son Patroclus accidently killed a young boy, so Menoetius and Patroclus were exiled to live in Phythia, the home of his friend Peleus. Peleus' son, Achilles and Patroclus became best friends.

TELAMON – LEADER OF GROUP 4
Brother to Peleus. Father to Ajax the Great, a hero of the Trojan blockade. Second only to Achilles in strength. One of the Calydonian boar hunters. After the Argo returned, he helped Hercules on some of his exploits.

NESTOR
Calydonian boar hunter. Became king of Pylos. Rose to fame as one of the wise, old advisors to the warriors at the Trojan blockade. Had many children, and died in old age.

IPHICLES

Twin brother of Hercules. Helped Hercules later with his many labours.

ANCAEUS

Returned to Samos. Planted a vineyard, but died from a boar wound before he tasted his wine.

ADMETUS

Boar hunter. Married Alcestis, a daughter of King Pelias. Became King of Pherae in Thessaly.

IDMON

Died on the voyage from a wild boar. Buried along with Typhus.

IPHITOS

Became King of Phocis. An ally of the Thebans in the war of the 'Seven Against Thebes'.

CALAIS AND ZETES

Twin brothers. Masters of reading prevailing winds. Returned to Salmydessus after the Argo reached Iolchus. Each married a local woman.

EUPHEMUS

Boar hunter. Later lived in Libya.

HYLAS

Hercules right-hand man. Died on the trip to Colchis when he fell on slippery rocks above a waterfall. His body was never found, and Hercules and Polyphemus looked for him while the Argo sailed onwards.

AUTHOR'S NOTES:

The story of Jason has been known for thousands of years. Archaeological discoveries dating to around 1500 BCE suggest people travelled from Europe to China and back as objects have been located in places where they are not normally found. No written evidence exists from this time, but as soon as evidence of early writing emerged, the story of Jason was already a thousand years old. Greek literature only began after the Bronze Age. We know that human sacrifices did occur, the use of a sheep's fleece in gold mining was real, and trade between geographically distant places in Europe and Asia was not uncommon.

There are many references throughout Greek and Roman history to the story of Jason. There were numerous stories written relating to his journey from Iolchus in mainland Greece to Colchis in modern day Georgia, but sadly, most of these stories have been lost to time. For example, it is possible that a reference providing a detailed description of the journey to Colchis by Jason and the

Argonauts was made in the epic poem *Corinthiacca* by Eumelus in approximately 730 BCE. Sadly, only fragmentary pieces have survived, which are references from Pausanias to a quote from the poem. Homer made a reference to a 'coursing ship' in around 700 BCE. It would be another 300 years until more references emerged, and fortunately, these ones survive in a much better format.

Today we have seminal references to the Argonauts from Apollonius of Rhodes (circa mid-3rd Century BCE), Vallerius Flaccus' Argonautica (70 AD), the Pythian Odes by Pindar (462 BCE), the Orphic Argonautica (5th or 6th Century BCE), Euripides play's Medea (431 BCE), Hypsipyle (411 BCE) and a myriad of footnotes. Of course, we have no way of knowing if the story has any roots in fact, but there is no doubt the story of Jason was known nearly three thousand years ago, as archeological evidence in the form of vase paintings, gold prospecting from Georgia and even some ancient coins testify.

Writing in 1925, Janet Ruth Bacon says that "In its original form, the Argonaut story was a narrative of a real voyage in the Euxine Sea, made by Minyans of Thessaly in the late fourteenth or early thirteenth century B.C." The story then became connected very quickly with other fairy tales relating to quests and journeys. Add in some existing stories about king's daughters, flying rams, gods and goddesses, human sacrifice, ancient trade routes and local traditions, it is not difficult to see how the story of Jason and the Argonauts came into existence.

The classical Jason stories have given very little narrative time to what happened before and after the voyage, preferring to focus on events during the journey. While this in itself is understandable, in this narrative, I wanted to devote some time to Jason's family and give some context to how and why he grew up away from his parents. In addition, what may have occurred after the Argo returned is equally interesting and deserves attention. Appolonius for example gives no time to this.

Placing Greek myths into a linear timeline is not an easy task, but that is not the case with the Argonauts. Mythologically speaking, the Argo sailed a generation prior to the great fleet landing on the shores of Troy. The two tales are inextricably linked however through not only time, but in personnel. Some Argonauts were present at Troy. Many of the Argonauts fathered sons who were major participants in the Trojan expedition.

From the ancient writers, there is no singular list of who the argonauts were or how many there were, or indeed how many oars were used at any time. I decided on forty-nine argonauts and twenty-four oars, for no other reason than it allowed for two lots of twenty-four rowers to operate the oars, with one (Orpheus) playing his lyre. Having only twenty-four oars allowed for the boat to be rowed all day, having the same number of rowers in reserve. I also liked the idea of including one female argonaut, Atalanta, who is present in some of the ancient stories as an Argonaut, and ignored completely in others.

When beginning a task such as this, it was impossible to focus on one, well known myth. Along the writing journey, it was difficult to ignore how many other stories were inextricably linked, such as the labours of Hercules, Hippolyta's belt, the Cretan labyrinth, the Calydonian boar hunt, the Lemnian deed, the Trojan war, the life of Medea, centaurs and minotaurs. These other stories hold up on their own, but elements of them fit neatly within the Jason saga.

In relation to the Calydonian boar story, some ancient writers

319

place this event prior to the Argo sailing, and some have it afterwards. Some have Atalanta as a boar hunter, some do not. Some say Meleager died on the hunt, while others do not. To me, it did not make much sense to have the boar hunt after the Argo returned, due to many of the Argonauts being desperate to go home. It made narrative sense for some of the future Argonauts to meet on the boar hunt, when they were much younger, and thus had already formed a bond.

What of the gods? In the original stories, the gods played an active, physical role in the narratives and lives of all participants. For Peter the storyteller, I did not want to have the gods play this role. Such was in the case of the story of Jason crossing the river and losing his sandal. What would my narrative read like without Hera's interference? How would the twins Helle and Phrixus leave Orchomenus in the area of Boeotia if not on the back of a flying ram? In Jason's early life on Mt Pelion, who was Chiron if not a centaur? With Theseus as one of the Argonauts, how could he explain the story of him killing a minotaur if there were no such beasts in existence? The use of gods in ancient Greek literature were a common technique to help explain the unexplainable. Today, we would defer to more scientific explanations of how famines come into existence, how lightning works, and how the sun appears to move across the sky each day.

I haven't ignored the gods entirely as they were an important component of everyday life in 1190 BCE Greece, and references to various gods do exist. What I have ignored is a supernatural explanation of an event, when a natural description would suffice.

Finally, my narrative is different from the more traditional telling of this story insofar as I do not have the Argo returning from Colchis via rivers in Europe, hugging the Italian coast, travelling overland in Africa, and circling for no apparent reason around many islands on their way home. They simply come home the way they went!

ADDITIONAL READING

Appolonius of Rhodes (1971) *The Voyage of Argo, The Argonautica*. Translated with an introduction by E. V. Rieu, Penguin Books.

Bacon, Janet. R (1925) *The Voyage of the Argonauts*, Small, Maynard & Company, Boston.

Barringer, Judith, M (1996) Atalanta as Model: The Hunter and the Hunted, *Classic Antiquity*, Apr 1996, Vol. 15, No. 1, pp 48 – 76.

Elderkin, G. W (1913) Repetition in the Argonautica of Apollonius, *The American Journal of Philology*, Vol 34, No. 2, pp. 198 – 201.

Flaccus, Valerius (1928) *Argonautica*, Translated by J. H. Mosley, Harvard University Press, London. https://www.theoi.com/Text/ValeriusFlaccus1.html

Fugard, Athol (2007) Jason – The End, *Arion*, 15.1, Spring/Summer 2007.

Gardner, E (1906) The Atalanta of Tegea, *The Journal of Hellenic Studies*, Vol. 26, pp 169 – 175.

Howe, Thalia, P (1957) Sophokles, Mikon and the Argonauts, *American Journal of Archaeology*, Oct, 1957, Vol. 61, No. 4, pp. 341 – 350.

Inman, James, A (2014) *Orpheus' Argonautica: Language, Tradition, Allusion and Translation*, PhD Dissertation, University of Texas.

Kalachanis, K., Preka-Papadema, P., Kostikas, I., Theodossiou, E., Manimanis, V., Rotolo, S., Kyriakopoulos, K (2017) The Argonautica Orphica Version for the Voyage of the Argonauts: A Geo Analysis, *Mediterranean Archaeology and Archaeometry*, Vol 17, No. 2, (2017) pp. 75 – 95.

Mackie, C. J (2001) The Earliest Jason: What's in a Name, *Greece & Rome*, Vol. 48, No. 1, pp. 1 – 17.

Marlow, A. N (1954) Orpheus in Ancient Literature, *Music & Letters*, Vol. 35, No. 4, pp. 361 – 369.

Nowak, Troy, J (2006) *Archaeological evidence for ship eyes: An analysis of their form and function*, Masters Dissertation, Texas A&M University.

Ovid (2000) *The Calydonian Boar Hunt, The Metamorphoses, Book VIII*, Translated by A. S. Kline

Rubin, Nancy, F (1983) Meleager and Odysseus: A structural and cultural study of the Greek hunting-maturation myth, *Arethusa*, Vol. 16, No 1/2 (1983) pp. 137 – 171.

Stephanidis, M. & Stephanidis, Y (2008) *Jason and the Argonauts*, Sigma Publications, Athens.

Whitefield, T (2020) *The Queen of Limnos*, Karpasi Press, Melbourne.

www.ingramcontent.com/pod-product-compliance
Lightning Source LLC
Chambersburg PA
CBHW020328120726
47904CB00002B/326